First Printing, 2009, Second Printing, 2022
ISBN 978-1-61539-474-6

By Arrangement with Lightning Press
Painting by Joanie Karnowski
Layout and Design by HMDPUBLISHING
Printed in the United States of America

ISBN: 978-1-915147-70-7 (Paperback)
ISBN: 978-1-915147-71-4 (Ebook)

Nighthawks

Lee Adams

Prologue

The year is 2002.

Berle's Promenade had been deserted for a long time before I showed up. Even now, except for my diner, it's nothing but leveled floor plans of asphalt and gravel with an occasional dirt parking lot breaking the monotony. Dirt parking lots hold up pretty well.

Swirls of burgundy, blue, and gold still peek through on some of the weathered cement, cement that will take you all the way to Vincent Highway if you walk its length. When this city was conceived, the Promenade and Vincent Highway were the two main arteries designed to pump life into Berle, my hometown.

V Highway runs parallel to the ocean for many miles. A famous, durable, well-traveled strip of road that remains, after all these years, a contemporary means of getting from one place to another. But the Promenade buckled under the city's growth spurt in the late '70s with the introduction of strip malls and an endless list of faceless franchises that began to surround it.

Berle's attempt at modernism eventually encircled the Promenade's antiquated allure like a chalk outline around a dead body. And it just went all the way down one shop at a time, leaving behind a ghostly stretch of memories, three abandoned blocks of faded glory and apathy and decay.

In the '50s and '60s, by all accounts, this was the real end. A crackling neon Mecca assembled for and catering to the after-hours set: musicians, writers, guilty lovers.

You had Monte's for cigars and cigarettes (and pot, if you knew who to ask), a coffee/juice bar called Roxanne's, a bookshop called The Barn, a Woolworth's, a magic shop, and the all-night diner that I eventually rebuilt. The rest, the way I hear it, were all clubs. One suited to every taste. Swank Jim's, The Orbit Room, Ozbourn's, Friar Tuc's. The legendary Candy's Can Can not only delivered top-of-the-line artists on the weekends but also boasted topless dancers on the off nights.

The Majestic Palms was the only hotel for a couple of miles, conveniently situated at the end of the strip facing Vincent. It must've been a godsend for the musicians who worked those clubs, renting by the month, week, and hour.

By the time I was old enough to walk the Promenade by myself, these forgotten palaces were boarded up, falling down, or gone. And the atrophy was thrilling through my young eyes. I loved to walk the Promenade when I was a kid. So did my friends. It was the coolest place to hang. Purgatory had an amusement park and we had year-round passes.

The neon carcasses that remained stared blankly at one another like zombies from either side of the concrete stroll. Each crumbling edifice provided our teenage imaginations a world of adventures – dark, dangerous adventures.

I remember The Majestic Palms standing crippled and vacant with a flaking wooden billboard girdered to its partial roof espousing former virtues such as "A Telephone In Every Room" and "Kitchenettes Available." A rusted fire escape clung to the hotel's side, and we shinnied up and down that rotted metal time and time again.

You could walk right into Woolworth. No fixtures remained but the vacuum-operated money tubes were still at the ready as well as some scattered hangers and moldy boxes cluttering the curling red linoleum floor. A painted Buster Brown advertisement survived against one dank wall and the staircase bore the most beautiful wood banister I'd ever seen.

The grave robbers who'd gutted the place had left part of the lunch counter, which we kids found very useful for everything from homework to Yahtzee.

I used to meet up with my pals there, Renee and Saul and Jackie, and Willie Dole, who never kissed me despite my charm.

It became our clubhouse, and the Promenade our turf. A bunch of loitering junior high school knuckleheads kicking around among the shattered glass, sitting cross-legged on half-chewed brick walls, looking to get into something. Looking for trouble that never came. Twenty-five years later, I'm staring out on that same Promenade and thinking how ironic it is that such grown-up trouble finally found me here.

The land the Promenade was built on is still owned by John Doherty's estate, John being one of Berle's founding fathers. Contractors and councilmen alike have tried to pry this land from Doherty's grandson, the present-day executor of that estate, but to no avail. He's afraid, as were his forefathers, that if he gives an inch, the Promenade will be reborn as some monolithic McDonald's with a checkered past. I agree with John, III. So I had to ask him very nicely to let me rebuild the diner, promising to keep it as close to the original as possible. I even put the new one right where the old one stood 60 years ago, smack-dab in the middle of the strip.

The place used to be called Chordeilettes. I don't know what that was about. When I was growing up, folks pronounced it Chordettes. However you cut it, it wasn't right. So I coined it Nighthawks. That seemed right.

I made every effort to capture the original cachet, but the only authentic feature, which I bought for $5,000 from John's warehouse of Promenadien treasures, was the dilapidated neon sign his granddad had retrieved before the walls were torn down. It was found crashed and resting on one end in the gravel, this garish, brilliant monster of a thing featuring a wide-eyed blinking owl clutching a coffee cup. Honestly, how could a place with that out front be called anything but Nighthawks?

Now I'm wondering if that old adage is true. You can't rechristen a ship. It's always bad luck.

CHAPTER ONE

When the last of the construction crews left and the gas and lights were turned on, I stood in awe of the masterpiece. Nighthawks is more than a diner, it's a monument. A street angel's Valhalla, a shimmering slice of American enterprise excavated from Berle's sleepy collective consciousness. Building-length fluorescent bands of cherry red electricity light up the darkened stroll like a beckoning roadside attraction, a vibrant *something* insulated by a comforting stretch of nothing to either side.

I was crouched down behind the counter, stocking the shelf under the glass cutout to the left of the cash register. Ashtrays and mugs sporting the same blinking owl that graces the neon out front share space here with Hershey Bars and Dentyne.

As Jesus came out of the Ladies' Room, I hailed him over to hand him the remaining box of coffee cups. "Jesus, can you put this back in the storage room before you hit the Men's?"

He nodded and took the box. "Sure, Julie."

Just then a car backfired in the parking lot and without any hesitation, I went from crouching to a completely prostrate position on the black industrial mat beneath me. At least I didn't scream.

Only Jesus and Debbie saw my overly theatrical reaction. I caught the look of quiet concern that passed between them as I lifted my head. Deb hung a couple of tickets, making like nothing odd had just happened. Jesus helped me up, his black diamond eyes calculating my stress level without comment. I was shaking so hard that he had to steady me, his hands on my arms, my hands on his elbows. Ultimately, he couldn't hold his tongue.

"Ay! Let it go for one minute, boss! Put it out of your head! It's not going to happen twice. Go have a smoke or something. I've got things under control."

I pulled away from him. "Oh, I'm…I'm okay. Feel better working"

"Yeah, I can tell."

"Did you fill the perfume dispenser in there?" I was pointing to the room he'd just exited. The Ladies' Room boasts a 1957 perfume dispenser stocked with My Sin, Emeraude and Chantilly. I'm a Tabu girl myself but I don't want every beatnik baby who wanders in for a piss to smell like me so I don't include it with the other classics.

"Sure. Toilet paper, perfume, feminine protection, everything."

I resumed fumbling with the Dentyne boxes as I switched my tone from public to private. "Oh, and don't forget to stock the condom machine when you get in the Men's Room. Okay?"

His more typical playfulness emerged momentarily. "Oh, si! Si, senorita. I keep it full." He speaks perfectly good English but there are certain Spanish words and pronunciations he seems to cling to for safekeeping, or to mock me, one or the other. Interestingly, his name is not among those Spanish souvenirs. He insists we call him Jesus, King James version, as opposed to pronouncing it Hasuse, which I believe we would've all embraced more comfortably. He's deep.

I rang up a trucker then turned to see my dark knight still behind me standing at attention. "I'm okay, Jesus. I really am." He relaxed but didn't move his feet. He simply leaned against the salad bin. I decided to refocus him.

"So, what's all over your apron today?" His snow-white T-shirt, glimmering crucifix, and crisp straight-legged jeans are never less than impressive. But his apron…I don't know. It always looks like he just slaughtered something.

"Oh, yeah. I was helping Heffe with the grill. Maybe I should take it off." He doesn't like wearing the apron. "You want me to take it off?"

Debbie, who was now sitting at a deuce marrying ketchup bottles to one another shouted, "Yeah, take it all off." Crew and customers twittered. Jesus smiled.

"You want me to take it off, Julie? 'Cause I'll take it off for you if that's what you like." There was a suggestiveness to his suggestion. Now the whole joint was listening. I didn't feel like providing a floorshow.

"No. No, that's okay," I muttered, fumbling with receipts.

Once again, Debbie piped in. "Yeah, keep it on, baby. I like it better dirty."

Dorothy Parker, she's not. Nevertheless, Debbie ceaselessly pitches this sort of weak sexual innuendo like a used-car salesman pitches guarantees. Everyone laughed but me. I appreciated that they were trying to lighten the mood but it would've taken more than a feigned laugh to do that.

I slipped into the turquoise tuck-and-roll booth in the corner with a notepad and owl-embossed ballpoint pen. I had every intention of working on an outline for my novel. That's why I built the diner, so I'd have a swinging place to write. The popularity of my first book, non-fiction, is what allowed me to build the place and I'm currently under contract to write another smash. Right then my literary obligations were pressing against me like a whore on a sailor and I just wanted out.

The corner booth had become my unofficial office by then, eight days after we'd opened for business, nine days after the murder. Feeling spent and uninspired, I put the pen down to regroup.

Here I could see everything from the cigarette machine between the bathrooms to the sleek, well-stocked jukebox at the far end of the gold-flecked Formica counter. Coffee perfumed the air, and a toaster oven cast the sweet smell of Danish out among the hipsters and lonely hearts for whom the diner was reborn. While taking in the perfection that surrounded me, my anxiety turned to a bitter sadness as it had many times over the last several days. "This is God's little acre, damn it. How could something so horrible have happened to such a wonderful place?"

Recognizing my tenuous condition, Rhea brought me a cup of coffee, the smell of Lava soap and chicory wafting up from her young, chapped hands.

"Try to forget it, Julie. God, I can't stand this." She was trying to forget what had happened, herself. Neither of us could.

I dabbed my tired eyes with both pinkies and readjusted my glasses while trying to speak. With uncharacteristic assertiveness, she ground both fists into the table, leaning forward to get in my face. "It's not your fault. The only thing that's your fault is that you built this place in the middle of frigging no-man's-land. I mean you've only got drag queens and drag racers as neighbors here. I'm surprised they don't have shit like this happen all the time on the Promenade."

She was right. This wasn't the safest part of town, somehow desolate and removed from the city that surrounded it. I thought I'd be insulated here. Turns out I was wrong. I smiled a cursory smile. "Thanks for the coffee, Rhea."

She shifted her weight from one long stem to the other while picking at the chipped black polish on her index finger with her thumb. "You're welcome," she whispered, then slowly shook her head in an 'I give up' kind of way, and did.

Rhea's a good waitress and a good kid. I'm no restaurateur, you understand, just a hack who owns a coffee shop. But I do seem to have a knack for hiring good help. Those first several days, however, nobody was worth a shit. We were all just getting by.

As I dipped into the hot coffee Rhea was good enough to bring, there was this God-awful clatter from the kitchen accompanied by the sound of hot oil sloshing and sizzling. Everyone at the counter locked into a kind of suspended animation like pausing a TV show midstream.

"Doris! Doris, get in here!" Carroll was barking from behind the pass-out window. Jesus lurched into the kitchen before I could even get up. "Get away from me kid! Vamoose! Doris!" Carroll is my lead fry cook. He's also a drunk.

I made it into the kitchen before he could yell again. "Carroll, are you okay?" The evidence lay before me. Something had gone into the fryer that didn't belong there and a little grease had shot up onto my rummy friend. The fry basket was on the floor. A large bread tray was on the floor. Loaves of frozen sourdough bobbed like huge dumplings in the hot grease. Thousand Island dressing was everywhere.

"Oh, God, Doris, the pain." He spoke calmly but with great drama as he did when he spoke of Vietnam. (He spent his entire tour of duty in a naval hospital with an inner ear problem, but that's another story.) His arm up to the shoulder was in the sink, cold water easing the situation a degree or two.

"I'll get the salve." I got the salve. "What happened?"

"It was something the likes of which you have never seen, Doris."

"Tell me." I gently patted away the excess water and began rubbing salve on the tiny flesh bubbles peppering his skinny gray limb.

"Well, the fry basket was on the side of the fryer, you see. And when those frozen loaves of bread came sliding down that goddamn tray, I had to drop it. It was an avalanche!

There was no other way. Then the tray hit the handle of the basket and…"

"What happened to the Thousand Island?"

He observed the dressing that was dripping off of everything from cupboards to dishes as if for the first time. "I have no idea."

"Here, hold this end of the gauze. You need to sit down for a minute?"

"I better stay up. Fight the good fight. What do you think?"

"Well, I'd say you're a lucky man. You didn't get burnt very badly." My skin-grafted forearm was exposed and available as evidence that I knew from where I spoke.

"You know all about that, little missy. I remember. Now, you've got to stop making a fuss and go back to work. We've got a lunch shift to gear up for."

"Well then, try to stay out of the deep fryer and carry on, good soldier. I don't know what I'd do without you, Carroll."

His tiny bourbon-colored eyes squinted affectionately atop his road map of a nose. "Doris, you're good people. No dootabootit." I headed for the swinging door as he yelled after me, "Good people!"

Carroll's nerves were as shot as mine. After all, we were both still under investigation.

As I approached the booth, Rhea was topping my cup. "Julie, why does Mr. Sharkey call you Doris?" A fair question. I considered giving her the whole story then reconsidered.

"It's a nickname."

"Some nickname. You don't mind?"

"I've been called worse."

"You're feeling better now, aren't you? I can tell."

"Yeah. Carroll has a way of tempering things. I do feel better."

"Your friend Charlotte says he saved your life once. Oh, my God. That old fart? I'm so sure." The goofy thing stood there gossiping and giggling like we were friends.

"He did," I acknowledged soberly.

"Oh. He did? Wow." Sensing that she had crossed a line, she added, "Well, do you want a tuna melt?"

"That's a ridiculous segue, Rhea."

She considered that for a good three seconds then added, "But do you want one?"

"I think you've got a new down on table four."

She bounced away, relieved.

I know the kids laugh at him behind his back. He knows it. But he also knows they count on him. So do I. And as long as he works for me, they'll all call him Mr. Sharkey.

Drunks don't bother me that much. I understand addiction better than your average bear. My affinity for prescription medication has kept me centered and productive for many years now, on and off.

So as far as I'm concerned, Carroll's habit does nothing more than add to his humanity, the way he occasionally wets his pants, the way he sometimes can't make it to the bathroom in time to throw up what remains of the night before, or the shakes he suffers when he can't get to a drink for a couple of days.

Not appropriate behavior for the food service industry, you say? You'd only say that if you'd never worked in the food service industry. Besides, he did save my life once. I like having him around.

I dropped a nickel into the side slot of the fortune-telling napkin dispenser in front of me, the bobbing head of a grizzled gypsy attached by a small coil on top. There's one standing sentinel at every booth. I'm proud of that. And even though I'm the one who loads these machines with rolls of yes/no answers, I still invest nickel after nickel trying to illuminate the less illumined aspects of my life. In that I get the nickels back, it's a win-win situation. That afternoon, I gave my particular metal mystic quite a workout.

"Is the worst of this shit behind me?" I pulled the handle. CAN'T TELL YOU NOW was her pull-paper reply. I placed that unsatisfying answer in front of me and tried again. "Am I safe here?" NOT SURE and ASK AGAIN LATER came out before ABSOLUTELY. I did not stand convinced.

That afternoon and every afternoon since our Grand Opening eight days before, staff and management staggered around, professional and friendly, quiet and preoccupied. Ammonia couldn't cut through the tension. Eggs and onions couldn't mask the scent of fear each of us was throwing off.

My brand new crew had been shaken profoundly. Two of the girls I'd hired quit before starting. Who could blame them? If I hadn't owned the place, I might have done the same. Still, the rest remained either out of compassion or necessity or on a dare.

Some customers hadn't yet heard of our little embarrassment. Others came because of it, some sort of perverted draw like Bonnie and Clyde's death car or something. There's no comprehending how warped people can be. I stopped trying a long time ago. Now I just see people as a bunch of twisted, self-serving motherfuckers, all of us balanced between pointless struggle and imminent demise. But that's just me.

Reaching for another nickel, I landed on a cigarette instead. Putting the cigarette back, I fished around for my pillbox to better take the edge off.

I thought about walking out front for a smoke but I just didn't want to go through that door. I didn't want to go through it but I couldn't stop staring at the chrome handle, the scripted We're always open! painted across the front. It happened before we were open, one day before.

I was the one who found her; hands pressed against the glass of a locked door that one day later would seldom be locked again. Two of her nails had broken off, presumably from dragging herself to the door. Her throat had been splayed open with something jagged and thick. The cops thought it might have been a key. They intimated, in fact, that it might have been the key to the diner, which put Carroll and me in direct line for questioning.

Though the cut did her in, it was a bullet between her shoulder blades that took her down. She had been shot in the dirt parking lot. That's where the first splash of blood was found. That's where they found the bullet.

They say that she was shot from several yards away. Then someone got much closer, close enough to open her throat. She dragged herself to the front door after her assailant or assailants left her to die. The cops determine it happened around 5 a.m.

I got there around 6:00, parading right through the unnoticed blood in the dirt. By the time I neared the corner of the building where the cement sidewalk begins, I had the nightmarish realization that I was walking on a carpet of blood. I just continued taking slow baby steps through it as my brain offered every alternative it could come up with: it's paint, it's syrup, it's, it's…

When I saw her little frame pressed against the door my first thought was that she was hurt, balanced on her knees, one hand wrapped around the chrome, the other fanned out across the glass. But the blood-soaked Welcome mat informed me that she was more than hurt. She didn't move as I approached.

My stomach cramped and my glasses fogged with panic. I dropped my keys twice on the ghoulish walk toward the body. Cautiously, I sat down on the tiled planter box also stained by the tragedy. My hands were clasped over my mouth as I stared at the girl who was staring back at me.

Her eyes were big and blue with a gaze so direct it seemed she was still in there. One hand had left a bloody stencil print on the glass directly above the place where it finally landed. Her thin, inadequate sweatshirt was drenched with carnage and morning dew. It clung to her child-like frame. I was close enough to touch her. I didn't. I just sat fixed on the way the flesh zigzagged under her pretty face. Looked like someone used pinking sheers on her. A small trickle of fluid still oozed from the single black hole the bullet had left on her back.

I swallowed the bile clogging my airway and mechanically dug for the phone in my purse. Trembling from the cold as well as the circumstance, I attempted to describe the scene to an emergency operator on the other end. As I did, details came into focus; her matted hair, her dirt-stained cheeks. She was wearing tattered white pedal-pushers and a pair of slip-on Vans tennis shoes. No socks, no purse, no coat. No jewelry but for a blue plastic watch on one wrist and several black plastic tube bracelets on the other.

She looked like one of those skinny kids you see sleeping under freeway overpasses, the kind of kid you could imagine shoplifting at a 99 Cent Store.

I tugged at my beret, tightened my wool scarf, and buried both hands in the deep, warm pockets of my Army Surplus coat. She must've been cold, really cold.

I could hear a siren in the distance. We waited in silence for it to arrive. Nine days later, she was more real to me than when we'd met. For nine days, there had been two voices pounding in my head, one mine, one hers. It didn't matter which one I listened to. The question was the same. Why?

CHAPTER TWO

I decided on a smoke after all. Locating a cigarette and match, I plowed right through the door, just as if I hadn't watched those two ambulance drivers pry that little girl off of it. But rather than sit on the planter box, I ambled toward the shattered street in front of me, the one that used to be Berle's most golden thoroughfare.

Through the smoke ascending over my corrective lenses I could see him off in the distance, his shiny black head glimmering in the late-morning sun. Crow and I had only met on two other occasions. This ebony soldier of fortune was the kingpin of a group of drag racers that had adopted Nighthawks as their own.

Because of the diner, the Promenade has become a favorite hangout for the city's ever-burgeoning drag racing community. They don't race here, they gather and plan. Late at night when the competition is over, they pour into Nighthawks for beer and chili. I don't mind. They make me feel safer than the cops.

I could see the muscles in his shoulders and arms ripple in time with each calculated step he took. His jeans, wife-beater, and aviator sunglasses all conspired to make the man seem even more imposing than his girth. The whole persona was designed for intimidation. For some reason, it never read that way to me. I liked him straight up. He approached, gave a quick nod, crossed his huge arms, and planted his boots about a foot apart.

"Hey, Crow. Kind of early for you to be out and about, isn't it?"

"I could say the same thing to you. How you holding up, JP? They know anything yet?"

I'd flicked my butt into the gutter and was fishing around for another. He handed me one of his, simultaneously flipping open the hood of his chrome-plated lighter.

"Thanks." It was menthol but I didn't want to appear ungracious. "No. Nobody knows a goddamn thing. Guess we're just supposed to pretend it didn't happen. They haven't even figured out her name."

From behind the shades, I could sense his eyes veering in one direction, then the other by the nominal shift of his head. "You moved in up there yet?" He was referring to the apartment above the diner.

"I'm having the furniture delivered today. I'll be in by tonight."

He started walking so I walked with him. He headed around the side of the building, back by the stairwell that led to my new front door. "Is that the only way in?"

"Okay, now you're freaking me out. Yes, that's the only way into the apartment. There's a fire escape on the other side. So what? What kind of scary fucking question is that?"

He smiled a toothy smile at my curtness and started back around the front of the building. I stayed in tow. "Seriously, Crow, I want to know why you asked me that."

He placed one callused hand on my shoulder. "I think maybe I can help expedite this little drama."

"What do you mean?"

"Maybe. Let me put out the word and see what surfaces. This neighborhood's tight. Somebody somewhere knew that kid." He opened the glass door for me. "I'm on your side, JP. Don't you worry about that. You take care of my friends and they'll take care of you." We'd both cleared the door and were huddled for a moment between a couple coming in and a couple going out.

"Thanks, cowboy." I felt a brief wave of relief like maybe he really could make things better. "Debbie, get Crow whatever he wants. It's on the house."

Of course, I'd just set Debbie up with a very easy string of one-liners but she didn't bite. Instead, she made with a coy grin that made me think she'd probably already given him whatever he wanted on some other occasion.

Joanne, our resident grandma, must've snuck in while I was outside. She was tying on her apron as I walked by. "Hey, Joanne."

"Julie, I'm sorry I'm late. My daughter…"

"Tell it to Rhea. She's had her purse on her shoulder for the last twenty minutes." The old woman looked so disgusted with herself. "Jo, it's no big deal. Your nametag's on sideways, though." She grabbed the tag and readjusted it. "Oh, for heaven's sake," she muttered.

This one can really break my heart. With every turn, she thinks I'm going to fire her. Her husband of forty years had just asked for a divorce claiming they suffered a lack of compatibility. He left her with a bankruptcy, mobile home, and two cats. She realized in short order that her Social Security wasn't enough to live on, and both of her kids were back east. So she found herself, at sixty-three, in need of a job. This is where she'd decided to make her waitressing comeback because this was the last place she worked—forty years ago. Someday she'll figure out that I'm never gonna fire her. A gal with balls that big? It's an honor to have her around.

I dipped behind the counter to pour myself another cup of joe as a lovely Valium fog rolled gently over the back of my head. Thank God it was kicking in.

As I readjusted heavy plastic frames atop blurred, bloodshot eyes, I became aware that my hands stunk of nicotine and was comforted by that, as well. Back in the corner booth and ready to address the work in front of me, I fingered the pen and blank notepad with nothing but good intentions. "I'll pay you tomorrow," said the gambler to the loan shark.

The joint was already jumping well before lunch. All of my regulars were there; i.e., Charlotte and the four kids who hadn't left since the yellow police tape had been cut.

The kids are bandmates. Right then, the topic among them was, as usual, what to name the band. Options included Stroke, Swollen, and (the more romantic) Big Pink Tongue. There's a white kid named Chad, a black kid named Chad, an albino kid so bleached I don't know what he is – he's named Doug, and a Japanese girl named Tacaco but she makes them all call her Chad. Chad, Chad, Doug, and Chad had just ordered another round of fries and Charlotte was at the counter doing her usual thing; throwing missed passes at Carroll, the red-nosed fry cook.

My pal Charlotte is a round woman with chocolate skin and big tiger-yellow eyes that she keeps perpetually painted along with her nails and lips. Pretty in a blow-up baby doll kind of way. One of those big gals that make the rest of us look like we should try a little harder. She's probably about forty-five, forty-six. I've never asked. And when that girl looks at Carroll, you can almost hear the angels sing.

Carroll, on the other hand, wouldn't have any part of it. Oh, they'd talk, you know, talk about her childhood on the stage, his unexplored writing scholarship to Berle U. But when she got that naughty look in her eye, that Ann Margaret sex kitten thing going, he'd fly out the door. I've seen him up and leave the kitchen during a push. That's restaurant lingo for a busy time. Once, I found him staring intently at the Dipsey-Dumpster out back, his forehead and index finger gently pressing the metal bin. Crazy kids.

Charlotte and I go way back. She's a lounge singer who works at a couple of different houses on Beaumont Avenue, the Capri and Captain's Cove. She's good. She's a good songwriter, too, but I seldom hear her do original stuff. Felix sits in with her boys on occasion and vice versa. Felix Mint, God of the sax, Ruler of Clubland, my old flame.

When the rotary phone rang at the counter, she looked over her shoulder to see if I wanted her to pick it up. Charlotte answering the phone had become standard by then. She was perpetually next to it and had more time on her hands than the rest of us. I indicated that, yeah, she should. Upon hearing the caller's voice, she shook her head no in my direction. This was to let me know it wasn't Felix on the other end. Every time the phone rang I hoped that it was.

Felix and I had been apart for over a year. We initially stayed in loose contact with a few strained telephone conversations, a few unreturned calls left on answering machines. But that day at the diner it had been months without any contact, and I wanted to hear that bass-heavy voice more than anything.

Denied that comfort, I was at least able to keep tabs on him, mostly through my psychiatrist, Dr. Marjorie Stewart. She had first-hand information as she was currently sleeping on my old pillow on my side of the bed. They met while I was in the burn ward at Saint Mary's fifteen months ago. He held my hand while she tended to my emotional recovery and burgeoning pharmaceutical needs. Good thing she's a psychiatrist because when the gal who's keeping you upright is also screwing the love of your life, it can profoundly mess with your head.

We never actually broke up, Felix and I. I moved out to pen the book I'd been contracted to write and, well, the boy just has a hard time being alone. Marge was so helpful in getting him over that hump, if you will.

Despite the passage of time and new house rules, I was expecting him. I needed him. But it wasn't him on the phone. It was my agent, Richard Randall. Charlotte mouthed that info my way as I ambled toward her.

I didn't want to hear what he had to say. My inability to deliver pages for the new book was getting on everyone's nerves. I'd happily blame it on the murder but the problem had been going on for months. I guardedly took the receiver from Charlotte and adopted my best "Who, me worry?" attitude. Then I did the bullshit thing where you know who's on the other end but you make them tell you anyway. "Nighthawks. This is Julie. Can I help you?"

"Julie, it's Richard."

"Well, hi! How you doing? Gosh, I've been meaning to call. Things have been just..." I threw in a giggle. "So, how have you been? How's Patrick?"

"Fine and fine. Don't forget you have that interview with the Times in less than thirty minutes."

"Of course. Absolutely. I'm looking forward to it." I had totally forgotten. "Say, did you talk to the reporter about not hitting the murder thing too hard? This is purely about the next book, right?"

"What book would that be? The imaginary one on invisible pages?"

"Come on, Richard. I'll get the editor something in the next few days. Just tell her to unknot her panties and cut me some slack. I'm still under investigation, you know. Things have been pretty intense."

"She needs pages, Julie. And you need this interview to go well so give the guy what he wants, whatever it is. And be nice."

"I'm nice."

"Not really. So if murder is what's making you newsworthy, give him the details. If they want an exposé on diners, give it to him. Forget the literary elitist malarkey and vie for as much print space as you can."

He was starting to piss me off. I've never been an elitist in my life. Or literary, for that matter. "Is that all?"

"No. I also don't want you to get into some tedious discussion about Maxine this time. We need to keep you relevant. That's yesterday's news, all right?"

"Sure, Rich. Hey, one more thing before you go..."

"Yeah?"

"You kiss my ass, okay?"

"That's my girl. Now go make me proud." Click. He was done.

I turned to Charlotte for validation. "There have been plenty of occasions when I've been nice."

A ruby glimmered from one puffy finger as she fluffed her bangs and hair to enlarge the overall effect. "You go, girl."

"But I'd better shit a book in the next few months or I'm in real trouble."

Relaxing both arms from preening her colossal do, she placed one hand over the other, ruby up, and addressed my concerns. "Stay true to your school, Julie. That's what I always say."

I leaned in close enough to smell the Aqua Net. "Do you really say that all the time?"

"No, I never really do." We exchanged weak grins.

"Where is that tall sonofabitch? Why won't he call me? He must've read the paper or seen the news by now. Should I call him?"

"Oh, hon, I don't know. I told you I haven't seen him in months. Ask Doctor Blondie. She should know."

"Yeah, but man, I hate that she does. Why won't he show up on his own?"

"Well, Julie, my man is right there and I can't get him to call either."

I glanced over at Carroll who was trying to remove something from the underside of the ticket wheel with a spatula. The foreign object hit the pass-out bar and started to scurry away but the spatula won.

"Charlotte, truthfully, why Carroll?"

"You've got him managing your kitchen. You tell me."

"Well, it's complicated."

"Exactly."

Just then the glass door swung open and a crumpled, sweaty fellow swung in.

"Shit. There's the reporter – early. Man, I'm not ready for this."

"How do you know that's him?"

"I used to work at a paper. I know the look."

She gave him the once over then turned back and whispered, "What do you call that look?"

"Nondescript."

CHAPTER THREE

I stepped forward to greet him before he even had a chance to scope the place. His hand extended automatically when he saw mine. "Hi. I'm Julie Page."

"Steve Hillerman with the Times. Nice to meet you."

"Same here. Can I get you a cup of coffee or anything before we get started?" I was guiding him to the corner booth.

"Sure. That would be great. So this is Nighthawks. It's fantastic. Did you go by old photos or did you just wing it?"

"Old photos, oral histories, and personal taste. The place came together so easily that I think the ghosts of the Promenade were just waiting for somebody to bring in building materials so that they could reassemble it. Have a seat."

We both slid into the booth at right angles from one another. I hollered to Jo for the coffee as the guy whipped out a recorder from his backpack and placed it at an equal distance between us on the Formica.

"You believe in ghosts, Ms. Page?" He hadn't hit the record button yet and I was already on the defensive. Do I believe in ghosts? What was that? Was he just chatting or was that some loaded, leading question designed to undermine my integrity? Everything I said could and would be used against me in the court of popular culture. He might be a fan. He might be a foe. And I wouldn't know which until I read it in the paper.

But we were on my turf. I was in control. I could spin this interview any way I chose.

"Ms. Page?" he repeated.

"Julie. Call me Julie. Everyone does."

"Doris! Doris, can I see you for a minute?"

Okay, we were off to a rough start. When I unclenched my jaw enough to turn my head, I saw Carroll's eyes and nose peeking around the frame of the kitchen door. He looked like Kilroy after a bad night. "Can you excuse me for a sec?" I exited the booth and pushed the kitchen door in so that my cook was forced to let me through.

"What is it, Carroll?"

"I don't have a good feeling about that guy. What do we know about him?"

"This is what you called me in here for? Jesus!"

"Si?" Jesus pulled back from the automatic dishwasher far enough to see what I wanted.

"Nothing, Jesus. I was just... Sorry. Look, Carroll, we don't know anything except that he's a reporter and he wants to do an interview. It's no big deal."

"Well, you look like you just saw a ghost. What's he asking you about?"

The irony was too great for discussion. "You wouldn't believe me if I told you. Now, please hold down the fort for the next hour or so. This thing needs to go well, okay?"

"Aye aye, captain." He started back toward the grill. "But I've got a bad feeling, Doris. Something's rotten in Denmark!" He busied himself with nothing as I cautiously reentered the dining room. Admittedly, I had the same feeling.

The reporter was opening an individual creamer for the coffee that had arrived in my absence. I repositioned myself next to him and manufactured a smile. "Sorry about that. Running a diner is a full-time job. Now, where were we?"

"No problem." He took a drink and wiped his mouth. "Must be hard to handle all this and write."

Bastard! That's not what I meant. I wondered how I might fish out another Valium without him noticing. "Well, writers write regardless. That's our curse."

"You believe in curses? Julie?"

My eyes remained pleasant as I sipped from the cup in front of me. When I finished taking a sip, I took another.

"Man, I love these napkin dispensers. Where did you get these?" He popped the gypsy on the head so it bobbed playfully.

"I bought some of them on ebay and had the rest made to order."

"Do they work?" He looked like a kid all of a sudden, an annoying kid.

"Yeah, they work. Would you like anything to eat?" I was hoping to discourage him from asking the gypsy questions so we could get on with the task at hand.

"No thanks. May I?" Too late. He was already groping for pocket change.

"If you like."

He deposited a nickel and placed his hand on the lever. Fixing me with a Houdini-like gaze, he asked his question with all the artificial apprehension of a teenager approaching the entrance of a funhouse. "Are there ghosts on the Promenade?" The handle went down as my eyes rolled up. Maybe this guy didn't work for the L.A. Times. Maybe he worked for the Paranormal Times or something. I should've asked.

And then, as luck would have it, the handle stayed down. It wouldn't budge. I tried to jostle it myself but no go. This delighted him. He placed his hands close to the napkin dispenser as if warming them and added, "Ommmm. Clearly, a message from beyond."

I grabbed a butter knife and started poking at the slit the arm rested in. "There may be a little peanut butter stuck in there." Finally, the lever popped back, but no fortune appeared. He coughed up another nickel and dropped it in before I could protest. Glancing at the chrome and neon clock on the wall, he asked, "Is it noon?" This time, the handle went down and an answer came out. BETTER NOT TELL YOU NOW was the verdict.

I shrugged turning both palms heavenward. "Apparently, the cosmos is no respecter of time. Shall we get started?"

"Good idea. I could play with that all day." He hit record. "You've got to forgive me but I'm supposed to ask you a couple of questions about the murder. Boss' orders."

I was picking at my cuticles under the table. "Well, I probably shouldn't talk about that, not until the police say it's okay."

"What have they come up with so far? Anything?"

"Look, Stan…"

"Steve."

"Steve, I can't talk about the investigation. The authorities have asked for my cooperation while they sort everything out."

"But some of the information is public record, like how you found her and how she died."

"Oh, yeah. It's been in all the papers. Say, why don't you pull something from one of those articles to give to your boss? Would that work?" His boss, my ass. This young buck just wanted to add the tragedy to his bleak little resume.

"So, you are still under investigation?" He was resilient.

"Well, yeah. They're just following protocol, you know. I'm the one who found her, it's my diner, etcetera. I'm certain they'll have it taken care of in no time."

"It's been nine days."

I became aware that I'd drawn blood by digging into one of my cuticles a little too diligently. Casually, I slid the unsullied hand to the tabletop and pulled a napkin down to semi-tourniquet the wound. "Right, only nine days."

"So, let me get this straight. The murder happened a day before you opened and the cops let you go ahead and open on schedule? Why?"

That was a question I'd asked myself. "Well, the Berle Police Department felt they had all the forensic evidence they needed. They said I could go ahead and open, so I did."

"What forensic evidence did they find?"

"I don't know."

"Gosh, nine days and no leads. No motive or anything?"

"Not that I'm aware of. I really can't talk about it."

From one booth over, the four bandmates were intent on their sandwiches and my interview. "God! She told you she can't talk about it, like, one million times," Chad hissed audibly while continuing to focus on her grilled cheese. I made a mental note to comp them all next time around.

The reporter acknowledged her jibe. "There's the word from the peanut gallery. Well, I tried. Let's talk about books."

"Sure. As far as I know, the cops don't have a problem with that." He ignored my attempt at humor.

"Your book, For the Record, which beautifully chronicles the adventures of Maxine Montego, has remained at the top of the bestseller list for the last twelve months. This thing is still going strong after a year on the shelf. To what do you owe that success?"

"Maxine," I answered, without reservation. "She was my muse throughout. Some stories insist on being told. Hers is one of them."

I always feel less insignificant when I'm talking about Maxine, so I embrace every opportunity to do so.

"What an unbelievable story."

"Yeah. Truly amazing."

"I understand the book is being made into a movie as we speak and her music catalog is still selling gangbusters here and in Europe."

"She deserves it."

"But you're the one making all the money. What's that like? Ever feel guilty about that?"

And the happy moment was over. This piece of shit had gracefully plunged me back into the self-loathing I'm most accustomed to.

"I've tried to do right by her," I said, wondering if I had. "Could you excuse me for one more minute? Too much coffee." I leaped up and headed for the bathroom as he hit pause.

"Sure. Take your time."

When I was safely inside a bathroom stall, I located the pillbox tucked in one of the pockets of the men's sport coat I had on and took another pill. I figured one more wouldn't kill me and, hey, if it did, we'd be done with the interview. Then, I unzipped the side zipper of my capris and peed. When in Rome…

While urinating, I attempted to figure out how to proceed. Richard wasn't going to like how this whole thing was coming down. I didn't like it one bit. Being nice was making me very tense.

I took my time washing my hands and rearranging my burgundy mop. Then I cleaned my glasses with spit and toilet paper. When I returned, he was frantically taking notes on a pad that had not been there before. He looked up, smiled, put the pad in the back pocket of his jeans, and waved. I waved back as I climbed into position for another round of Spin the Grenade.

"Here we go." He released the pause button. "So, I'm wondering if you're suffering any second book jitters? I mean, it would be almost impossible to deliver another book that would capture the public's imagination as completely as For the Record. No one could blame you for dragging your feet on your next project."

What made this guy think I was dragging my feet? For all he knew, I had another book ready to print. How much did he know?

"Oh, I'm not dragging my feet. I'm working on the next book presently."

"Aw, that's great. What's it about?"

I gave him a coquettish wince and purred, "I'm not ready to talk about it yet," as my stomach made a loud rumble that we both chose to ignore.

"Is it about the girl who died nine days ago at your front door?"

He continued to casually push each button on my dash to see which one operated the emergency lights.

"No. It's fiction. It's a novel."

"Maybe you should reconsider. You can bet somebody's going to write about it. Abandoned promenade, brutal murder. Come on, now. If that isn't a recipe for a bestseller, I don't know what is. You know you'd do a brilliant job. You rocked us once, you could rock us again.

"Thanks but For the Record was different. I was a part of that story."

"And you don't think you're a part of this one?"

Heavy eyelids fought to remain open behind my corrective lenses as Joanne poured more coffee for my assailant and me. I attempted to regain my vacillating composure and took a long swig. I could almost watch his words evaporate from my conscience as, thankfully, the pill taken earlier banged me sideways and the most recent waited its turn. I must've answered the last question because he was asking another.

"So you don't want to talk about the murder and you don't want to talk about your next book. I don't know…How's your health?"

I stared blankly at the guy as my pupils dilated and my breathing slow considerably. Boy, did I want a smoke. He reached across and patted my hand. I'm not sure what the gesture meant, although he may have simply been trying to bring me back, which he did.

"Hey, what convinced you to build this diner? And why here? There's quite a large drag racing community around this part of Vincent Highway."

"Really?" Never so loaded I'd rat on a pal.

"What made you choose this spot?"

I rallied my tongue and lips and gave him a decent canned answer. "Oh, I remember hearing such great stories about the Promenade when I was a kid. I'm too young to have dined in the original, in Chordeilettes, but the gal who brought you that coffee was a waitress there. Having her here adds to the authenticity of the joint, don't you think?"

"Wow. A ghost incarnate."

"No, she's very much alive." Asshole. "Listen, could you stop with the ghost shit? It's starting to get on my nerves."

His eyebrows shot straight up and his mouth fell slack. Then he laughed. "Aw, hey, go easy on me. I'm just looking for a good story, same as you. I didn't mean anything by it."

"It's kind of creepy."

"Well, sure it is. My bad. If I had people dying on me, I wouldn't like it either. I'm sorry, Julie."

Now, was that a friendly response? I had my doubts. But the thick fog drenching my better judgment was providing him ample room to explore my limits.

"Listen, I want to talk to you about what's going on with Random House. I know that when they signed you, it was for a two-book deal, For the Record and the one you're writing now. But there's talk about them terminating that contract. What's going on? Are you shopping for another publisher?"

What the fuck was he talking about? I didn't care if this guy actually knew something or if he was just playing a hunch based on some rumor. Either way, it was time to start lying through my teeth.

"No, we're very much on love, Random House and me. They're already talking about a sequel to this book. But I want to explore my options. Maybe write some short stories. I don't know. The publishing house has been very sweet about allowing me space."

"That's good to hear. The press was so unkind to you after Maxine's biography came out. I thought that was unfair, calling you a one-trick pony, making it seem as though your success was some big joke. I'm glad to hear that your publisher didn't buy into any of that."

"Thanks."

"Oh, hey, in fact, I've got a couple of those reviews right here."

"Why?"

"Here's one. 'This sophomoric attempt at writing is rescued only by the import of the story. The trials and tribulations of Maxine Montego make for a significant read even written with an insignificant hand. This material, in the care of a legitimate author, would have transcended the constraints of a mere biography to become as immortal as its subject.'"

My mind wandered while he read. I own this diner. I don't have to write at all. Maybe next year I should expand the place and add more booths.

"Here's another one. 'A monkey could've written this book and it would still be a bestseller. Julie Page deserves a whole bunch of bananas for her human-like accomplishment.' Man! Don't you feel unjustly maligned by that stuff?"

"I try not to feel much at all."

He calmly checked the recorder when I said that, making sure we were still rolling.

"Why do you think the critics were so cruel when the book was—and continues to be—such a huge commercial success?"

Finally, a question I could answer.

"There's commonly a great distance between commercial success and a well-written book, don't you think? I mean, our culture isn't clamoring for Melville and Joyce. This culture doesn't even want to read. We just want to see a nice clear shot of a celebrity without their underpants on occasionally. My little opus was shocking and brutal and very easy to digest. That's all you need to be successful. Success doesn't have a fucking thing to do with quality, artistic integrity, or talent."

He stared at me hard. "Well, I won't argue with that," he added thoughtfully. "But I'm not sure that wisdom applies to your particular success. Don't underestimate yourself."

Every word he'd uttered up until that moment felt like a poke with the barrel of a loaded gun. Then, in an instant, it was as if he put the safety back on.

"Think about somebody like, say, Shakespeare. Something like As You Like It was just viewed as cheap pop entertainment at the time. But give it a century or two, and it's a masterpiece. It's too soon to know how history will remember your work."

"Did this guy just compare me to Shakespeare?" I thought. "I must've missed something but at least it seemed friendly."

"Well, it's true you never know how things are gonna play out. And the play's the thing." Oh yeah, I still had it.

He hit the stop button and slid the machine into his backpack. "You know what, Julie Page? You just gave me a hell of an interview. Thank you. And thanks for seeing me. I know a lot is going on here right now and I appreciate it."

Did I give him a good interview? Really? I still couldn't tell how things had gone but it was over. It was over.

"It may not seem like it but I'm a big fan of yours, you know."

How could I know?

"You're the quintessential pop heroine of the day, a... something, something...sad clown... something....something...survivor...blah, blah, blah."

He may have called me a sad clown. I'm not sure. I had stopped listening looking past him to a new down at the counter. Somebody seemed to be creating quite a commotion.

As the reporter went on to tell me that he thought the piece would come out in a couple of days and how they always cut his work mercilessly from the bottom and how he was going to fight it this time, an electric blue sharkskin jacket was speaking to me clearly from across the room.

Cecil Valentine (whose real name is Cecil Valente) was sitting at my counter. Cecil hosts a show on cable called "Hearts from Beyond." Contacting the dead has made him extremely popular even though these days it seems you can find somebody to contact your dearly departed in every cab and cafe.

I met him years ago when I lived in New York. I was only there for eleven months. Just long enough for the weather and rent to send me back home. But I gave New York a try. I figured if I was going to be a writer, you know.

Cecil wasn't communicating with the other side back then. He was working Coney Island, barking in front of the freak tent. He let me stay at his place for the last of those eleven months so I could save up enough to get back to Berle and my unopened pile of rejection slips. Apparently, he had moved to the West Coast a few years later, not only to pursue the dead but also to distance himself from an expensive acquittal he's not comfortable talking about. And there he was, sitting at my counter, running his middle finger over his pencil mustache and signing autographs.

We had run into each other a couple of weeks prior to the murder. That's when I told him I was about to open a diner on the Promenade. He liked the idea.

Even though his show is huge, it is cable. And because he has always enjoyed keeping a low overhead and staying as mobile as possible, he'd rented a room at the Sea Nymph down by the old pier. That's the same motel I'd been staying at while the apartment was being built. It was there in the adjacent coin-op Laundromat that he filled me in on the improbable transition from carnival to cable. But, of course, to hear him tell it, the transition was nothing but logical. It was all showbiz.

I rose to greet my old friend. "Excuse me, but I want to say hello to someone."

The reporter rose in turn and fell in behind me. I think he was still talking. A few steps further and he grabbed my arm. "Is that Cecil Valentine?"

"Yes, it is. He's an old friend of mine."

Cecil caught me approaching and made a little kiss face as he continued listening to a middle-aged couple practically hanging on his shiny lapels.

"Now there's somebody who definitely believes in ghosts, huh, Julie?"

Wasn't this guy gone yet? He reached Cecil before I could get through the crowd. "Cecil Valentine? I'm Steve Hillerman with the Times. Nice to meet you. I'm a big fan of yours."

Sure, that's what he says now.

"So nice to meet you, Steve." When they shook hands, Cecil didn't get up and he didn't let go. He looked pensive and sincere as he spoke in hushed tones. "Someone is telling me that you're troubled, Steve. Is that right?"

The reporter was flummoxed. He didn't know whether to laugh, run or take notes.

"I'm hearing… I'm hearing a male figure now. Father? Grandfather? Uncle? He's saying that you try too hard to please him. Don't try so hard, Steve. He wants you to know he's very proud of you. Now I don't mean to keep you. You go on about your business. We'll talk more at a later date, I'm sure."

The guy practically fell over himself getting out the door. It took an exorcism to get rid of him and Cecil was the man. I placed my flaccid arm around his overly padded shoulders as he put his arm around my waist.

"You smell like cherry lip gloss, my brother."

He pulled a napkin from the counter gypsy in front of him wiping his mouth and neck then slid the paper under a saucer.

"I'm a lucky man. What have you been up to, little girl?"

"I've been dodging bullets."

"Real or metaphorical?"

"Probably metaphorical, but they feel very real."

CHAPTER FOUR

Charlotte extended one ample leg from the stool she was perched on. When both pumps were firmly on the ground, she straightened her mini skirt and walked down the counter a few stools to where I was standing. "Jules, I gotta go, honey. I've got a fitting this afternoon for a new outfit. That club wants me in something different every night." She was referring to the Belmont Capri, and a fine dinner house it is. "They've got me in so many outfits the boys in the band are starting to call me Cher instead of Char."

She offered her rubied hand to Cecil. "Hello, Mr. Valentine. I'm Charlotte Vaughn. I enjoy your show."

Cecil's Puerto Rican but grew up in the South (I'd tell you where but he's never said) and, therefore, has a faint Southern accent - or maybe a Southern approach is a more accurate way to put it. Still seated, he released my waist to take her hand.

"Charlotte. What a perfect title for such a lovely work of art." He chose to kiss it. "I am so truly delighted to make your acquaintance."

And Charlotte, having been around the block and to two county fairs, knew everything she needed to know about this particular television celebrity by that greeting.

From the pass-out window, Carroll observed this exchange with grave interest. She gently pulled her hand away and made busy getting keys out of her pocketbook. "See you later, lover," she purred to the pickled object of her desire. Carroll, having been caught staring at what he claimed not to care about, straightened up and spun the ticket wheel as if looking for checks. There were no checks. It was an embarrassingly empty gesture. She gave my forearm a little squeeze and strutted out the door.

Her flirtatious goodbye brought color to Carroll's lackluster cheeks. "That dame's crazy," he growled, seemingly disgusted.

"Crazy for you, you big stud," I answered in defense of lovers everywhere.

The look of horror that immediately drenched his face quickly vanished and he lurched into one of his infamous laughs, which consists of a series of hard, toneless wheezes.

"Doris, you lay me out!"

Cecil, never being one to ask questions, ignored the fact that Carroll had just called me Doris. There are so many things I appreciate about this carny. I played the diplomat. "Hey, Carroll, come on out here for a minute. I want you to meet an old friend of mine."

As he stepped into the dining room and headed toward us, he wiped his hands on his apron then pulled off the hairnet that contained his thin, pomaded locks and tucked it in his shirt pocket. "Well, there you are. Cecil Valentine, in the flesh."

"Cecil, this is my friend and lead cook, Carroll Sharkey."

Cecil gave him a real man's handshake. "So, you've seen my show, Carroll?"

"No. No, sir, I haven't. But your mug is plastered on the bus bench in front of the Cat's Meow over on Vanguard. Must be pretty famous to have your mug plastered on a bus bench. It's a privilege."

Cecil seemed genuinely charmed by Carroll's candor and retired his usual bullshit for the moment. "Well, my brother, I'm doing all right today. Tomorrow could be another story."

"If you don't mind my asking, where did you get those mother-loving shoes? Bertha! Those are something."

Cecil was wearing Cuban heeled ankle boots, green, with taps on the toes.

"From a gentleman who had to go away for a little while. He loaned them to me, indefinitely."

Carroll's dim bourbon eyes closed and reopened in cartoonish exaggeration. Not wanting to appear unsavvy, he added, "Well, they're impressive. They make a statement." He started back to the kitchen while reapplying the hairnet. "I'm going to have to keep my eyes peeled for a pair of those puppies. Impressive!"

Cecil tossed Carroll some male encouragement. "Guaranteed to drive the ladies wild."

Carroll smiled and chuckled as he disappeared back to his workstation. Cecil politely waited for Carroll's exit then put both hands on my waist and turned me so that I was facing him. With a knee to either side of my hips, I was now standing between his seated legs. He pulled me close for some intimate conversation. "I hear there was a little disturbance on the Promenade since last we met." The position he had me in felt less consolatory and more personal in nature. I pushed him a few inches back, removed his hands from my capris, and leaned on the counter.

"She was just a kid. Who would do a thing like that?"

Taking my lead, he leaned on the counter along with me. "It is my unfortunate experience that a person is never too young to have enemies."

I looked at him squarely. "She was trying to get in here, Cecil. She fought so hard. Anyone else would've died in the parking lot but this one, this one dragged herself all the way to that door."

I didn't look at the door. Neither did he.

"Well now, some things we get to understand, some things we don't. And sometimes, my sister, we should just leave things alone. You know what they say, what you don't know can't hurt you."

"I don't know, man. I don't know if I agree with that philosophy."

From a booth across the way, the kids were yelling at me. "Julie! Hey, Julie! Come here! We want to tell you something."

"Customer is king," I whispered to my philosophical buddy as I went over to see what the deal was. "How may I serve you?" They all chuckled.

The albino, Doug, was sitting on top of the tuck-and-roll booth, hands in both pockets of his gas station jacket. "We've come up with names and we want you to be the first to know."

"Oh, happy day. I've lost sleep over this. What are they?"

"Okay, we're going to call ourselves 'The Chads,' okay? And, like, he's going to be black Chad (he referred to the white guy) and he's going to be White Chad (he referred to the black guy) and she's going to be China Chad and..."

"No!" his bandmate screamed. "I'm Girl Chad. I told you a million times. And I'm Japanese! You're so stupid." He seemed unscathed by her jibe.

"So what are you going to call yourself, Doug?" I tried to help him pick up where he'd left off.

"I'm Dangling Chad. What do you think?"

Girl Chad chimed in. "I'm going to call you Stupid Chad." Doug did not acknowledge the tomato slice Girl Chad had thrown onto his plate in anger.

I crossed my arms and placed one hand on my chin to convey interest. "But are you sure Dangling Chad is catchy enough? For fame, I mean. After all, this may be how the history books remember you."

He considered this seriously. White Chad reiterated my advice. "It ain't' catchy, dog. Besides, nobody's gonna get that shit anyway. Dangling Chad. Shit."

Black Chad entered the conversation. “Dude, we’re gonna have to hand out literature before every show explaining what it means and why it’s supposed to be funny.”

We all fell silent for a moment. Then, Black and White Chad, respectively, started tossing out suggestions. “Big Chad, Flat Chad, Dumb Chad, Pale Chad…” This went on for a bit when finally, the Chad under scrutiny looked like he had a brilliant idea.

“Hey, Julie, what about this? Doug.” He flopped down into the booth, smiled at me, and nodded his head slowly like he knew he had arrived at something truly great.

Girl Chad needed clarification. “You mean Doug Chad?”

He looked over at her briefly then back at me, took both hands out of his pockets, and held them up as if seeing something on a marquee. “No. Just DOUG.” The kids grumbled and sniffed at this ridiculous suggestion.

I nodded slowly in agreement. “Wow. Perfect. Now that’s unique.” Five seconds later, they were all laughing and cheering and lauding him for being so clever. My work there was done.

As I started to walk away, Girl Chad called me back. “Julie, that’s that guy from the dead people’s show, isn’t it?”

“Yes.”

“Why don’t you get him to contact the dead girl? Then she could tell you what happened.”

I inhaled then exhaled wistfully wishing it could be so easy.

“Well, Mr. Valentine isn’t working right now; he’s visiting and drinking a cup of coffee. Whenever he’s here, he’s off the clock. Okay?”

I turned in time to see Detective Francis DiAngelo walk in and my heart skipped a beat. Frank was the detective assigned to the case and every time I saw him I was sure he was going to tell me that they’d caught the creep. That they knew, unequivocally, who did it and that that person would never be able to hurt anybody again. But he just came in for coffee.

He and I had met some eighteen months prior during another sordid chapter in my scaly, blemished life, and he told me then to call on him if I ever needed to. So, after surviving the first round of cops that arrived the morning of the murder, I called Frank. He finagled whatever he had to, was assigned the case, and had been around ever since.

Detective DiAngelo is a fine man, but he has an annoying habit of doing everything by the book. And he's even willing to rewrite this book occasionally when he believes a rewrite will protect the greater good. I suppose this is approbation for most cops but the guy parts his hair a little too straight, if you know what I mean.

He acknowledged me then positioned his penny loafers a foot apart, clasping his hands in an "at ease" fashion, waiting to be seated.

He's built like a boxer. And the white cotton button-down adorning that brutish physique always carries the comforting scent of spray starch. Seems he had inadvertently attracted some mischievous attention from three teenage girls huddled over by the jukebox. They tried to make eye contact and he tried to ignore them, holding his attention front and center.

"Frank."

As I approached, he relaxed a bit and almost smiled, running a hand through his short Italian locks.

"Julie. I'm just patrolling the neighborhood, as usual. Thought I'd drop by, and see how you're doing. Everything good?"

"Tell me you've found something, Frank, anything."

"Not yet. Forensics is still at it. We're going to figure everything out. You just need to be patient. Hi, Debbie," he managed as she passed us with an arm full of plates.

"Hi, Frank," she cooed and went on her way without further comment.

"So, have you given any thought to getting that curb painted red out front? I can help you with that, you know. The City Engineer is a nice guy. He'll do it if I ask him to."

"Frank, can you get off that?"

"You need to consider it, Julie."

"Okay, you understand that the joint is in the middle of nothing. There is no parking congestion, Frank. Nothing is congested but my lungs."

"That's the point. There are no boundaries. You need to set boundaries. You don't want people parking right in front. It would be a deterrent.

"A deterrent to what? Business? Let's sit down. And, like I keep telling you, you don't have to wait to be seated."

"I can wait like everybody else."

"Nobody waits to be seated, Frank."

While guiding the big Boy Scout toward a table, I saw Crow stand up. He, along with two of his cohorts, had been holding court in a booth near the front for a couple of hours or more. When he saw Frank, he placed a wad of bills on the table and headed for the door. They don't both fit in the same room. The girls at the juke had finally made a selection so over the strains of "Pink Poodle" by Sam Butera and the Witnesses, Crow, Frank, and I met by the door. His work associates split but Crow remained, reticent yet capable of taking on whatever Frank wanted to dish out. And Francis was loaded for bear.

"Where you going, big guy? You need to get back to the Bat Cave to finalize plans for the next big event?" The detective's voice never rose above his usual discreet conversational tones but the import of his delivery changed dramatically.

Crow slid on his aviator glasses. "Detective."

"You remember the last conversation we had? Remember how that went? Be a shame for that to happen again, don't you think? No gangs in this neighborhood. Not this neighborhood. If you and your sorority sisters insist on killing each other, and by all means, I don't want to discourage that, you need to do it somewhere else. You need to take it a couple of towns over. Out of Berle and past Wilmore."

Crow bent his head to look at me. "Take care, JP. We'll catch you later." He started out but Frank wrapped a paw around the kingpin's generous bicep to finish his thought.

"It's adorable how you like to ignore me. You go ahead. Ignore me. But I promise you that = when you so much as jaywalk I'll be there. When you blow your nose on the sidewalk, I'll be there. And if you don't flush and wash your hands after every single piss, I'm the one who's going to be there, pal, reminding you."

Crow maintained an indifference throughout these threats that was not making Frank happy, at all.

"Thanks, detective. It's comforting to know you'll always be there for me. Now, may I leave, or do you want to kiss me goodbye?"

Frank let go of Crow's arm.

"Yeah, I can be very devoted. Just remember that's how it's gonna be until you move your little gypsy caravan elsewhere."

Crow gave with a toothy grin as he reached for the door handle looking back in my direction. "Girl, you ought to consider who you're spending your time with. You *can* refuse service, you know. I'm gonna get you one of those signs."

Crow's laughter was conservative but audible and Frank looked like his head was going to pop off the end of his neck.

"Yeah, don't let the door hit you in the ass, pal. See you real soon." He put his hands on his hips and shook his head in disgust. "I'm sorry you had to hear that, Julie. He's around here too much. You shouldn't cater to that crowd. It's no good. Not good for your reputation. Is he bullying you in any way? You can tell me. I'll take care of it."

"Frank, you need…an Advil. Let me get you a couple of Advil."

I got him to a table and into a chair then sat down next to him.

"I'm fine. I can't stay. I just wanted to check in on you."

"Coffee?"

"Sure. Okay. That would be nice. This is a nice place, Julie. You shouldn't cater to that crowd."

Joanne was filling salt and pepper shakers next to the malt machine. I interrupted her meditation.

"Jo, could you get a coffee and heat up a Danish for Detective DiAngelo?"

"Oh, that would be nice. Thanks. Are the Danish fresh?"

"No, but I hear the Finns can get real frisky."

"That's not funny."

"It's almost funny. You are in a shitty mood, Frank. Honestly, you're way too uptight lately. You're going to have to pull that big stick out of your ass. It's going to cause an infection."

"Why do you talk like that? Nobody wants to hear you talk like that."

"Frank, the thing is we've got real trouble here, real trouble that deserves your undivided attention. I know you've got a personal thing with Crow but he's not the bad guy."

Joanne served him the coffee and Danish along with a look of concern. "Detective DiAngelo, you don't look well. Are you feeling all right?" She

placed the back of her hand on his forehead, checking for fever.

"I'm fine, Joanne." He gently brought her hand down for her. "Thanks for asking. And thanks for the Danish." He loosened his tie and unbuttoned his collar as Jo went back to her side work, still frowning.

"How do you know he's not the bad guy? Huh? How do you know? These aren't just people who drive over the speed limit, Julie. These good neighbors of yours run drugs and stolen cars and all kinds of colorful things. You think they're above murder?"

"It doesn't add up, Frank. Besides, I have pretty good instincts about people and he just doesn't smell bad to me."

"He doesn't smell bad to you? Did you just say that?"

"Whatever. You know what I mean."

"This isn't *West Side Story* or…or *Guys and Dolls*, Julie. These people are real live criminals who commit real live crimes. You've got to start thinking."

"You know what I'm thinking? I'm thinking you watch too many musicals for a straight boy."

He softened up a bit and attended to his Danish as the joint thinned out. Cecil sauntered over sliding his hands down both shiny lapels as the detective put down the Danish to shake his hand. I started with the introductions but Frank usurped the script.

"Jeez. Cecil Valentine. You know, my mom watches your show all the time. She'll be thrilled I met you."

"The pleasure is mine, detective. Are you taking good care of this fine-looking woman? I do hope so." He massaged my neck as he spoke.

Usually Frank doesn't like to see men handle me. It's purely territorial, not sexual. Paternal, really. And everything Cecil says to anybody sounds like a come-on – because it is. But on this occasion, Frank didn't mind at all, starry-eyed and flushed with delight at the nearness of a real live television celebrity. Frank and his mom watch a lot of TV.

"I am. The whole BPD is. Say, would you mind signing something for me? For my mom. She'd be thrilled." He pulled a napkin from a gypsy and produced a ballpoint pen from his shirt pocket. "Her name's Rosaline."

Right behind Cecil's ready smile was a dose of ambivalence. "Why, certainly, detective."

Frank dropped the pen, which rolled under the table, and both men attempted to retrieve it. When Cecil bent down, a knife fell from his jacket. The retracted blade hid behind a smooth mother-of-pearl handle about four inches long. I froze, Cecil froze, but Frank didn't miss a beat.

"Here, let me get that for you." He handed my duplicitous buddy his shiv along with the pen and the napkin. Cecil signed the napkin and graciously handed it back to Frank while slipping the knife inside a pocket along with the pen. "There you are, detective."

"Call me Frank."

"Why, thank you, Frank. Now, I didn't mean to interrupt you two but I'm going to have to dash. Julie, Nighthawks is perfectly delightful. It's my new favorite bistro. Break a leg with the move and I'll be in touch." He leaned over and kissed my cheek, his pencil mustache brushing across my temple in the process. Then, he shook Frank's hand a second time as he tossed a wink and baby kiss across the room. I thought at first he was winking at one of the girls. Turns out it was Jesus, much to Jesus' chagrin.

"Boy, you know Cecil Valentine. That's nice."

"We're old friends."

"Can he really communicate with the other side? I mean, I think some people do have a gift like that. Is he on the square?"

I couldn't quite wrap my head around the idea that a guy who solves crimes for a living was asking me if I believed in my friend's psychic abilities. It was unnerving. But there was something so childlike in the question that I didn't want to just blow him out of the water.

"I don't know, Frank. I haven't asked him. Everybody has to eat."

"Gee, Mom's going to be over the moon with this. She watches that show all the time."

"Frank, I gotta go. I've got to meet the movers at the storage unit and get the rest of my things out of the Sea Nymph. If you hear anything…"

"I'm on it. Forensics has been dragging its feet but if they come up with anything, you'll know about it. Try not to worry, Julie. I know it's hard but everything's going to be fine."

I got my purse and brand new army surplus peacoat from a hook on the other side of the kitchen door. Carroll was peeling potatoes at the sink.

"Frank need anything out there?"

"No. Jo got him coffee and a roll. He's happy. I've got to go meet the movers, Carroll. Tonight's the first night I'll be completely in upstairs. Isn't that exciting?"

He continued peeling. "You need to watch your p's and q's, Doris."

I pulled down a paper towel to clean my glasses.

"What does that mean?"

He made a vague gesture with the potato peeler. "You just be mindful when you get in here. Is the phone connected?"

"Yeah. Yeah, the phone was turned on this morning." A small shiver ran up my spine. Then, to encourage the both of us, I added, "Hey, I'll be fine, Carroll. This is a 24-hour diner, you know. There's always going to be somebody downstairs if…if I was to ever need anything."

Still peeling, he attempted to shift the mood a little. "Now, you make sure those movers do what you're paying them for today. Those guys always try to screw you out of something. Nothing but a bunch of drunks."

"I will. Thanks. So, do I have you working a double, or is somebody going to relieve you pretty soon?"

"I'm out of here as soon as the Chinaman shows up."

He was referring to Domenic. Dom works nights, usually. Sometimes splits. He's a three-hundred-pound Hawaiian but that doesn't dissuade Carroll from calling him the Chinaman.

"All right, Mr. Sharkey. Catch you on the flip side."

I returned to the dining room in time to see Frank staring longingly at Debbie who was fighting a grin from behind the counter. I understand I have enough on my plate but I worry about these two. I like Debbie. She's not a liar and she's not a phony. But, goddamn, she's as loose as a Goodwill girdle. Of all the broads in the entire world, why would this sweet, uptight lug decide to put his eggs in that basket? Everybody's put their eggs in that basket. On the other hand, she is different around Frank, softer, more controlled. She monitors herself around him. Maybe he looks like something steady she could lean on. Maybe she looks like somebody he could take care of. What do I know? Maybe this is the real thing, a true love, a holy love. And if it isn't love, there is that condom machine in the Men's Room.

I gave them both a wave on my way out into the punishing light of day.

CHAPTER FIVE

Fall was in the air. A crisp, seductive breeze had several discdarded candy wrappers and potato chip bags dancing crazy across the broken concrete. I could smell the ocean amidst fumes from the soybean plant down in the harbor. The late afternoon sun was hinting that if we all played our cards right, it might go down early again that evening. I took out a cigarette and struck a match against the whitewashed brick of the diner.

Tugging my beret in place over disheveled tresses, I headed toward the Cadillac in the back of the joint. As I walked through the same dirt I'd been walking through for over a week, I could still see her blood, blood that was no longer there. Her presence was so strong. Made sense. After all, this is where it happened. This is where she'd been gunned down on her way to…to me. I ran my right hand along the bricks as I walked, wishing they could talk.

The Cad needed a bath. So did I. Maybe after the move I'd get around to driving one of us through the car wash. The guys there love it when I drop by. They don't see '55s very often. I'm infinitely more popular at the car wash than I am in literary circles.

The big, black door squeaked painfully open as I threw my purse on the passenger seat and climbed inside. The AM radio still works like a charm but I didn't turn it on. Newscasters were still rehashing tidbits about the murder, each robotic commentator programmed to give the kid's last moments all the depth and relevance of a pre-recorded Dial-A-Prayer. I couldn't take the chance. So, in self-imposed silence, I turned the ignition over and steered the great beast out of the dirt and into the alley.

One side of the alley faces the Promenade and the other faces the store backs and parking lots of the businesses on Bartelle. Bartelle is one of those funny streets in the city that's half old and half new. It's an uncomfortable thing to see happen. Nothing fits. There's an accountant next to a dentist's office which is next to Felipe's Bridal Boutique. This is followed by the Two Cousins Taco Den, the old Berle Watch Repair, and a Bank of America. They're all dark after 6 p.m., even the Taco Den. If I wanted privacy, I chose the perfect place.

I turned left at the Tuk-U-Inn Motel on the corner of Damien, and headed south, toward the pier.

It's not a long haul from the Promenade to the Pier, maybe five or six miles, and I arrived in front of the Sea Nymph around 3:30. I'd decided on the Sea Nymph as opposed to the Tuk-U-Inn because the latter is primarily reserved for prostitutes and squatters. Not that I have anything against working girls, on the contrary. Rather, out of courtesy, I thought I shouldn't be taking up valuable workspace. They do a whole lot of business for a six-unit facility and it seemed to me the machinery supporting this subterranean commerce was fragile enough.

So, the Sea Nymph had been home for the last few months. Little did I know it catered to half-baked celebrities other than myself. But I wasn't that surprised to find Cecil staying there. If someone had told me he was in town, I could've made the leap that you'd find him at the Sea Nymph, or somewhere similar. It's the kind of place Cecil would be drawn to. We have a lot in common, he and I. I'm not necessarily proud of that. I'm just saying.

The small parking lot nestled in the middle of the courtyard was crowded to capacity when I arrived. Seems a situation over at Van Dyke's Billiards and Pasta was causing the neighborhood concern. There were two cop cars and a paramedic congesting the nearby driveway, so I pulled around back to the ocean side.

The surf rocked rhythmically down below and the boardwalk looked empty, as it usually does on any given Tuesday afternoon. I took a minute to soak up the stillness.

On the beach, a family of four, each with a bucket, was collecting shells and other treasures that the tide had left behind. At the mouth of the pier, a couple of fishermen were gutting the day's catch in a rusted metal sink. Sometimes life is so beautiful it's almost unbearable.

I located my room key and walked toward room #7 located at the far end of the court. It wasn't a bad room. It had taken care of me and the maid had never stolen so much as an aspirin. No mints left on your pillow at the Sea Nymph, but a fine motel, just the same.

I pulled down my suitcases from the shelf in the doorless closet next to the sink and packed. Then I tucked some unused typing paper inside the cover of my Hermes 3000 and snapped the lid in place. This all went in the trunk of the Cadillac including the clothes I'd left on hangers.

With the loading completed, I walked over to the lobby to square up with the desk. The clerk, Hans, was eating marshmallows in front of a small portable TV. It was tuned to a repeat of California Gold, the one where Huell Houser interviews the Del Rubio Triplets, and I didn't want to interrupt him but I had places to go.

"Hans, hey. Sorry to bug you but I'm out of here. What do I owe you?"

He looked momentarily stunned. "Somesing wrong vit da room, Julesy?"

"Oh, no. No, it's been great. But the apartment's ready for me now. I'm moving in over the diner, my diner, the new one on the Promenade."

Bringing both pink satin pumps down off of the file cabinet, he walked over to where I was standing at the counter. He didn't have his bridge in so his jaw hung a little concave over a notable five o'clock shadow. "Oh, Julesy. Ve gonna miss you somesing awful."

"I'll miss you too, Hans. You come see me at the diner, okay? First meal's on me. Will you do that?" I offered up what I thought I owed. I must've been right. He took it.

"Oh, I sure vill. May I bring da missus?"

"Please. I think Sheila will like the place. But you gotta bring your teeth to fully appreciate it."

I grinned and he touched his mouth with the second and third fingers of his right hand. "Oh, Julesy. You is awful!"

"You come by, Hans. I'll look forward to it." I was in the doorframe. "Hey, those shoes are gorgeous."

He yelled through the glass as I climbed inside the Cad. "I got zem half-price at Felipe's! Bye-bye!"

I took off to meet the movers at the storage unit a few blocks away. The oil pumps on Daisy were idle as I passed and while enduring a broken traffic light at 46th, I watched a guy in front of Scott's Tool and Die pull down the heavy corrugated shop door for the night. The movers showed up a cigarette after I did.

"Hi, I'm Julie."

"Hi. How long you think this is going to take?" one of them asked. These titans of industry were ready to call it a day before leaving the van.

"Uh, well just an hour or two, I suppose. I don't have very much in there but I do want you to get it upstairs for me and assemble the bed."

"Wow! You want us to set up a bed?"

"Yeah. That's why I went with you guys; because your boss said you'd assemble the bed."

"Upstairs? Lady, we didn't hear anything about setting up a bed."

No. No, this wouldn't do. I called their boss. We talked. Then I handed the phone over to one of his employees so that he could explain my position to them more clearly than I had. This guerilla tactic of mine garnered great admiration and affection from both movers. Neither of them spoke for the duration of our brief relationship. I ended up moving most everything myself and had to pay them overtime. But they did assemble the goddamn bed.

Because I am anal-retentive, I had marked all the boxes so I would know where everything went. I didn't have much. Between promoting my book and building the diner, I'd been in rented rooms since leaving our house – Felix's house. I took very little when I moved out of the house on Poppy, just my personal things, the typewriter, a radio, a record player, and some records Felix said I could have.

So, in anticipation of my new home, I had purchased what I thought would be needed. There was a box of never-before-used dishes on the never-before-dirtied Spanish tile floor and a second box of brand-new pots and pans. Another contained silverware, a can opener, coffee machine, coffee, paper towels, like that. One was a box deposited in my sparkling white bathroom and several more placed on the unscuffed hardwood floor toward the front of the apartment.

The two stuffed chairs from LeRoy's Furniture fit nicely by the front window and the radio sat on a small incidental table against the wall. The new Ikea dining room set and bookcase looked too empty to seem terribly inviting but were positioned appropriately for future adornments. Everything that was in the car went in the bedroom for the night. Once that was accomplished, I was ready for an inaugural cup of coffee and a smoke in my new, swinging, bachelorette pad.

I hadn't bothered with curtains yet so the large picture window in front stood naked and inviting. I leaned against one side of the cool turquoise frame and sipped steam from a plastic Hello Kitty cup as twilight bathed the city. I stared out onto the Promenade and beyond, watching Berle gradually flicker on, lights twinkling up and down the streets and out across our little portion of the Pacific.

The oil islands situated twenty miles offshore always look so cheerful and inviting from this distance. A tiny slice of a silver moon hung like an exclamation point in the approaching night.

While I stood there bewitched and sedated, the huge owl riveted to the diner lit up, as did the red neon bands that encircle its circumference. That was an interesting first. I pushed the window open and leaned out. The apartment was above him by several feet but this was going to take some getting used to. Each time his great lids close, there's a flash. Each time his great lids open, there's another. It's relentless. Open, close. Open, close. At least it strobes the front room and not the bedroom. The bedroom is at the back, over the alley.

From the bedroom window, the one housing the fire escape, you can only see part of Bartelle and some of V Highway. I decided it would be fine. Besides, I could turn him off manually if I wanted to. The automatic timer was in the apartment over by the kitchen counter. But I knew when we met that he would be the thing that would bring in the crowds, guiding them all the way from Vincent through the dirt to a table. I could get used to the flashing.

I leaned back in and closed the window, walked over to the radio, and flipped it on. My favorite jazz station was coming through loud and clear but the DJ was contributing some particularly tired, watered-down tunes. Lifeless, e.g., without life. I placed my butt in one of the new easy chairs for the first time and sat the cup down next to the flamingo lamp. As the room went red then gray then red again, I thought how the DJ must not have been feeling terribly inspired that evening. It wasn't hard to put myself in his shoes. I hadn't been truly inspired for quite a while.

I have yet to solve the riddle that is inspiration. Sometimes it's a kiss goodnight, sometimes it's rape, but when it hits you, it slaps like an open hand.

As consuming as addiction. Omnipotent. Then, ready or not, your muse evaporates in front of you like a character being transported from the Enterprise and you're left to figure out what you said or did that pissed her off.

It was inspiration that lead to the publishing deal that brought me here. Funny how that went. There I was, a struggling, artistically hungry working stiff burrowing a spoonful at a time to escape my 9 to 5 existence. Then the money and fame showed up and my burning desire to express myself flew right out the window. Well, that's also when Felix and I took a time-out. To be fair, that event might have bruised my creative spirit more than the celebrity that rained down upon me like shard glass confetti.

Felix Mint defined the worth of my life simply by allowing me space in his. The tallest man I've ever known – in every way. He, too, understands what notoriety can do to an artist. The hip elite do not merely take this sax player's calls, they call him. In demand. Hot. But he can balance it. He has a way of modulating the grace notes to whatever pitch he wants. Or at least he used to, when we were together, when I was *his* muse.

But I took care of that by moving out to write a book about Maxine Montego. I just couldn't do it there. Whatever it is I call "artistic integrity" always implodes in his presence. My self-hatred is the only thing greater than his brilliance. And that worked for me until I *did* have a story to tell. Then something had to give. And I will forever feel responsible for pushing him right into the arms of the first woman waiting her turn in the wings. The same woman keeping my medicine cabinet sweetly stocked and my wallet drafty. My pretty psychiatrist, Dr. Marjorie Stewart.

This charming, supple, back-home blonde waited patiently during my stay in St. Mary's, waited for my complete physical recovery, waited until I had the last box out of the Poppy house before she made her big play for my lanky Buddha. Oh, she'd done the homework prior, been the supportive one for him, the concerned friend, but she only brought out the big guns when she knew I was gone. Her ethics intact and dainty hands clean. And it didn't take long at all.

I tried to stay focused on my writing, tried to ignore what was taking place just a few blocks across town. But psychiatrists won't refill your prescriptions unless you go see them. So I saw her. And with every visit, just like the junkie I am, I could never fight the urge to ask about him, and she always graciously complied.

She even added wonderful details now and then. Not in a cruel, gloating way, just matter of fact. I'd think I wanted to know and then I drive away sick to my stomach with the knowledge.

I don't mind scars, which is a good thing because I have quite a few. They remind us of where we've been, that we healed, and that part of us is a little tougher for the experience. But losing Felix left me with an open wound that never toughened up. A blackness that never lifted. And I did it to myself.

Are there ghosts on the Promenade? You bet. They're with me wherever I go.

CHAPTER SIX

I decided to take a shower and go to bed. Not that I was tired necessarily but I was dirty. And if not bed then what, unpack? Bed sounded better. The shower was almost too bright for me to stand in having no mold or scum on it yet. I could've ordered colored tiles but I ordered white. White, white, white. Everything in the bathroom is white. What was I thinking? I dried and threw on my large chenille robe while wrapping a towel around my head. Usually, a shower brings me around a little bit but this one didn't.

I poured another cup of coffee and lit another cigarette bringing them into the white bathroom to pluck my eyebrows under the piercing light. The ashtray balanced precariously on the white porcelain sink. Yes, these walls would soon be brown and all would be well.

Stepping back into the bedroom, I crossed to look out the large side window, the one with the fire escape attached. It's pretty cool having a fire escape, kind of like a terrace without the patio furniture. I opened the window and threw my lotioned legs out onto the metal, bringing the cup and ashtray along. I kept the fire escape retracted but it was there if I needed it. Made me feel a little safer; having two ways out and only one way in.

A thick marine layer rolled in blanketing the darkness. Because the Promenade is predominately flat and barren, the fog loves it here. And it flooded over the long stretch of concrete like something out of a gothic novel as I sipped and sucked. When I could no longer read the billboards on Vincent and the coffee was gone, I crawled back inside.

It took a good ten minutes to locate the blow dryer but the feat was ultimately accomplished and I blew my chin-length mop into its usual unkempt configuration. I turned the coffee pot off and leaned out the front window again, this time to see if I could sense what was going on downstairs. With the window open, I could hear the jukebox blowing greasy licks of "Head Snappin'" by Red Prysock out onto the walkway and up past the Owl. I watched a gal leave and two guys walk in. Seemed business was good.

I turned off the flamingo lamp and with only the aid of the blinking Owl, made my way back to the bedroom and my brand new bed. Squirming out of the robe and into the Amazing Criswell T-shirt reserved for sleep, I pulled down the sheets and crept inside. And there I lay.

I lay there staring at the ceiling and walls that eventually came into view. Something was wrong. Felix should've called. He might not have ever been the most monogamous ape in the zoo but he loved me. On some level, I knew he still loved me. If for no other reason than to alleviate his own need to see that everything was all right, he'd have called. Then I did the scariest thing a woman can do. I reached for the phone and dialed his number. If he answered, if I got the answering machine, or if Dr. Jekyll picked it up, I'd just have to figure it out when I got there. My fingers were trembling and my palm was damp. It rang once, then twice, then three times. No answering machine, no answer. I let it ring fifteen times before giving up. Well, he was never any good with answering machines and he was probably at a gig or in the studio. It was 10:00.

I shot out of bed relieved that I hadn't made a fool of myself and more worried than ever, but I wasn't sure why. As it turns out, pacing is a ridiculous exercise. I didn't want any more coffee. I was too wound up. Fishing for the number of the Capri in the book on the kitchen counter, I called the club hoping to get a hold of Charlotte. She could find him. If she wanted to badly enough, she could find him. I'd just have to relay my concerns more assertively than I had.

"Thank you for calling the Belmont Capri. May I help you?" a sophisticated female voice intoned.

"May I speak to Charlotte Vaughn, please?"

"I'm sorry. Who did you say?"

"Charlotte Vaughn. She's singing there in the lounge. I need to speak to her."

"Oh, Charlotte. Yes. I'm sorry but Charlotte is on stage right now. She's in the middle of a set. May I take a message for you?"

I closed my eyes in momentary defeat. "No. No, that's all right. Thank you." The phone again in its cradle, I stood motionless in my blinking red living room trying to decide what to do. A woman ought to look better than I did if she's going to walk into the Belmont Capri. I was fairly certain they wouldn't let me in wearing just underwear.

Though I couldn't go the college mile to manage stockings and heels, I did put on pants. Remembering I'd tucked a blue sequined shell in the big suitcase, I fished that out, as well. Black flats and a handful of Bakelite bracelets and I was ready to hit the road.

The new army surplus peacoat was going to have to do, as I didn't know where my dress coat was at present. I hit the porch light, locked the door, and made my way downstairs.

Driving Vincent in the fog is no easy task but it's a short haul from the Promenade to Champaign. Once on Champaign, you're driving in from the ocean so the fog thins out in short order. I applied some lipstick with the aid of the clip-on cosmetic mirror on the visor as I turned onto Lyle Avenue. That's where the club is.

The lights on Lyle were inviting. Not that I need an invitation in this town. The Shell Station on the corner had a full complement of cars at each pump, and the old PhilCo Five and Dime was still open after 10:00, and after sixty-five years, I might add. Incandescent bulbs lit the sidewalk in front of the refurbished Atherton Theatre. The Atherton had taken to showing kitschy teen flicks from the '50s and '60s as well as foreign films and indies. There's always a market for an art house, especially if it's the only one.

I passed Captain's Cove, the other club where Charlotte works, while trying to remember where the Capri sat on the boulevard. And there it was, Charlotte's name out front.

I pulled the Cad into the lot and allowed the Valet to take the keys. I could hear my pal singing as I hit the foyer. This posh establishment still offers the nearly obsolete courtesy of a cloakroom but I wasn't in the mood to use it. Stuffing my bulky coat under an arm, I made my way toward the empty hostess station, as they were done serving dinner for the night. To the left was the lounge, and it was respectably full for a Tuesday night.

I stood at the back for a moment and took in the cool that is Charlotte. There she stood; a chubby, powder puff diva in a chartreuse velvet boom-boom gown that draped the floor and cut up past her dimpled knee. Oh, to be more like dear Charlotte. Her hushed version of "Blue Gardenia" had the room mesmerized. I wouldn't even take a seat, as this interpretation deserved undivided attention.

When the boys concluded the outro and the crowd gave up a gratifying round of applause, I furthered myself into the room and over to the polished oak bar. The bartender wanted to know what he could get me.

Liquor has never been my poison and besides I had taken a couple of pills earlier. Then I considered how my nerves were shot to shit and ordered a Manhattan, up.

As he mixed it and Charlotte leaped into a spanky version of "Teach Me Tonight," I glanced across the room to see a man sitting by himself at a deuce against the wall. It looked like he was crying. I took off my glasses and wiped them with a cocktail napkin to determine if I was correct.

Yep, it was Carroll. Having paid for the drink, I gathered my things and walked sideways between tables to make my way over. He wore his thin brown gabardine suit and bolo tie, the same outfit he reserves for weddings and funerals.

"Carroll, hi. What a surprise. I didn't know you ever came out to see Charlotte sing. That's great." He didn't even attempt to hide the tears streaming down his weathered face. "Hey, you okay?"

It seemed I didn't surprise him nearly as much as he surprised me, and he just shook his head as if we were already in the middle of a conversation. He was clearly in his cups. "Oh, Bertha. She slaughters me. Have you ever heard anything so beautiful in your mother-loving life?"

I situated my things in the empty chair to my right and took a drink without comment. This was the sweetest scene I could ever imagine. My Carroll had fallen in love with one of the best women I know, and she with him. I got a little misty myself so I took another drink. I'm not good with touching moments.

The set ended and Charlotte sashayed over smiling and shaking hands as she maneuvered through the cheerful crowd. When she approached the table, Carroll jumped up and started to applaud. She gave him the dirtiest look I've ever seen her give and he stopped on a dime, pulling out the chair next to him for her to sit down, which she did.

"Julie, honey, what are you doing here? I thought you moved today."

Just then, a waitress delivered a Mint Julep to Charlotte saying it was from the gentleman in the tux. She pointed to where he and his party sat. Charlotte nodded in appreciation, finding the straw with her lips. Carroll was not amused.

"Good thing that so-and-so has a tux." He started to rise, as did his volume. "Yes sir, that's gonna look real good in your casket, buddy." Charlotte grabbed his arm and muscled him in place.

"Sugar, I told you, this isn't the Cat's Meow or the Alibi or the Why Not. This is the Belmont Capri, and if you make a scene in here you'll lose your visiting privileges – and I don't mean to the club."

They both melted and leaned their heads together, nose to nose. So, their relationship had taken a turn over the last 24 hours. I missed that memo. And though I was glad to see them so happy, watching it was kind of icky.

I removed the cherry from my Manhattan, took a serious gulp, and gargled with it as the whole point of my visit started to drift away on a sea of whiskey and bitters.

"Julie? Julie, honey, are you okay?"

"Not so much. Could I see you in private for a minute? Sorry, Carroll."

He partially rose and reseated himself, very George Sanders. It was all too absurd. I grabbed my things and we took off toward the foyer for a private moment.

"Charlotte, I need you to find out where Felix is."

She crossed her arms real imperial-like in front of her heaving bosom. "You came out here to talk to me about what we talk about all day at the diner?"

"Look, something's wrong. Don't ask me to explain it but I'm sure something's wrong. You know a lot of the same players he does. Somebody knows where he's working."

Her face went a little softer as she sat us both down on the bench near the door. She crossed her legs and leaned in. You got a reason to think he's in some kind of trouble?"

"I don't know. I know I am. Just ask around, okay? I can't do it myself because I don't want it to look like I'm hunting him down. I called him tonight."

"Oh, my Lord! Did she answer?"

"No. And no answering machine, either. He's probably just working on something that's kept him underground for a while but I won't find the courage to call again and I need to know. It doesn't add up that he hasn't called. Just do this for me, Charlotte, please."

She stood up, as did I. "You got it, sugar. I'll put out the word."

"Promise?"

"I promise. Now go home to your new shiny pad and get some sleep. You've been running on empty for too many days."

"Yeah, nine days. Thanks, Charlotte. Thank you." We hugged.

"Bye-bye. Get some sleep."

On the drive home, I tried to figure out why one Manhattan had me so looped. Letters on the street signs were floating to and fro and I had to swerve to miss the curb twice. Somehow I made it back, parked the car, and got myself up the stairs. Once inside, I perused the fridge for sustenance. That's what it was. I hadn't eaten since the tuna melt. But there was no food in the fridge. I thought about calling Dom to have him bring something upstairs but that seemed lame and I wasn't about to go out again. I foraged around in the box of dry goods and located the saltines and peanut butter. Leaning against the kitchen counter, I ate until I felt some better and retired to the bedroom.

I got my clothes off and slid under the covers. The room was moving around me. I clutched the sheets for balance but to no avail. From behind closed lids, lights were still whooshing by, like I was still driving. Then sleep. My dreams are often fractured and unsettling but this one took the cake.

I was at a bus depot in the middle of the desert sitting on a bench by myself. The place was abandoned and I knew I didn't have a ticket but I sat there anyway. Nothing happened. Seemed like the dream went on for hours.

Then, I thought I woke up. I was in my new bedroom, in my new bed, musing over the desert dream, when I heard something across the room. I sat up. Through the shadows I could make out a form, a human form, moving slowly into the doorframe. I reached for the nightstand and produced a gun, a gun I don't have, and sheepishly asked, "Who's there?" There was no answer but the form continued to move around from just inside the bedroom. I called out again, more energetically this time. "Who's there? What do you want?" As the form began to make its way to the bed, my heart stopped and I tried to shoot but the trigger wouldn't budge. I finally found the courage to grab the light above the drawer where the imaginary gun had been, and flick it on.

She was standing next to my bed, looking down at me with the most beautiful blue eyes I've ever seen, large and clear, just like I remembered them. She wasn't dead. There'd been a mistake. She'd finally found me like she was trying to do that morning. I went to put the gun down but there was nothing in my hands. I motioned for her to sit on the bed but she attempted to shake her head no. I knew that she'd come to tell me something in that dream way you know things that are not articulated. So I waited. It was hard for her to move her head because her throat was ripped apart, mangled and swollen.

She tried twice to speak, her eyes shining peacefully above her dirty cheeks then realized it wasn't going to happen and smiled. She did what she could to move her lips so I could read them, slowly, carefully. She was saying, "Thank you."

I started to ask her what she was thanking me for but before I could, her eyes started to bat and twitch and a different expression came over her, one of concern. I heard a sound coming from the front room, furniture being moved, and I had the gripping realization that we were not alone. When the second form hit the doorway, the girl's face turned ghoulish and twisted into an expression of sheer panic as she spread her arms and protectively dove on top of me.

I woke up for real this time, shaking so hard that I'd managed to push the bed against the wall when it had been a good three inches from it. The sheets were wet. I rolled over, face down on the pillow, and screamed until I went limp.

CHAPTER SEVEN

I lay there until the nightmare faded and I could breathe normally. Then I pulled myself together and got up. Coffee beckoned but not as loudly as the shower. Prepping the pot to brew in my absence, I tugged at the Criswell T-shirt stuck to my sweaty frame. In one fell swoop, it was off of me and in the sink.

As I watched it there in the hot sudsy water I read the caption under a picture of the infamous predictor; a line he spoke at the preface *of Plan 9 from Outer Space*. "Can your mind stand the SHOCKING truth?" The ominous implications almost made me smile.

On the way to the shower the phone rang. I picked it up on instinct, disallowing the answering machine to do what I pay it to do.

"Julie, it's Richard."

"Hey, Richard. Listen, I'm really on a roll with these pages. May I call you back when I'm at a decent stopping point?"

"Have you seen the paper?"

Didn't sound good. "Nnno. No, I haven't."

"Well, you've been busy writing. I understand."

"Don't start with me, Richard. If you've got something to say…"

"The article came out this morning, and I must say they did give you plenty of space."

I felt as naked as I was.

"The kid said the interview went well. He said he was a fan." Silence on the other end. "Richard?" Okay, how bad is it?"

"It's pretty bad."

"Like move to another city bad or there's no such thing as bad press bad?"

"The headline reads, 'Julie Page attempts to summon the past.' Isn't that catchy?"

"What's the spin?"

"He makes comparisons between you rebuilding the diner and your attempt to rebuild your career, and that both were better the first time around. Oh, and there are a couple of quotes here. Here's one, when asked if you feel you've been maligned by the literary community you say, 'I try not to feel much at all.'"

Had I said that out loud?

"He goes on to suggest your flailing bid to recapture some artistic footing isn't completely your fault; that you have been dogged with unfortunate circumstances and that you are a kind of Pagliacci of print."

So the bastard did call me a sad clown.

"But the part the publishing house is enjoying most is this line, 'Her ability to hold a conversation is as limited as her ability to hold her liquor.'"

"That's just bullshit. I don't even drink."

"Maybe if we tell the paper that it's prescription drugs, they'll post a retraction."

I leaned my bare butt on the back of an easy chair and lit a smoke. "Look, pop culture's funny about this sort of thing, Richard. The piece might even garner more interest. Let's not panic."

"I might be more encouraged by that wisdom if you were a rock star. But you're not a rock star, Julie, you're a writer. And your current employer isn't happy about this at all. You're on very, very thin ice."

Drag, blow, flick. "So, what should I do?"

Several seconds passed before he spoke.

"Julie, when you wrote *For the Record* you were so disciplined, so focused. You allowed your gift for storytelling to shine through that entire book."

"And…"

"And that's what I want you to do."

There was an almost inaudible click and I knew he'd said everything he had to say. I stood there pressed against the tweed upholstery, the receiver still at my ear, and thought how that was good advice.

In the shower, I rocked back and forth with my arms raised as if receiving God's healing power while water cascaded over my head and body in a baptism of the flesh, if not the spirit.

Dressing to impress loomed paramount, as I had decided this was a good day to go see Dr. Stewart. No, I didn't have an appointment, but between her guilt and money-lust, I knew she would allow me entry. I opted for a vintage Lilli Ann suit, drop earrings made to look like television sets, a brand new pair of white bobby socks, and my Mary Janes. Once, in an uncommon moment of candor, she suggested I might consider wearing shoes more age-appropriate. Since then, these have been my favorite shoes. Not because of the age insinuation but rather because, on some level, they pissed her off, and that was good enough for me.

Slipping on the Timex and dabbing on the Tabu, I felt prepared to meet my nemesis eye to eye. It had been over two months and though the refills weren't empty, I like to plan ahead. Maybe she'd tell me where he'd been without making me ask. And maybe I can walk in and out of other dimensions just by concentrating.

It was noon and the diner smelled great as I popped into the kitchen from the back door. Jesus was at the grill. "Hey."

"Hey."

"Where's Carroll?"

"He didn't show. Don't worry, I've got it under control. Man, boss, you look hot. Muy caliente! You're not going out like that, are you?"

I unbundled some industrial towels while he complimented me. "Why, yes, I am."

"You better wait until I'm off duty so I can escort you because you could get in trouble looking like that."

"You're sweet."

He put down the two fry baskets he had been shaking and turned toward me, his black eyes twinkling with mischief. "I'm not that sweet."

As this subtle invitation further rouged my cheeks, I virtuously veered the conversation back to the matter at hand. "Has anybody called Carroll?"

He picked up a bag of shrimp and emptied it into a third basket. "I have not. He's no good when he's drunk. Let him sleep it off."

I thought about scolding him for making such an unsubstantiated accusation then decided he was right and let it go.

"Jesus, could you whip me up a couple of eggs and a pancake? I'm starvin', Marvin."

"Si. I'll bring it to you."

I entered the dining room in time for Rhea to hand me the phone. "It's Charlotte, Julie. She's been calling all morning."

"Thanks, Rhea. Charlotte?"

"Julie, honey, I didn't want to call upstairs in case you were still sleeping. Carroll's right here. Now, honey, don't be too mad at him."

"Is he all right?"

"Oh, he's fine. He just gets himself so worked up over the silliest things."

"Okay, listen to me, Charlotte, you tell that old sot that I don't pay him to show up when he feels like it. This is a real live, grown-up job. And if he doesn't want to take care of it, I can sure as hell find somebody who does. Will you tell him that?"

"Did you sleep at all last night?"

"I'm serious, Charlotte. I'm sick of this shit. You tell him I want him in here when he's scheduled to be here. This isn't a fucking volunteer situation. Christ! He makes me so mad."

"…You feel better now?"

"Little bit. Listen, I'm going to see Dr. Stewart today."

"Oh, my Lord. Girlfriend, don't say or do anything you're gonna regret later, you hear me?"

"Yeah, I know. I'm not going to make it a big, drawn-out thing, just find out where he's working these days, real off-the-cuff."

"Well, you be careful. I left a few messages around town last night. He'll turn up. Honey, for all you know he walked through his front door an hour after you called him."

"I know."

"But, Julie…"

"What?"

"You need to not be too disappointed with what you find when you find it."

"I just can't believe he'd be around and not feel any need to check in. It was a murder! If he is around and just doesn't think he ought to check in, well, that...that would help me get over him, I'll tell you that."

"Uh-huh. Are you going to get your prescriptions filled today?"

"I figure as long as I'm there, yeah. Why?"

"Sugar…"

"Charlotte, please."

"All right, just take care of yourself."

"Come on, it's me. I'm fine. I'm always fine."

"Uh-huh. Call me later."

"Bye."

I was sitting at the counter so that's where Jesus put my plate. The butterball on the pancake was melting and the eggs were steaming and the aroma from the coffee smelled like a call from the Governor on my way to the Chair.

Of course, the Chads were behind me talking over each other so furiously you could hardly hear the juke. When they stopped to take in oxygen, one of them spotted my silhouette and hailed me over. "Julie! Julie, come here!"

"I'm eating," I hollered, unprofessional-like. Before I could further prove my point, Doug had plopped himself down next to me with a flyer in his chalky, pink hand.

"Julie, I don't want you to get too excited but I have news."

Between chews, I bit. "What is it, Doug?"

"You thought this day would never come, I know, me too, but it has. It's finally happened. Are you sitting down?"

"What is it, Doug?"

"Guess."

"Don't make me use the butter knife."

"Okay. We got our first gig. We're playing tomorrow night at the Bait Shack. Can you stand it?"

"Well, I very nearly can't stand it. That's great! The Bait Shack, huh? That's 18 and older, right?"

"Oh, yeah, it's very 18 and older."

"Well, rock on, Doug. That's fantastic. How many songs do you get to do?"

"We've only got eight, but I thought if we did the first song again at the end we'd be playing to a different crowd by then and it should work. I don't think anybody will mind. You think that's punk?"

"I think it's ingenious. I'm very proud of you. Are you nervous?"

"Not too much. Hey, stage fright's part of the deal. That's what they say."

"You're going to be great. I can't wait to hear all about it." I swallowed the last of the grease and washed it down with the end of the caffeine. He looked sort of timid all of a sudden. Not at all the Doug I'd grown accustomed to. I swiveled to face him straight on and waited for clarification. He glanced over his shoulder at his cohorts, so I did, too. They were all staring at him, wielding little gestures of encouragement his way.

"We…everybody in the band would love it if you could make it tomorrow night. But we know you're, like, so busy, and you're trying to write that book, and the diner, and the…the other thing. We totally understand if you can't but we wanted to invite you. You're kind of like our mascot. Or, no, more like a touchstone or something."

"I…Oh." My life just wasn't about fun right then, what with trying to write that book, and the diner, and the other thing.

"I swear to God, it's okay if you can't. No pressure. You can come see another show. There'll be lots of other shows."

But I was their mascot.

"I'd love to, Doug. Thank you."

"Are you serious? Are you sure? I mean something could come up between now and tomorrow. You don't have to promise or anything."

"I wouldn't miss it for the world. I'll be there with bells on."

Cocking his head as if he wasn't sure he'd heard me correctly, his expression quickly dissolved to one of appreciation making him look like an old man for a split second, fragile and introspective.

"We won't let you down," he pledged solemnly. Then he turned to the other kids and made with a screeching cowpoke kind of whoop that nearly broke the windows. When he yelled, the other three yelled. A man dove under the table next to theirs and a baby started to cry from a booth by the door. I could've reprimanded him but I didn't want to.

"Okay, here's the flyer. You know where the Bait Shack is, right? Down on third?"

"Yeah."

"Okay, we start at 10:00. There's a $5 cover but we'll have you on the guest list. And remind the guy at the door that you're there to see us because they note those things." He put the flyer on the counter under my purse.

"I'll remember."

I rose and we both walked over to their booth. "Everybody excited?" I asked enthusiastically. Girl Chad bounced up and down, her pigtails swinging gleefully from side to side. Black Chad smiled broadly from above his dyed green soul patch and White Chad grinned slyly, too cool to show teeth.

"So, Julie, you are gonna come? That's awesome! You rock so hard," Black Chad gushed.

"Yeah, Julie, that's most excellent. It's gonna be da bomb. Da Bomb, dog!" White Chad addressed the first half of that opinion to me and the last bit to the entire table. Abbreviated high-fives all around.

"I'm looking forward to it. If I don't see you before, break a leg, okay?"

Girl Chad piped in as I hit the door. "We love you, Julie!"

And that was the greatest moment I'd had in weeks.

CHAPTER EIGHT

I was invigorated by the autumn chill, or maybe by the kids. Something had jump-started my confidence. As I pulled the Cad out onto Vincent, turning right toward Wilmore and the doctor's office, I braced myself to deal with the woman head-on. I knew I was at the precipice of something, an ending or a beginning. I had that feeling you get when you know you're truly ready to let something go or take something on. I suppose it's conviction. Very liberating, conviction. Takes so much of the guesswork out of things.

Vincent was unusually busy for a Wednesday afternoon and the drive unromantic. I passed the small, innocuous sign suspended on a short metal pole that reads "Welcome to Wilmore – A Nice Place to Live." Ironic that the city's slogan is what it is because most of Wilmore isn't zoned for residential use; it's almost all industrial, though a few old neighborhoods remain. A close relative, Wilmore shares Berle's Port and industry. But where we have the oil and machine shops, Wilmore has the big factories and plants: water, electricity, petroleum, and a full complement of Dairy Queens and Winchell's for your dining pleasure. It's also where most of the drag racing takes place. After all, the streets are pretty barren at night, not a lot of foot traffic. However, because of recent police intervention, the draggers relocated across city lines to the unsullied roadways of Berle.

If you make straight through Wilmore past the aqueduct and train tracks, you eventually arrive in Peavemont. That's where the doctor hung her shingle.

The façade of the office (a façade shared by three adjoining medical buildings) is colonial in design. White columns and mock window shutters dress the entire facility with only slight variations between the suites. The parking lot is typically filled with Jaguars, Lexuses, Mercedes, and the like. My vintage Cadillac looks mighty conspicuous when visiting this parking lot, like a toothpaste lid strung in the middle of freshwater pearls. Though my car is in top-notch, cherried-out condition, the other cars stand united in their efforts to belittle and judge. Yes, I need counseling.

The foyer is always a little too frigid and that day was no exception. A woman sat reading a copy of *Psychology Today* under a medium-sized watercolor print of the seashore in a peach-stained wood-veneer frame. The receptionist hung a medium-sized watercolor smile on her peach-stained wood-veneer face and asked me to sign in. Upon completion, I asked if I could use the ladies' room and she granted my request. I went. Back in the foyer, the woman who'd been reading the magazine was gone.

"Excuse me, Mrs.…Mrs. Page?"

"It's Miss. Yes?"

"I don't have you down for an appointment today, Ma'am."

Let me just say something here, and this is an aside for those of you who work in the public, salespeople, like that. If you want a woman to be receptive to whatever you're about to say and you don't know her name, don't call her anything. Nothing pisses me off more than some idiot who's probably no more than three years younger than me calling me ma'am. The only women who should be called ma'am are under seven or over seventy-five. And I'm not even going to get started on the *Mrs.* thing.

"No, I don't have an appointment but I'm hoping Dr. Stewart will see me for a minute or two."

"Well, ma'am, the doctor's planning on leaving when she's finished seeing the patient she's with right now. We discourage walk-ins."

"Call me Julie."

"Right. I can put you down for two Wednesdays from now. How's that? Around 3:00 work for you?"

"Not really. Today is better. Just check with her and see if she can see me for a minute today, would you?"

"She's with a patient, ma'am. I'm not going to interrupt her when she's with a patient."

"Please call me Julie. I'll just wait until she's finished with that patient. Then maybe she'll see me, okay?"

She grew weary of my persistence.

"No ma'am. No, that's not okay. You're not understanding me. You're going to have to make an appointment if you want to see the doctor. Now, may I make an appointment for you?"

I was born weary. Keeping my voice intimate and relaxed, I elucidated.

"Look, you drab little cow, I don't think you're understanding *me*. You need to let the doctor know I'm waiting and you need to stop calling me ma'am or I'm going to need to pull your tired, worthless ass up through this tiny window and discuss it with you further out here."

She slowly dropped her head, placed the pen on the blotter, and spread both hands out in front of her like a gal checking her manicure. With a notable amount of resentment, she rose slowly, pushed in the chair, and repositioned a small bud vase on the desk a hair to the right. She made no eye contact but did walk in the direction of Marjorie's office. I stood poised and tense, wishing life was easier and that I was nicer.

Upon return, she did look at me briefly while repositioning herself at her post. "Doctor will be happy to see you when she's finished with the patient she's with. Please have a seat."

Winning can be such a hollow victory. "Thanks."

I sat in one of the plush leather chairs and flipped absent-mindedly through an issue of *Field and Stream.* The pill I'd taken on the ride over wasn't offering the consolation I sought and an hour can be an insufferably long time. I thought about stepping outside to have a smoke but decided I should guard my position, having fought so hard to gain it.

When the door leading into the office corridor finally opened, I felt a wave of relief that was almost tranquilizing. Then, nervous anticipation took over as Doctor Stewart and her patient came into the waiting room. I remained seated but did nod at the doctor who nodded back acknowledging my presence.

"You consider what we talked about, Virginia, okay?" The woman confirmed that she would. "All right, I'll see you in two weeks. Now go have fun on your vacation. Take care."

With Virginia cleanly out the door, Doctor Stewart told the girl at the desk she could go home and gave me her full attention. "Julie."

I rose. "Thank you for seeing me, Marjorie. I know I didn't have an appointment and I appreciate it."

She guided me to her office and closed the door. "Tanya tells me you're being difficult." She winked and smiled. "I'm sorry she gave you a hard time, Julie, she's new. She was working as a receptionist at a talent agency before this. Please sit down."

Her office is like a little gallery: sculptures, paintings, and European knick-knacks gracing every inch. There's a beige leather couch and two like chairs as well as the high-backed, ergonomically correct one behind her desk.

She never sits at her desk (at least not when I'm there), always opting for one of the other two chairs. This is an attempt, I believe, to create a sense of equality. It breaks down the wall of authority allowing her to *really* listen, and for the patient to *really* share.

Her blonde locks were backlit by sunlight filtered through vertical blinds, and the pale pink jacket of her pantsuit hung open over a diaphanous blouse accentuating her petite, polished exterior to great effect. I considered what I was wearing. All at once, I didn't feel so caliente. I felt like an extra in a community theatre production of "Bye Bye, Birdie."

I'm surprised it's taken you this long to come see me. I read about the murder. Are you okay?"

"I'm trying to be."

"I called to check on you at the number you'd given me but the desk said you hadn't been there for some time."

"Oh, I've been…" Did I want to tell her I'd been staying at the Sea Nymph? "…with a friend." No, apparently not. "They were finishing up my apartment over the diner and I wanted to be closer to it through the process."

"Like you wrote in your book, it's all about the process." She grinned an I'm-such-a-big-fan grin.

"It's true," I chuckled humbly, bowing to the flattery that she knew my work so well.

"What a horrible thing you went through." Her tone quickly shifted to one of sobering concern. "How did that make you feel?"

"The kid being murdered at the front door? Well, it's troubling." I was going to have to do better than that. "You know, it happened right before we opened. Honestly, these last few days have been very hard, Marjorie. I'll admit it. I'm not having an easy time at all."

"Well, I'd be worried about you if you told me differently. Julie, it was a heinous murder. You have every reason to be shaken to your core."

This is always a dance on coals, seeing the good doctor. I have to tell her enough that she continues with the medication and information but, of course, I don't want to tell her anything too personal or revealing. It's a delicate balance. Sometimes I do well, sometimes I talk too much. But like a chicken pecking at a toy piano, I keep on plunking until corn falls through the chute.

"Yeah, I'm all messed up. I'm not sure the medication is working as it should."

"How much are you taking?"

"Well, I haven't taken anything for about a month. I think I lost them in the last move, but they weren't working all that well before that. I'm having a horrible time sleeping since the murder. Maybe you can give me something to help me sleep, something a little stronger than the last prescription."

She gave me a dour look. "Julie, I gave you extra of everything last time you were here. You've got to be more careful."

She scribbled out a refill good for two more bottles of Xanax and handed me the paper. I unclasped my purse and slid it in as if it meant nothing to me at all, as if it were no more important than a receipt from the market. Then she walked over to the cupboard of delights to fish me out some more Valium. She always wrote a prescription for the Xanax but just gave me the Valium from her personal stash, buddy to buddy, so as to not red flag the insurance people.

"Marjorie, I am sorry. I've lost so many things over the last year what with all the moving around. I was too embarrassed to tell you. But now I did need some help."

She came back with three small bottles of Valium (five milligrams instead of two) and handed them to me.

"This is older stuff but it should still work for you. I'm in the process of cleaning out this cupboard for some new shipments. Julie, I want you to keep one bottle in your purse, one in your bathroom, and maybe one somewhere in the diner where no one else can get to it. And don't lose them! If you don't start monitoring yourself, the anxiety attacks are going to come back. Have you had any lately?"

"No, I've done pretty well, considering." I threw the pills in my purse without questioning her generosity. "I'm going to be fine. I'm just having a little trouble sleeping."

"I think you should talk about how you're feeling, Julie. It sounds like you're not addressing your feelings about the murder at all yet."

Crossing her legs, her Jimmy Choo's were now in a direct face-off with my Mary Janes.

"It was horrible, Marjorie. She was just a kid. I've never seen anything so awful."

"Are you feeling guilty? Responsible in any way?"

"Maybe, yeah. She was trying to get in. I wasn't there."

"But you know that you, of course, aren't responsible at all. There was nothing you could've done. The fact that it took place at your diner was purely coincidental."

As soon as I started thinking about the murder I found myself answering her honestly, despite myself.

"Yeah. But it's like she's still trying to get in."

She leaned forward in her chair. "How do you mean?"

"I can't stop thinking about her; about it. I had this wild dream the other night."

"Good. Dreams can be very telling. What did you dream?"

Just on the offhand chance that she was good for something other than pills and Felix updates, I gave her a try.

"She was trying to thank me for something."

"Wow. What do you think she wanted to thank you for?"

"I don't know. I can't imagine. And there was someone else in the dream."

"And who was that?"

"I woke up before I saw who it was, but I know it was the murderer."

"How do you know that?"

"Because the kid's eyes told me so. Isn't that crazy?"

"No, it's not crazy. It's normal that you would be trying to process what happened; that your subconscious is attempting to work out the details. What were your emotions during the dream? Were you scared? Calm? Detached?"

"I was really happy to see her. But then we heard someone in the front room and I felt as scared as she looked."

"Where did it take place?"

"In my new apartment over the diner."

"You feel violated by the murder. Something has come in that has threatened the sanctuary you've built for yourself."

"I suppose so."

She sat looking at me like I was supposed to say something else. I had nothing.

"Haven't the police come up with anything?"

"No. No motive, no name, nothing. Detective DiAngelo is working overtime on it. He'll come up with the solution. I just have to be patient."

"You just said the detective would come up with the solution. That's an odd way to put it. Most people would've said he'll come up with the answer, but you said solution. What did you mean by that?"

"Gee, I don't know. You tell me."

"Well, instead of just wanting him to find the murderer or murderers, you may be hoping somebody will be able to make this whole thing go away; to relieve your guilt and insecurities instead of just to solve the murder. Does that sound right?"

"I don't know. Sure."

"Wait...Detective DiAngelo. I remember Detective DiAngelo. He helped you out of that other situation, didn't he? A little over a year ago when you were in the hospital?"

My composure was on the decline. “Yes.”

“Good to have friends in high places. And, as I recall, he’s not a bad-looking fella.”

I already had the pills. It was time for us to discuss the other subject I’d popped in for.

“You do have an eye for the fellas, don’t you, Marjorie?”

Her lips parted but instead of speaking she clamped them back together and crossed her legs in the opposite direction. This feeble attempt at girl talk had gone terribly awry and the conversation shifted irreversibly. Nevertheless, she tried to rein things back in.

“I guess what I’m getting at is have you gone out at all since I saw you last? As of two months ago, you hadn’t since…since…”

“Since Felix left me for you. No, I’ve been busy.”

“Julie, it’s been over a year.”

“Thirteen months.”

“You should try. You get so fixated on things and this murder can’t be an exception. You should go out, have some fun, get your mind off of it. As your doctor, I’m advising it.” She smiled. “Probably doesn’t seem like very professional advice but I’m serious.”

“Get my mind off of the murder or Felix?”

She folded her arms and lifted her chin to the sky.

“I don’t know what to say to you anymore about that. I don’t. We’ve been over it and over it.”

“Was he surprised to hear about the murder?”

Shaking her head and throwing her little arms up, she rose. There’s a small refrigerator built into a wall-length bookcase to one side of her office, out of which she pulled a bottle of Aquafina. She offered me one, as well. I declined. I watched as the doctor bought a little time while considering what she would and would not discuss.

“Julie, I’ve tried to be supportive of you. I’ve given you the very best of my expertise since taking you on as my client. And I think we've made some good progress. I do. But talking about Felix every time you come in just isn't healthy. What can I do to help you get over that chapter of your life? You're going to have to tell me because I've run out of thoughts on the subject."

"I'm sorry, Marjorie. I haven't meant to make you uncomfortable."

This was a new tack on her part, the I-can't-do-this-anymore angle. I deduced I should step carefully through this unswept minefield.

"I guess I don't really have a sense of closure about it. The connection between the three of us, well, that's been a difficult dynamic for me to deal with, having to see his girlfriend every time I need – emotional reassurance."

Pecking, pecking.

She rushed over to the couch and gestured for me to join her. Reluctantly, I did.

"Julie, I'm the one who's sorry. I should have never thought this situation could work. Of course, seeing his girlfriend every time you need advice has made the transition more difficult." And there was the corn.

This is how the game is played: I say "his girlfriend" and if she repeats back "his girlfriend" then that means she is still "his girlfriend." A piece of valuable info had been gathered.

"Look, Marjorie, I am over it. It's ancient history. But every once in a while I just want to hear that he's well and happy."

She was looking at me like I was a Downs Syndrome baby. I let her look at me like that for a few seconds. Then, "I haven't seen him in any music magazines lately and he's not in any of the club listings I've noticed. So, is he, Marjorie? Is he doing well?"

Her hands were to either side of her knees. "I certainly hope so, Julie. He's been on the road for the last month and a half. He won't be home for another four weeks or so."

"On tour?"

"Asia. It's not his usual band either. He's traveling with, with, I can't think of the man's name. I'd never heard of him before. Felix was very excited about going, though. You know, he loves to travel."

I happen to know he hates to travel. "That's great. He must be having a ball."

She considered her next question carefully. "Do you want me to tell him anything when he calls? Do you want me to tell him about what happened on the Promenade?"

That was nice of her. She was being so fucking nice.

"No. No, that's okay. Why drag a rain cloud over his good time? Thanks anyway."

"You're welcome."

I got up and straightened out the Lilli Ann, glad to know he knew nothing of the murder but angry that I'd once again stooped to conquer. As I walked toward her door, I offered some salient advice.

"You ought to keep him on a shorter leash, Marjorie. He might possess the allegiance of a dog but he's as faithful as a politician."

No reason she shouldn't be worried. We stood at her office door eye to eye.

"He's faithful to me, Julie. That's all behind him now."

"How can you be so sure?"

"Julie, I'm a psychiatrist. I can read people pretty well. What he and I have is something special. Not like… He doesn't feel the need to… He's changed, that's all."

This gal could slap me fifteen different ways, and did. I smiled broadly.

"Oh, Marge, be careful. You're sounding like a fool in love."

"I don't think so, Julie." The sincerity in her face made me want to puke. "Besides…" She started to tell me something then swallowed her words.

"No, go on. It's all right. We're both grownups."

"Okay." Her voice got softer and gentler as she reached into my chest and yanked out my heart.

"Before he left, he and I decided to try and get pregnant, and now I am. I'm pregnant."

> She couldn't contain her joy, beaming ear to ear and cradling her womb. "He doesn't know it yet but he's going to be a daddy. I should be starting to show by the time he gets home. Julie, please be happy for him. He's matured so much over the last several months. And he's going to make a wonderful father, don't you think?"

My knees buckled and I grabbed the wall for balance, retracting my hand quickly so as to not seem affected by this furtive attack on my psyche. She dialed back the happiness a little and moved in close for some fortune cookie advice.

"Julie, you have a new diner, you're working on a new book, and you have a new home. You've got everything in front of you, a brand new beginning. Seize the opportunity. You're a wonderful person. Make a wonderful new life for yourself."

All I could do was stare blankly into her sun-kissed face; into the abyss; into the black hole that was my future without him. No, she was not worth my tears. It was time to go.

CHAPTER NINE

The next thing I remember is being in the Cad driving back through Peavemont. By the time I entered Wilmore, it was 5:00 or so and the sky began to dim with factory smoke and early twilight. I pulled into the Tommy's Fat Burger #3 just to stop driving. My eyes were black with wet mascara and swollen from the cathartic cry I'd allowed myself once out of her queendom. A malt sounded good.

I walked up to the pass-out window and made my request. The young employee seemed concerned with my appearance yet reluctant to pry. Back in the great beast, I brought out one of the bottles of Valium the good doctor had provided. I placed two pills under my tongue and knocked them back with the thick vanilla elixir before remembering that these were five milligrams instead of two. Oops. Climbing back out of the car, I did what I had done on a couple of other similar occasions, sticking a finger down my throat far enough to hopefully extricate the drugs. I could see one of them in the bile and ice cream spewed on the asphalt and perhaps part of another. I couldn't be sure.

The young employee watched from the safe side of the counter. Again, I mounted the front seat, this time turning the key and finding the road.

Between Wilmore and Berle there's one of those new drive-through pharmacies that are all the rage, and that's where I'd gotten my prescriptions filled since they opened. The mascara was blinding me and by the look on the employee's face back at the Fat Burger, I knew I was no longer fresh. But I wanted those pills. A drive-through was the perfect solution.

I pulled up to the window, gave my pertinent information, and handed the girl the sacred paper. She tried the office number, then came back to the window.

"I'm sorry, but the office is closed for the day. Can you swing by tomorrow?"

"No! No, I can't! I have a business to run and I need the prescription tonight! I need to sleep tonight! She must have a number for emergencies. This is an emergency. Get that bitch on the phone and tell her I need them now!"

"Excuse me?" The girl at the window leaned down to better look inside the car. I was geared up to yell more but when she looked at me, she pulled back with the calm of a bank teller who'd just been passed a stick-up note. She punched in some data on her computer screen and then picked up the phone again. Her conversation with the doctor was brief and quiet. She left the window and returned with a bottle of Xanax. I paid.

What low point had become level ground for me now? How bad was this habit of mine?

That brief pang of self-examination was easily defused after only short consideration. After all, I remained functional, lucid, mostly. And I just didn't feel able to take on the challenge of limiting my absorption right then. The chasm it would leave would be vast and I would need to be stabilized, at least in some aspect of my life, to successfully dry out again. I'd been here before. It takes work. Finishing the end of the malt, I entered the Promenade.

I had a burning desire to call Charlotte, tell her to call off the dogs, tell her we should start knitting booties, but seeing Cecil sitting at my booth in the corner quelled that instinct. I'd call her later when we could talk.

"Hello, my brother."

"Well, hello, little sister. My my. You are looking a bit wrung out."

"Wrung out, strung out, and hung out to dry."

"Yes, sir. That sums it up. Why don't you take a load off, Fanny, and tell Uncle Cecil all about it?"

Was Cecil my first choice as a confidant? Hey, he was there.

"Yeah. Okay. Let me go freshen up first."

"You do that." He fingered the handle of his coffee cup methodically.

I hit the Ladies' Room and nearly squealed in horror at the ghastly sight reflected back at me. My powder puff proved to be an insufficient tool. I hurried back out into the diner, threw my purse next to my worldly guest then darted into the kitchen to grab a shop towel. Jesus was coming out of the walk-in freezer and Jesse stood at the grill. "Hey, Jesse. You helping cover for Carroll?"

"Yeah. It's cool. I need the money. You okay?"

"Couldn't be better. Hey, Jesus."

"Que pasa?"

"I'm, I'm just gonna go wash my face. I've had a rough day."

"Ay! Who did that to you?" He tilted my melon with his icy hand, examining the damage. "Shit, I thought you got beat up for real."

"A verbal beating. I think there might be some internal bleeding."

"You threw up, too. You got throw up on your little outfit."

"Oh, no, that's, that's malt. Calmante, muchacho. I'm A.O.K."

He picked up the 4" deep stainless steel bin filled with turkey patties and started back to his business. "I'm leaving in a few minutes. You want me to do anything for you, boss?" He had fire in his black diamond eyes.

"No, I'm good. Thanks for working overtime."

I had one hand on the swinging door and he had one hand on my shoulder, keeping me from a clean get-away.

On the Q.T., he rephrased the question. "I'd like to beat the shit out of whoever made you look like that. You want me to beat the shit out of anybody, boss?"

I was touched to know that he would beat the shit out of Doctor Stewart whenever I finally weakened and asked. "That's okay, Jesus. I can handle it."

I didn't even look at Cecil as I swooshed past on my way to the bathroom. There, I let the water run forever until it finally got hot, held the towel under the faucet, then under the push-dispenser of soap, then onto my distended face. When I was sure I had all the makeup off, I ran the water cold, dipping the other end of the rag through and applying it to my eyes trying to bring the sockets back into some semblance of shape and order. Finally, I splurged for a little more soap to scrub the vomit off of my vintage wool collar.

There were only a couple of downs in the diner, no dinner crowd to speak of, as I crawled into the booth next to my fancy company.

"Why, there you are, darlin'. Now, that is some better. Yes, indeed."

"Yep. I'm back in the saddle, daddy-o. Have you eaten?" My stomach was still sore but for whatever reason, food sounded like the remedy.

"I'm always willing."

Jasmine and Joanne had split the floor and because neither was occupied presently, they both came over to the table in tandem. "Jasmine, sweetheart, this is my table," Jo calmly explained. Jasmine retracted her bid and slunk over to the juke.

"These kids think I'm just working for fun. What can I get you two?" Taking in my "before the make-over" appearance, she added, "Julie, are you all right?"

"Hey, Jo. Yeah, I'm fine. I'd like a turkey Ruben and my friend here would like…what would you like, my friend?"

"I haven't looked at a menu."

"It's a diner. With that said, what would you like?"

"That sort of existentialism could dramatically reduce a business' printing costs. Very forward thinking, Ms. Page. I'll have a burger and fries. And do hold the onions, precious. You never know, I might get lucky tonight."

He winked at Jo, which both embarrassed and amused her.

"Well, you look some better but your voice lacks its usual bravado."

"Felix is going to be a dad."

"Better him than me. Do I know Felix?"

"No. You don't. He's my…my..." Tears resurfaced from some tear reserve I didn't know I had. Cecil put his arm around me without saying another word. I stopped crying soon enough but remained silent and sniffly until the food came. He never asked me to explain, and I never did.

Once our bounty lay before us, he squirted on the ketchup, I squirted on the mustard, and something like equilibrium was established. I knew I had to get on with my life. I'd been living with the hope that Felix would come back for way too long. Cecil ate and I tried to while mustering some resolve.

"Julie, my sister, I do marvel at your good taste. This establishment is perfectly delightful in every respect."

"Yeah. Thank God for this place. It's all I've got."

"Now, you didn't simply stumble upon it. No! You didn't buy it from somebody else. You built it. You *designed* it. This glorious arcade is a product of your profound fortitude."

I grinned at his theatrical delivery. "I suppose it is."

"Why, I believe you could build anything you desired to – out of sheer will."

My mood wanted to lift but I couldn't get it to stay up. I needed some spiritual Viagra. "Well, my brother, I'd like to rebuild a few things, that's for sure."

"For instance."

"For instance my crumbling career. Maybe my health."

He pushed his shoulder against mine and whispered, "Isn't it fortunate that everything you wish for is within your grasp?"

"Not everything," I countered.

"Everything worth your time—and tears."

"Yeah, you're right. You are right. It's time for me to start over. Make some fresh mistakes. Bigger mistakes."

He laughed. "Absolutely. You don't realize it but you have a very powerful aura, Julie. There are angels all around you."

"Am I dead?"

"No. But you are in a divine transition."

I ate some of his fries. "Because if I'm already dead, that would take a lot of pressure off."

I was looking to get lost in some frivolous camaraderie and Cecil was the perfect foil. He helped me eat his fries.

"You truly ready for the big sleep, little sister? Wonder what it's like on the other side?"

This sinister snakebite of a question rattled my otherwise road-hard demeanor. But I stayed passive while considering the lily. "No. I'm content to kill myself off a little at a time."

"Be careful what you wish for, as the saying goes."

"You're creepy. And you have ketchup on your mustache."

He dabbed at the thin band of hair across his upper lip. "There's poetry even in your nonchalance."

"Yeah? Well, I'm no novelist. Maybe I'm a poet. I'll be like, *Maybe if I continued things would please me more but now I have no hope and I am tired.*" I snapped my fingers in mock beat applause.

"Who are you channeling?"

"Ginsberg."

He looked off into the distance. "Yes, there he is, smiling upon your efforts from the otherworld."

"Tell him I don't want him hanging out here. He's going to attract the rowdies."

He held a hand to his forehead and closed his eyes, then went back to eating.

"Did you tell him?"

"I told him there's a Denny's on Elm."

"Cecil, do you think there's such a thing as artistic death? I mean, can something die that is, by nature, divine?

"May I have your pickle?" While chewing my pickle he played along. "You can't kill what is divine, but you can be a discourteous host."

"I dig. So, do you think money and celebrity rob an artist of their edge? I mean, can you stay inspired and be well-fed?"

"I don't believe you can. You might have food on your plate but somewhere there's got to be something missing. I think that's what ignites inspiration, don't you? The quest to fill some void?"

"Yes, I do. So where's my inspiration?"

"It's right around the corner, darling Julie. Guaranteed."

"That's a relief. So, it's just you and me here, Mr. Other-world. Tell me the truth. Can you see ghosts?"

He set his napkin on his now empty plate and pushed it away. "Lord, Julie, no, I can't see ghosts. It's a parlor trick. Now, are you disappointed?"

"No, I'm not. I figured that was the case. But you want to know something?"

"What's that?"

"I think I can."

CHAPTER TEN

He bonked the gypsy in front of him with the back of a spoon as a half-assed grin spread across his smooth leather face, a grin broad enough for me to see that gold-capped tooth of his. "You a little creepy your own self, ain'tcha?"

I put down my sandwich. "I swear to God, I can feel her, Cecil. It's like she's still here. I dreamt about her the other night, and man, I don't think it was a dream. She's trying to tell me something."

"Joanne, darlin', could we get some more coffee over here?"

Jo delivered. He produced a black onyx flask from… from somewhere. I watched as he blithely unscrewed the cap, the clear polish on his well-kept nails glinting under diner lights. "May I?"

"Go ahead. I should pass. I might have taken something earlier."

"You're not sure?"

"It's hard to tell sometimes."

"Well, we gonna be sure this time." He hit his cup and then he hit mine. "So, what is it you think that little girl is trying to tell you?"

We both took a swig. "I don't know. I think she's trying to thank me."

"Trying to thank you. Fascinating."

"There is a certain irony to it. It doesn't matter. I'm all fucked up. Hit me again, brother." He did. "Entertain me, Cecil. Do something like when I was staying at your place and you'd do that…what do you call it?"

"A bally? From the sideshow?"

"Yes! Yes! Do that!"

"Oh, my goodness, I don't know, chérie. It's been some time. Is there no better way for me to entertain a pretty thing like you?"

One hand remained wrapped around his cup while the other slid under the table, initially undetected by me until it landed on my knee. I shot him a playful look of mild disgust as if he'd told an off-color joke as I placed my hand over his to remove it politely. But he laced his fingers through mine and held them there.

"Anything you want, darlin'. Anything you want."

He took another sip of the loaded coffee. So did I. My head began to whirl comfortably, all bottle-rocket emotions snuffed out by liquor, pills, and exhaustion. But I could still feel, and therefore wanted him to take my mind further way – across the great divide.

"Go on, brother. Sell me something."

His eyebrows rose and fell back into place twice in quick succession as he brought our joined hands up from under the table then rubbed his lips slowly over my knuckles before releasing them.

"And so, I shall. You know, Julie, darlin', the bally is a very intelligently constructed bit of marketing. It might sound like light entertainment but actually, its framework is formulaic and its boundaries, finite."

"Really? I had no idea."

His hand made a return engagement to my knee. I knew it was there but it didn't seem all that important so long as he kept talking and stayed with me for a while.

"It's broken down into four equally important parts."

A mustached mouth hovered close enough to tickle my cheek as he divulged this trade secret in whispered tones. "You got to build a tip then freeze the tip. Once you've done that, you hit them with the opening, and finally, the jam."

Hot breath and a gin-coated tongue moistened my ear and neck. And though I could still feel, it was something less like pain coursing through my body.

It brought me back to the time I'd spent at his pad all those years ago. Cecil comes on to everybody with the ease and indifference of someone saying hello. He puts it out there. If you're into it, cool. If not, that's cool, too. But when I moved into his brownstone, it was hands-off. He never so much as winked at me. And I appreciated that. He knew I was at his mercy and wasn't going to, in any way, take advantage of it. Besides, that would have diminished the thrill of the chase. He does have a code.

Not until the day I was leaving for Berle did he once again make a bid for my virtue. I had thought about saying yes but didn't. So in a hurry to get home, I chose to keep him in the friend file instead of reappointing him to fuck buddy status. Now, here we were again, and again, a decision had to be made.

I wasn't feeling all that sexy but I was spent and high and with someone I knew, someone who'd proven himself to be a good friend. I remained open to the possibilities.

"Tell me more."

"Building a tip means gathering a crowd. Lots of ways to do it. I always used the dollar ruse."

His hand slid lightly up my thigh like he was straightening wrinkles out of a tablecloth. "What's…what's the dollar ruse?"

"Oh, I'm gonna show you. Yes, I will."

Shifting position, he exchanged the hand that was on my thigh for the other, placing the free arm around my waist, and crossed his legs in my direction.

"Next, you got to freeze the tip. That's carny for get them packed in real tight."

He pulled me to him with one hard tug and held me there for a moment, lips to lips. I did try to retract but he had a firm grip on things. Maybe it sounds cheap but I was digging it. What he lacks in GQ looks he makes up for in technique.

Then he loosened his hold a little and got that other hand up and in my drawers so fast I didn't even have time to argue as my jaw fell slack in amazement. His palm molded to my body, cupping mon petite juju like a skilled artisan spinning a terracotta bowl.

"This is where you show them part of something but you don't finish it, so they want to come inside."

Because no one had ever done that to me, I didn't see it coming. Between the casualness in which he got up there and the sensations playing over my belly, I was locked in admiration.

"Oh, my God. You didn't just do that," I murmured.

"Next is the opening."

The artist's fingers gently worked the clay as my breathing became irregular and small sighs escaped into the turquoise tuck-and-roll of the booth.

"Now you've got their attention so you can tell them all about how great the big show's going to be once they get on the inside."

"Cecil, stop."

"Then comes the jam."

He entered me with precision and a great deal of expertise, as one skilled digit spoke more eloquently than his words.

"You drop the price for a limited time, for the next three minutes, something like that, convincing the marks that they've got to act fast before they miss a golden opportunity. In other professions, they call it 'closing the deal.'"

"Okay," I heard myself gasp. "Right now, or I'll change my mind."

He was out of the booth and buttoning his checkered jacket before I finished the sentence. In a dazed flurry, I fished out a ten and tucked it under my plate for Jo, then joined him in front of the booth. "You got a condom?" I queried quietly.

"Honey, I own stock in the company." Then he turned to Joanne. "Jo, darlin', thanks for taking such good care of us."

Jo seemed unable to look either of us in the face but muttered that we were welcome. He was holding the door for me.

I grabbed his arm, whispering, "I mean do you have one on you."

Fixing me with a quizzical expression, he jibed, "Not yet."

When the fresh air hit me, I began to rethink what I had just said yes to. I

attempted to renegotiate, throwing out weak objections like, "Cecil, maybe we should talk about this," and "I'm not sure I'm ready."

But the barker drowned each protest with a booming side-show voice quite unlike his own as he practically carried me through the dirt lot, around the building, and up the stairs to my apartment. "Step right up! Step right up! Gonna be a big show under the Big Top tonight!"

I used to love to hear him do his bally in front of the tent on Coney Island. And I found myself loving it again. So, while I'm spitting out these feigned misgivings, I'm laughing. And that gave him all the assurance he needed to proceed. I could only let him in.

The front room blinked red in time with the Owl God that lit it. "Nice touch," he chuckled, as I locked the front door behind us. Once inside, he backed me up against the front room wall, pinning my arms above my head, and purred, "Oh, precious girl, oh, little baby, there are so many things I want to do to you. Yes, indeed." His lips and tongue were making it very difficult to get a word in but I managed.

"Cecil, seriously, wait." He let go of my arms, wrapping his around my waist. "I don't think I can do this. I haven't been with anybody since..."

He gently squeezed my hips, waiting to speak until he'd calculated his next move.

"...Since you were with the father-to-be? Julie, honey, let me help you get over that. Let me help you move on. It's time. It's time."

I could feel his demanding cock pressing against my wool skirt and thought how, even though the offer to help me was mercenary, ultimately, he was right. And it would feel good. And Felix was going to be a dad. I stepped back and started to unbutton my jacket.

"Julie, darlin', what say we move the party into the bedroom?" Upon determining where it was, he held out his hand and waited. "Now you're gonna need to invite me in. Only with an invitation."

I took his extended hand and brought him to my new bed. Did I want to turn back? Should I? Well, I'm not that kind of girl.

Naked, I started remembering that bally he barked all those years ago. It used to kind of turn me on. I don't know why, the rhythm, the sheer magnitude, his commanding presence making it clear who was in control six shows a day, seven days a week. And now he was on top of me. And I could see the tent. And I could smell the popcorn. And I could hear Monsieur Valente as I stood transfixed somewhere deep within the captivated crowd.

"We're going to do a little pre-show on the outside here, give you a taste of what it's all about on the inside. Let's bring out the sword-swallower, the human blockhead, the fire-eater, and that little lady with that giant snake while I get things started. Look at this dollar. Watch the dollar. It's fun with money but it's not funny money. You can tell it's real by the smell of it. Young woman, step right up here. Can you smell it? Can you smell the mint? Know what kind of mint that is? That's govern-mint. Now watch the maestro. Watch what I'm going to do. I'm going to wrap it once, wrap it twice. I don't know if you folks in the back can see this so everybody move in nice and close. That's it. Now I'm going to give this dollar a pull. That tiny twist is the most important part of it. Watch the maestro. This is something that was taught to me by a master magician. In fact, he's one of the ten acts and attractions we've got live on the inside. Watch the dollar. Come in nice and close and I'll show you what it's all about. See this little end here? Nice and tight. Now the reason that little twist is so important is because that means nothing goes in and nothing goes out. So if anything's going to happen it's going to happen right there. And to make things more interesting, I'm going to put it right here and I'm not going to touch it again. It takes a moment for this to work so I'll tell you what I'm going to do. I'm going to enlighten you about the big show we've got live on the inside. This is the world's greatest gathering of human curiosities, commonly known as the sideshow. You can't truly say you've been to Coney Island until you see the big show. I can tell you about each and every act and attraction on the bill. The master magician will amaze and amuse and confound and confuse you. Lately, his best trick is walking down the street and turning into a bar but that's another story. Also on the inside, you'll see the sword-swallower. Watch as he slips two feet of steel down his gullet from the tip of his lips to the bottom of his belly. The fire-eater will sit down to a meal of flame and brimstone. Why, he practically makes an ash of himself each and every performance. You'll enjoy the high-voltage lady, Madame Electra, as she's strapped into a real electric chair. Volts will be shot through her system and electricity will shoot from her fingertips as she lights bulbs with her bare hands. It's positively shocking. And there's more. Bathsheeba will enchant you with a giant Balinese Python with which she will be performing the Dance of Death. You won't find one in a zoo but on the inside, we've got two. Lady, do you like snakes? Of course, you do, look at the guy you're with. Joking, my good man. We're here to have fun. And speaking of fun, you'll have plenty on the inside with Two-ton Tessy from Tuscaloosa. Five hundred and fifty-three pounds of feminine fun. She's so big she was born on March 10th, 11th, and 12th, that's how big she is. And she, too, is going to do a little dance. And when she does that dance, she gonna shake it like a bowl of grandma's jelly. And you know that it's jelly 'cause jam don't shake like that. It's an act that will put a smile on your face or there's something wrong with your smiling apparatus. In that I truly want you to see all ten big acts and attractions, I'm going to do something. See the sign that says three dollars for adults, two dollars for kids? Forget about it. Because right over there, the ticket taker is going to put away those three-dollar tickets, he's going to put away those two-dollar tickets, and he's going to put them in retirement for three full minutes. And while those three minutes tick away, he's willing to let every man, woman, boy, and girl, he's going to let you all in for a dollar. One dollar gets you on the inside but you gotta do it now. Start the timer! Now's the time to do it. Take a dollar out of your pocket. Get a ticket from the man. It's wild, wonderful, and one of a kind. You've got to see it to believe it. Once seen, never forgotten. Get your ticket and come inside our air-cooled, comfortable theatre of curiosities and see the show that put Coney Island on the map. You've heard about it. Now, you've got to see it. Don't go get yourself a hot dog. Don't go get yourself some cotton candy. If you want to take advantage of the dollar deal, the dollar steal, you've gotta do it now. One dollar, one dollar, one dollar, I don't want to holler. Folks, it's only a dollar. Now, I've got to make my way to the inside and start the show. And when I start the show it's goodbye to this good buy so do yourself a favor and take a dollar out of your pocket. There's no better buy or bargain on Coney Island. Hurry, hurry, hurry! *It's show time!*"

CHAPTER ELEVEN

The basics were accomplished effectively enough. And it felt good. I may have been rusty but Cecil was well-oiled. It's true what they say; it comes right back to you, like riding a bike. And when it was over, he slapped me on the ass and made for the shower.

Lying there, I flashed on the day I discovered, early in my relationship with Felix, that he had been with other women. And how it got some easier to live with over time, once I determined they were nothing more than stage whores and celebrity suckers, and by the time his pants were zipped he'd forgotten their names. It's just sex. Sometimes, it is just sex.

Hiding in my big robe, perched on the side of the bed, I sat staring at the floor when my houseguest reappeared. While he preened, we chatted.

"This is a nice place, sister. You've done well for yourself."

"It is a nice place. I haven't even sat in all the furniture yet."

"One day at a time. Relish the process. Fresh environment, fresh start. Yes, ma'am, I'm in love with fresh starts."

We talked about him giving up the brownstone in New York, about playing the long shot that he could parlay his particular talents into this "in vogue" cable idea, and how those dice had, indeed, rolled seven on the come-out. And we talked about what a freakish turn of events found us at the Sea Nymph simultaneously after so many years. By then, he not only had his tie knotted but his tasteful pompadour set nicely, as well.

At the front door, he kissed my cheek. “Well, Julie Page, you certainly make a bad boy work for his supper.”

“Sorry. I have a way of making everything harder than it needs to be.”

“Yes, ma’am. Plenty hard.” He winked while adjusting his cufflinks and stepping onto the stairwell. “Now that we’ve established the dance, next time maybe we’ll lower the bar a little, see how we do. Explore some other avenues toward our mutual fulfillment.”

“Next time?”

“Oh, there’s a whole world of discovery waiting for you out there, precious. Next time we’ll try our hand at something more exotic. How’s that?”

“Hey, Cecil, remember in the bally you used to do, you had that whole bit about the dollar? You set it up at the beginning but you never come back to it. How come?”

He seemed confused but flattered by the question. “Well, honey, the barker doesn’t have to. He’s already directed the marks’ attention somewhere else. They forget all about it.”

“I didn’t.”

He was at the bottom of the landing heading off through the pitch-black lot. “No, you didn’t. And I’ve made a note of it. Sweet dreams.”

I locked myself in for the night. Stepping carefully into my still slippery bathroom, I placed the stopper in the drain and turned the hot water on full blast. The towel Cecil had used was draped over the shower railing so I removed it and threw it in the hamper by the bedroom closet. It took a second for me to remember where the other towels were. When I located the box, I drug it to the door of the bathroom and folded the box flaps back for easy access. I didn’t want to figure out where they should go right then.

While water filled the tub, I wandered over to the front window to see if I could assess what kind of business the diner was drawing on this Wednesday night. I leaned out in time to see two fabulous vintage cars drive slowly past the front and turn toward the lot, one T-Bird, one DeSoto. It amused me to think that these same two cars might well have turned into that same lot on that same dirt sixty years ago. You never know. History has a funny way of repeating itself.

The twang of Ned Miller singing "From a Jack to a King" wafted up past the Owl and into my apartment.

I found my glasses and scribbled myself a note to buy a blind or some drapes the next day. Enough with the flashing.

Even over music and running water, the phone startled me when it rang. I did not, however, grab for it as I had when it startled me earlier in the day. This time, I allowed the answering machine to pick up.

"Julie, this is Frank. I was hoping to catch you."

I snatched the receiver out of the cradle before he could continue.

"Frank, hey. What's up? Do you know anything?"

"Julie, I'm sorry to call so late but I'd like you to come into the precinct tonight if you can. I've got something I want to talk to you about."

The running water was starting to concern me. "Frank, hold on for a minute, okay? I've got to turn off the bath water. One sec."

I made a mad dash for the tub, landing there just in time to stop the water from flooding over onto the new white tile. Short trip but I was panting by the time I got back to the call.

"Frank, what is it? Did you arrest somebody?"

"No. No, we haven't arrested anybody yet. Julie, I'd rather talk to you about this in person."

The fact that there had been no arrest was disappointing but something was up. Something crackled in his voice that I had not heard before. Something disturbing.

"Okay. I'm just going to take a bath and throw some clothes on and I'll be right over."

"Maybe you should skip the bath."

My heart contracted then went back to its usual rhythm. I bit hard into a cuticle trying to funnel this newfound energy into some familiar tic. And I became instantly sober, stone cold sober.

"I'm on my way." I didn't wait for any pleasantries that may or may not have followed. I doubt he offered any.

With shaky hands, I threw on some clothes and laced up my All-Stars. Grabbing for the peacoat that rested on the back of an unused dining room chair, I found my keys and made my way down into the dirt and darkness.

There are no lights back there, back where I park the Cad. An exposed bulb hangs over the delivery door on the other side but not at the back. The fog rolling in and around the blackness altered my depth perception in such a way that it almost seemed like there were walls around me instead of a dirt lot and the vast night sky. I had a hell of a time getting the key into the keyhole.

Once inside, I pushed in the lighter and unclasped my purse feeling around for a smoke. My elbow locked the door while the bright orange glow of the lighter made contact with the tip of a cigarette, illuminating the area around the steering wheel for the moment it remained. Popping the wind-wing, I put her in gear. Dust mixed with the heavy air creating low clouds that only the high beams cut through.

It remained touch and go until the streetlights on Vincent brought some clarity to the situation. As I turned onto Bartelle, the filmy fog curtain that hugged the waterfront grew distant in my rearview mirror.

The precinct was across town on 61st and Rose. I had a good ten minutes of drive time ahead of me. The radio static sputtered and scratched as I jostled the knob, finally locating an ambiguous pop station to keep me company. But the music sounded like screams and each passing streetlight burned into me like a long receiving line of judging eyes. What did he know? What did he want? A stoplight at Crescent forced me to hit the brakes.

While the car raced idle, I saw a crippled woman on the corner start to make her way down into the crosswalk. I kept thinking *Don't do it. Don't get in front of the car.* But when the light turned green that's exactly where she was, belligerently forcing me to deal with her problem. Like being stuck at a bad drive-in movie, I sat glaring at her as she took her time with one cane and then the other. As soon as I could swerve around her, I hit the gas and peeled out, nearly hitting a car coming in the opposite direction.

Once the moment passed, once the honking horn of the other car and the angry yells of various passers-by faded behind me, I reevaluated my current state of mind. I could've hit that woman. She wasn't trying to piss me off; she was crippled, for Christ's sake. And I could've hit that guy's car. I'd come dangerously close. What was wrong with me?

I wanted to take something but told myself I could fight the craving a little longer until Frank and I had a chance to talk. I wanted to hear him. I wanted to remember what he had to say.

Turning into the parking lot at the police station, it seemed I'd accomplished something arriving safe if not sound. At the opposite end of the lobby, an officer in uniform sat at the check-in desk. The walk toward her felt like the walk toward the Principal's office when you've been summoned out of class. "Hi, I'm here to see Detective DiAngelo."

"Your name?"

"Julie Page. He's expecting me."

She got a hold of him right away and said he'd be out in a minute. She also asked if I wanted to sit down but I told her I'd rather stand. Hands stuck deep in both pockets, I brushed a loose hair from my cold face by rubbing my cheek against the stiff wool collar of the coat while staring into a trophy case filled with medals and awards for things I didn't care to read about.

"Julie! Man, you got here fast." Frank was at my shoulder already guiding me back through the lobby and down the long hall to the squad room.

"Really? It felt like hours." I adjusted my frames and tried not to make eye contact with anyone until we finally arrived at his desk. Lots of activity in a squad room, lots of desks, lots of noise. Kind of like a newsroom. I never liked newsrooms.

"Have a seat. Can I get you anything? You want some coffee?"

"Frank, what is this about? What did you find out?" My words were barely civil as I hunkered down in the cane-back chair at the side of his desk.

He saw the stress on my face and dropped his head a little while leaning in.

"Forensics came back with their findings this evening."

"What did they say?"

He searched for words while shuffling his chair at an angle. Legs spread, he folded his big paws, placing both forearms on his thighs. The desk was no longer between us.

"She took a bullet between the shoulder blades before her throat was cut."

"I know that."

"Here's something we didn't know, there were fibers left in the bullet wound. They found a couple of fibers, dark blue fibers, like maybe from a navy peacoat."

My eyes started to blink uncontrollably and my mouth fell open slightly. I could feel tears approaching before I even grasped what he was telling me. Frank placed a hand on mine and when he did, the tears fell easily clouding both lenses.

"Where's your other coat, Julie? When did you get this black one?"

That's why I felt so scared. I was a serious murder suspect now. That's what he was trying to tell me.

"Francis, you know I didn't kill that girl. Jesus Christ. You know I didn't do that. Oh, my fucking God, Frank. What am I going to do?"

"Hey, hey! Watch the language and the volume, okay?" He still had one hand over mine and grabbed my chin with the other as he spoke softly a few inches from my ear. "I know you're scared. Panic isn't going to help you right now. Do you understand me?" I sat motionless but for the whimpering. "Julie." He now had my whole face in his hand, shaking it a little to force a response. "Julie, do you understand me?"

"What do we do?" Gravity and fear brought me back to the moment in an almost mechanical fashion. You get real pragmatic when your ass is on the line.

He released my hand and face, leaning back against his chair.

"Where's your old coat?"

"Frank, that coat had burns all over it, you know that. I should've gotten rid of it when I left the hospital a year and a half ago. I just couldn't part with it. After all, it saved my life."

He took on this ultra grisly expression, half angry, half frustrated.

"Did I ask you for an essay? I don't want you to wax nostalgic about the coat. I want you to tell me where you put it, and when."

All at once, it was like I was in a tunnel, my peripheral vision gone, as the distance between us seemed to elongate. It looked like he was much further away than he was. I closed my eyes and rubbed them from underneath my glasses trying to bring things into perspective. When I reopened them, he was sitting just inches in front of me, patient and intense.

"I threw it out."

"When?"

"Two, maybe three days before the murder."

"Where?"

"In a dumpster. The construction crews were still packing up and there were dumpsters in front of the diner. Most of them were removed before that morning, the morning she was killed. The other two were brought around the back for us to keep."

"When's trash day?"

"I don't even know. I haven't noticed."

The muscles in his face relaxed a little as he nodded, looking off to the side of me.

"Okay. You're gonna need to answer some questions for another policeman tonight. I wanted to talk to you first. He's just gonna ask you the same things I did."

"Frank, are they actually going to arrest me for this?"

He tried to smile. "No. Nobody's getting arrested tonight. You've got no motive. Those fibers don't make you any more of a suspect now than before tonight."

"How do you figure?"

"Julie, me and the fellas have a theory and you're not going to like it. I don't like it either."

"What is it?"

"Those fibers were in the wound. If you're wearing a coat like that and you shoot somebody, it's fairly difficult to get fibers buried in the bullet hole. Now, maybe when the murderer was slitting her throat, maybe then. Closer contact, some kind of struggle. It has to be looked into but it doesn't hold much water. The chances are slim to none. On the other hand, if you were wearing a coat like that and somebody shot you, those fibers could very easily make their way into that hole."

"Help me out, man. My Nancy Drew days are behind me."

He rubbed his big neck and once again leaned toward me.

"I think she was wearing your old coat."

"Like she dug it out of a dumpster?"

"Yeah, street kids do that."

"Okay, she's wearing the coat. What else?"

"Well, up until about two weeks ago, you were wearing that coat, had been for a long time. That coat was pretty identifiably yours. How tall are you, Julie?"

"I'm five-four. Why?"

The look in his eyes made me think he wanted me to fill in the blanks like it would be better if I figured it out myself. The lightning bolt struck hard when it landed and I realized just exactly why I'd been so preoccupied with this whole sordid affair. Because it wasn't supposed to be her at all. It was supposed to be me. And somehow, somewhere in my subconscious I already knew it.

"I'll bet she was about five-four, too. Right, Frank?"

"Yes, Julie, she was."

We were both very still for a minute. Then Frank got up and poured us both some water from the cooler, bringing two paper cups back to the desk.

"You got any enemies that you know of?"

As I thought, I couldn't come up with a prospect.

"Lots of people don't like me but I can't think of anyone who wants me dead. It could've been a random act of violence like we talked about at the time."

"That's starting to seem less likely. Okay, listen to me, I want you to tell the other officer exactly what you told me and then I want you to go home and go to bed. I don't imagine it'll be all that easy to sleep tonight but do your best.

You're going to have to be on your toes and in good shape so you can help us with this. Can you do that?"

"So, where is the coat now?"

"That's the million-dollar question. The killer might have taken it."

"But why?"

"Well, I'm no psychic like your Mr. Valentine but I'm thinking whoever laid open that kid's throat could see it wasn't you. So maybe they took it hoping things would look more random than they were."

"Frank, she had blonde hair, mine's burgundy."

"Yeah but you usually wear a hat outside." I fingered the beret that was rolled up in one of my pockets. "Maybe she was wearing some kind of hat that morning. It was cold, remember?"

"I remember."

He rose then I rose. "Now, I don't want you to talk about this to anybody yet, okay? Not Charlotte, not Carroll, nobody. Got it?"

"I won't."

"Good. By the way, where's that deadbeat ex-boyfriend of yours these days?" They never got along, Frank and Felix.

"He's on tour somewhere in Asia. I haven't seen him in over a year." All the while I'm thinking how much I wish I could talk to Felix and how my promise to Frank would mean nothing if I got that chance.

"Well, don't talk to anybody, okay?"

"Yeah."

He started to lead me across the room then stopped short, taking my shoulder and turning me to face him once again.

"Julie, I'm going to catch whoever did this. Please don't think for a minute that I won't. I will. And when I find the creep, I'm going to take care of it so you don't ever have to worry about it again. I promise you."

His confidence was somehow frightening in its sincerity. We continued walking, eventually landing in front of another desk with another cop sitting at it. "Julie, this is Officer Darnell. He's going to ask you some questions about the coat and then you can go on home, okay?"

"Thanks, Frank."

Officer Darnell was fairly brief and to the point. Not rude, not delightful, just to the point. He suggested they might want to talk to me further and asked that I remain accessible. I said I would.

On my way out of the precinct, I made a pit stop at the bathroom. There was a large frameless mirror screwed to the wall next to the sinks. I stood there looking at myself in this new coat, a coat I'd purchased a couple of weeks ago from the Army Surplus on Grayson. At the time I thought it looked pretty much like the old coat except this one's black and the other one's blue, and this one doesn't have any burn marks on it and the other one does.

Now, as I saw a full-length image of myself in the coat, it didn't look right at all. Almost like it didn't fit. I unbuttoned it on my way back through the lobby to the double glass doors in front.

I took in the night, letting it fill my lungs with thick, wet air. The Cad looked as inviting as one's own bed after a long trip away from home and I climbed inside ready to call the evening complete.

But with every inch that separated me from the police station, as lights fell away and I drove back into the heavy fog that had by then become an integral part of my life, consolation turned to concern. And as I pulled into the dirt lot off of the alley, concern turned to fear. And when I climbed the concrete steps to my front door, fear turned to dread.

Somebody tried to kill me. Somebody wanted me dead. And odds were pretty good that somebody still did.

CHAPTER TWELVE

I turned on every light that wasn't already lit and opted for instant coffee instead of brewed. It was close to midnight. After draining the tub, I refilled it with hot water as the microwave heated a cup in the kitchen.

While drawing this long-overdue bath, I fished out the Valium from my purse, leaving the Xanax in there. Was I about to divvy up the three bottles of Valium between my purse, medicine chest, and diner, as the good doctor had recommended? No, certainly not. But I did need more room in my purse.

Procuring a vitamin bottle from the cupboard, I sat at my new dining room table for the first time. Emptying the three smaller bottles to the left and then the larger vitamin bottle to the right, I switched the stash. Now it appeared I had one prescription and a bottle of vitamins in my handbag. That didn't seem so bad. I placed the Valium bottles full of vitamins in the medicine chest. *So if I ever want a vitamin*, I thought, *there they are*.

I took one of each, a Valium and a vitamin, brought my weak cup of coffee with me to the bathroom, and climbed into the tub. My muscles made every effort to relax.

The washrag felt good against my skin but wasn't quite rugged enough to scrub away the burgeoning truths and deceptions clogging each pore. From the psychiatrist's office to the first sex I'd had in over a year to the supposition that someone wanted me dead, mister, it had been a big day. A day that started with a nightmare. And now here I was again contemplating sleep. Well, I couldn't afford another nightmare, not that night, not when I needed sleep so badly.

Once dried and clothed, I brought one more Valium to the kitchen counter and found a paring knife in the utensil box on the floor. I cut it evenly and easily right down the middle. But while performing this surgery, the first one took hold and profoundly kicked my ass. Yes, five milligrams. Excellent.

I dropped the knife, taking a moment to place both valuable halves on a Corningware saucer before hitting the lights. Once between the sheets, I gratefully allowed a magnificent numbing narcotic vacuum to suck out all remaining thoughts about my life for a few solid hours of zero.

When I finally awoke, sun-drenched the bed like a klieg light from hell, and I had the sense it was deep into the day but couldn't be sure as I had forgotten to wind the Baby Ben. My watch and glasses were right by the clock and I commandeered them both before assessing much else. It was 1:35 p.m.

I stumbled around bandy-legged and empty thinking how I really needed to buy some window coverings. My chest hurt. I lit a cigarette. It took another ten minutes of aimless shuffling before standard grooming rituals took place. Those accomplished, I felt ready for another day of mayhem and fresh complications.

I attempted to unpack that afternoon but continued to be preoccupied with my mortality. So basically this unpacking consisted of opening boxes, removing things, and returning them to the boxes as I just wasn't sure where anything should go. Twice during this unpacking rehearsal, I got a call from the publishing house. On neither occasion did I pick it up. And that's why God made answering machines.

Of course, I had to run into a framed photograph of Felix. I'd tucked it in with a suitcase of loose photos. It was from our only camping trip.

Felix has jammed with everyone from Eric Dolphy to Alicia Keys. His prowess on the sax has been well documented in every music rag from here to, apparently, Asia. But pitching a tent just isn't on his resume. Yet, that summer, he decided that's what we should do. I'm uneasy with the sun and nature, and he just isn't programmed for it, but there we were, big as life and twice as ugly.

In this particular pic, he's wearing goggles in lieu of the sunglasses he forgot at home and an orange floral fishing hat perched atop his crazy black Eraserhead hair while attempting to pitch a tent. The Power Ranger Bermuda shorts he'd chosen for this adventure displayed his ridiculously skinny white legs to full effect. Both long stems were braced a couple of feet apart as he tried to hook a large sheet of canvas onto a pole he'd managed to stick in the ground. There was a trash bag twist-tie around his goatee (because he thought he might need it) and he had both hands wrapped around the canvas, or vice-versa, while still balancing a Camel between his brilliant, elegant fingers.

I had only stopped laughing long enough to snap the picture. We stayed there for two nights, played Monopoly, made s'mores, sang songs, swam, and imitated the extremely loud birds that preceded us to the breakfast table both mornings. It was the best time. I placed the frame back in the suitcase and clasped it shut.

I took a Xanax.

When I found the box with the foodstuffs in it, peanut butter, saltines, etc., those, I took the time to unpack. They were displayed in plain view across the counter for heightened accessibility along with a box of wooden matches and a figurine of a glazed frog playing the banjo. The frog is delicate. I'd put him in with the food so I wouldn't forget where he was.

The garlic-stuffed green olives were difficult to open but I persevered. And the saltines were as rewarding stale as they had been crisp.

While feasting on olives and crackers cross-legged on the floor, I stared at the Hermes 3000 across from me on a small typing table I'd stolen from my last day job.

I'd dragged this typewriter with me everywhere I'd been for over fifteen years. It has sometimes served as a kind of oracle inviting me to communicate through it, other times sending me threatening letters, blank page after blank page. And right then, as I sat on the floor of my new kitchen wiping olive juice from my mouth with the bottom of my shirt, it began to talk to me.

I remained transfixed as it spoke. "Who would want you dead? Who killed that girl? You know the answer. Now that you know it was supposed to be you, you know the answer. What is it?"

I did know the answer, but I couldn't get it to come in clear enough.

Then this wave rushed over me, of destiny or ability or something. I had no intention of writing, not right then. But the typewriter looked, all at once, like the friend I know it is. For the first time in months, I didn't have that horrible feeling of impotence. Scenes and settings, textures and colors started to come into focus.

I stared at the tool that had seen me through a bad book and a best seller and began to feel the Buddhist-like oneness that accompanies a writing binge. And I knew that if I sat down in front of the Hermes 3000 the story would start telling itself now. And it would be her story.

But why? Why in the middle of such a dark chapter in my life would I get the itch to write again? Money and freedom and celebrity hadn't inspired me. Drugs hadn't unlocked any artistic passions, real or imagined.

And then, like getting on the freeway and remembering you left the stove on at home, it hit me. It hit me so hard I felt punch drunk sitting on the floor, my hand still soaking in the olive jar. The answer to the question I'd been asking myself for years finally presented itself in Technicolor clarity. It's desperation. Inspiration comes from desperation. Of course, it's so simple. And right then, I was as desperate as I'd been in a long while. My life was on the line.

Feeling greatly relieved at finally cracking the code that had dogged me my entire adult life, I sealed the saltines, screwed the lid back on the olive jar, and rose from my meditation. I gently placed the frog on the typing table next to my best friend. "Tomorrow, you and me, Hermes. It's a date."

The only thing I took the time to hang was the cat clock, which I positioned in the kitchen. According to him, it was after 5:00. The sun had, indeed, started thinking about going down and I reluctantly started thinking about going out.

It was cozy in my apartment. It was safe. Venturing outside didn't seem inviting considering somebody out there was holding a grudge. Besides, I had an outline to write. Nonetheless, a restaurant was operating without me downstairs. I should check in. And I told the Chads I'd make it to their first show. I'd given them my word.

For the next hour and a half, I contemplated what it would feel like to open the front door. "*Frank could be wrong. He's only guessing,*" I thought attempting to placate the strong inner voice speaking to the contrary.

Continuing to bargain with myself, I considered how Frank thinks Crow is a bad guy and that Cecil can, in fact, communicate with the dead. Frank's not always right in his assessment of things. I had no enemies; at least not the kind who want me dead. I could do this. I could go outside.

The painter pants and All-Stars were just too comfortable to change but I did manage that same blue sequined shell

I'd worn to the Capri. I even went to the trouble to apply some powder and lipstick. After successfully negotiating the clasp on a large charm bracelet, I gave myself a squirt of cologne and threw an extra pack of smokes in my purse while reaching for the peacoat. Wearing it had lost its appeal but my options were limited and it was too cold to go without.

I entered the kitchen of the diner through the back door around a quarter past seven. Though the dinner set was thinning out my crew remained in high gear. Carroll and Jesse busily pulled checks and passed out plates while the girls bustled around professional-like.

"Well, there she is! Doris, we figured you'd won the lottery and caught a plane to Reno!"

"Hey, this isn't your shift, Carroll. What are you doing here?"

I leaned against the prep table. Carroll put down the tools of his trade and joined me for a heart-to-heart. He's prone to sentimentality.

"Making up for lost time, my friend. Making up for lost time. Now, I know I disappointed you yesterday."

"Carroll..."

"No, let me finish. Charlotte and I had a talk about it, you know, like couples do, and when she's right, she is right." He leaned close so Jess couldn't hear us. "I think my drinking is starting to affect other aspects of my life."

Several varying retorts played through my head. I settled on this.

"Carroll, that's absurd."

"I'm serious as a heart attack, Doris. I truly think it is. And I've simply got too much to lose to let that happen. Too much."

With great resolve, he strode back over to the grill, picked up the tongs, and flipped a couple of Porterhouse steaks like he meant it.

"A couple, huh? You and Charlotte really hit it off."

"Hit it off? Hit it off? Oh, Bertha! That woman is the best thing that's ever happened to me. She's one in a million. You ever heard her sing?"

"Are you serious?"

"How do you mean?" he asked, his face twisted in confused concern.

"Uh, yes, yes I have."

"Then you know what I mean."

"So where is your better half, Carroll?"

"My better half! Man, Doris, you slay me. She's probably getting ready to go to work about now. That hair of hers takes some time you understand. Oh, I signed your name to a shipment that came in around 3:00, dry goods mostly, and several large cans of stewed tomatoes."

"Why didn't you sign your name? You're the manager."

"Hold the phone. Let me get this straight. You want me to sign my name on deliveries?"

"It doesn't matter. Thanks for covering for me."

"That's what I'm here for, little missy. You can count on me."

While prepping some kale on a couple of plates, I cautiously inquired, "What name did you sign?"

"Julie Page, of course. I'm not an idiot, Doris."

"Carroll, make me a turkey Ruben, would you? I'll be out front for a while."

"Aye aye, captain!"

Once clear of the swinging door, I popped my head back into the kitchen with an addendum. "Hey, why do we need several cans of stewed tomatoes?"

He stopped dead in his tracks, slowly perusing the room. "I have no idea."

The rush ended. There were only three tables occupied when I slid into my office. Joanne brought coffee and Lana was right on her hip as she approached.

"Julie, Mr. Sharkey says it's okay with him if it's okay with you if they break me off the floor now 'cause it's pretty slow and you've still got Jo and Tina and

Rhea scheduled 'til nine and ten and I don't think we're going to get another push in the next hour and that's when my shift is over anyway."

"Go."

"Thanks, Julie," she sang, dashing for the kitchen where the lockers are to grab her parka and backpack.

She never came back so I assume she exited through the side door in the kitchen. Now it was just Jo, Tina, Rhea, and me in the dining room and Carroll and Jesse in the kitchen. The customers remaining paid and left in quick succession. Because the joint was empty and the jukebox silent, I yelled across the room. "Hey, Jess, you want to go home early?"

He was behind the counter removing a bin of dirty dishes for laundering. "Thanks, Julie, but I need the money."

"Tina, you want to bail?"

"Okay. Can I get something to eat?"

"Yeah, whatever you want."

"Can I get a Denver omelet, Mr. Sharkey? With onion rings?"

Carroll placed the spatula to his hair net in a salute of agreement. "Tina, hand this to the chief, would you?"

She brought me my dinner, then went behind the counter to pour herself a Dr. Pepper. The quiet of the room seemed foreign, off-putting. Just the clink of the crew piddling around with side work and the sound of me eating filled the air.

I'm not sure I'd ever been in the joint without musical accompaniment since we opened but no one acted like they minded so I didn't complain.

Jo sat at a counter stool with her legs to the side. It was clear her feet hurt from the look on her face and the delicate way she retracted them from the linoleum. Semi-comfortable, she took the opportunity to ask about the topic du jour.

"Julie, hasn't DiAngelo come up with anything yet?"

Time to hear how this lie sounded when spoken aloud.

"No, Jo. Nothing. I guess these things take longer than you might expect."

Tina sat next to Jo at the counter and got busy with her onion rings. Jo went on.

"Well, it took thirty years to solve the last murder that happened on the Promenade." She guffawed, putting her feet up on the stool to her right while leaning her back against Tina's shoulder.

Everything went remarkably still. Jesse finished stacking clean plates, the steam still evident, and put his elbows on the inside of the counter looking out at Jo. "You going to tell us a ghost story, Joanna Banana?"

Rhea threw her apron in the dirty towel bin and hurriedly sat down next to me in the booth. And though Carroll remained in the kitchen, his bloodshot, bourbon-colored eyes were glued to Jo, focused and intrigued.

CHAPTER THIRTEEN

When she realized our attention was directed at her and her alone, she brought her feet back down and swiveled around, making eye contact with each one of us.

"Carroll? You don't remember the murders?" She quizzed the oldest member of her audience first. My fry cook had the same look on his face as when he asked me if I'd ever heard Charlotte sing. He knows he forgets things and it troubles him.

"Maybe. Bring it back to me Joanne. How did it go again?"

Jo looked at me squarely. "Julie, you don't remember your folks talking about the murders at Friar Tuc's when you were a kid?"

I shook my head no while spinning through a Rolodex of memories trying to recall any such stories. Though I was pretty sure I wouldn't have forgotten it.

By then, Carroll had come out of the kitchen and was standing with both skinny gray arms on his bony hips. Jess leaped up on the work counter waiting for details and Tina, through frantic chomps on onion ring after onion ring, stared at the woman next to her with the wide-eyed anticipation of a kid at a campfire awaiting the retelling of Bloody Mary.

Jo's mouth fell open, aghast at our ignorance, as she picked up Tina's Dr. Pepper for a pre-storytelling swig to clear her instrument. While Jo readied herself for the task at hand, Rhea piped in. At first, she spoke in this tiny un-Rhea-esque voice but in no time had it up to full throttle.

"Oh, my God, this is so weird. Like, three or four days ago there was this guy down at the 7-11 on Crescent. I was there with some friends and he was there with some friends and we were all hanging out in the parking lot talking."

It concerned me to know that she hangs out in 7-11 parking lots with strangers but I let her continue without comment.

"So, he asked me where I worked and I said Nighthawks and he starts rambling something about a murder. I thought he was talking about the girl who just died here but he goes, 'No, man. There was another murder years ago on the Promenade – a *mass murder*.'" Ending her dramatic sentence in a loud whisper, you could almost hear the incidental music leading us to a commercial break.

Jo produced a semi-smile while furrowing her brow. "Well, honey, it wasn't a mass murder, exactly."

"Whatever, Jo. I asked him what he was talking about but he was all, 'I don't know anything else,' so I figured he was making it up just to scare me. I was like, 'You're so full of it. There was not a mass murder on the Promenade, I'm so sure.' But now, just like two days later, you're totally bringing it up."

Rhea had been looking at Jo but then turned to Tina with a kindred spirit kind of head-shaking astonishment that her former classmate reciprocated.

Jesse attempted to amend the confusion. "Why don't you tell us, Jo? What happened at Friar Tuc's?"

Jo crossed her support hose and scratched the nape of her neck. Looked like she was gathering her thoughts so she could tell the story accurately and well.

"I was there that day."

"The day of the murders?" Tina asked too loudly.

"No, the day they found the body. I think most of you know they started ripping down the buildings on the Promenade around '76 or '77. Not all of them and not all at once. In 1976 I was still working at Chordeilettes, right here where Nighthawks is today. This was the very last place to close on the Promenade. Julie, did you know that?"

"No, Jo. I didn't."

"Well, it was. Chordettes is what everybody called it. And Nighthawks looks so much like it sometimes I forget where I am. Sometimes I think working here is like being on a movie set. Like somebody's making a movie about the old joint and I'm an extra. Isn't that silly?"

All three kids consoled their comrade with a chorus of "No, it isn't, Jo. That's not silly." It was sweet to see all of them jump to her defense.

Carroll finally had a memory that was vivid enough to share.

"I remember Chordettes. This place is the spitting image, isn't it?" The two oldsters smiled at each other in agreement. "Only this jukebox works and the AC is a hell of a lot better than those old fans."

Jo laughed. "Oh, Lord, yes. You know, they never got around to putting in an air conditioner, Julie. A controlled climate isn't very authentic of you."

"I chose not to authenticate the pain, Jo, just the pleasure." I smiled.

She and Carroll nodded and laughed again.

"Joanne, stop talking and tell the story!" Rhea's oxymoron somehow held water with all of us. Everybody settled back down.

"The buildings along the stroll were still standing but most were boarded up and gutted by then. Demolition crews had been brought in to start leveling some of the shops. I think the Dohertys were still thinking they might rebuild on the property at the time. So one particular day I'm working the counter, a counter that looked just like this one," she touched the counter, "and one of the demolition men came flying through the front door white as a sheet. Asks me if he can use the phone. We didn't have cell phones back then." She offered this aside to the three kids.

"Anyway, I told the fellow he'd have to use the pay phone by the cigarette machine," she pointed across the room to where our phone and cigarette machine are, "that the counter phone was off limits and such, but he just shook his head and kept saying, 'I need the phone lady. Let me use the phone.' Well, he looked so frightened I put the dial phone up on the counter for him."

Jo reached behind her and placed the dial phone on the counter, reenacting the moment. "He sat at a stool and called the police."

She gestured to the stool Tina was sitting at. Tina contracted her shoulders and visibly shivered like this Bloody Mary story was going to keep her up all night.

"What did he say to the police, Jo?" the waitress asked between chews and swallows.

"He said they'd found a body, a body of a woman, that it was standing upright and had been placed in one of the concrete pillars out front of Friar Tuc's. Somebody had buried her alive."

Tina stopped eating, Rhea scooted closer, and Jesse sat stony still, lips slightly parted.

"Oh, Bertha!" Carroll broke the tension, or, at least the silence. "How did they know she'd been buried alive?"

"They didn't know right away. Friar Tuc's had gone through some overhauling back when the war ended, World War II. The bar had an odd alcove in the front, sort of like an old movie house. When they renovated, they added the two large pillars to either side of the building, retiled the front walkway in a mosaic that spelled out the name, and expanded the bar. The body was inside one of those pillars so it had to have been in there since the pillar went up, almost thirty years prior. Because of the way the cement encased her, she hadn't decomposed much at all—like a mummy."

"Did you see it?" Jess asked in reverent tones.

"Yes. Yes, I did."

"Oh, my God, Jo. That's awful," I blurted out.

"I just couldn't believe what I was hearing the demolition man say to the police. So when he left, I walked over there myself before the police had a chance to keep me from it."

So she had balls then, too. Of course, she did.

"The demolition crew was so upset; all staggering around, mouths open, shaking their heads. And because they were so preoccupied I was able to make my way through the chaos and up to the broken plaster that had been the front half of the great column. And there she was, nestled in the back half, hands crossed over her chest, eyes closed, real peaceful. Looked like someone had lifted the lid off of a casket and stood it on one end. The corpse was covered in chalky concrete dust but you could still see everything. She was wearing a polka dot dress and platform shoes. Her hair was very long, but you know it keeps growing after you're dead."

She stopped to take another drink of Tina's soda while we all readjusted our butts, looking at each other in disbelief.

"Did they figure out who killed her?" Jess brought us back from intermission.

"Yes, they're pretty sure they did. The police opened up their missing persons files and dug back further and further until they discovered that the man who owned Friar Tuc's had reported his wife missing shortly after reopening the bar. She was never found. Conveniently enough, this man had also done much of the renovations on the place himself.

Once the police knew that, they got the idea that he probably drugged her first, so there was no murder weapon and placed her in the wet cement to get rid of the body. By the time she woke up, the cement had hardened enough that there wasn't even a way to scream."

Jesse choked out a nervous laugh, shaking his head. Rhea covered her ears like that would make the image in her head go away.

"Joanne, this is turning into a freakishly rough story. It isn't going to get any rougher, is it?" I felt, perhaps too late, like protecting my young crew from any additional baggage connected to their workplace. They were carrying quite enough already. She monitored her next bit of exposition.

"Well…well, there was another body."

Everyone in the room but me begged her to go on. I rolled my eyes and acquiesced. Jo continued but you could tell she was abridging and editing, leaving out details and picking up her pace.

"When they brought the rest of the building down they found a man buried in the same fashion in the other pillar. They were never able to trace his identity. The authorities figured the man and woman might have been lovers. The press speculated that they were and that when her husband found out, he killed them both and buried them in the front of his bar. The bar had only been open a handful of years which explains his decision to renovate so soon. No one would find the bodies and he would be able to enjoy his handiwork every time he went in or out past the pillars. I can't believe none of you have heard this story before now. It was in the paper for weeks after the bodies were discovered."

Carroll started waving his hands in front of him. "Hold the ever-loving phone! There were two bodies? The guy hid two bodies for thirty years and nobody got wise?"

"Isn't that something? But that's not going to happen now, Julie. Police investigations run some smoother than they did back then, DNA and all."

"Thanks, Joanne. You're very inspirational." She looked a bit sheepish but I threw her a grin so she knew I was ultimately fine with her terrifying history lesson.

"But they arrested the guy, right, Jo? He didn't get away with it." I wasn't grinning when I asked that.

You could tell she wanted to give me something other than what she was about to. But her role as tribal scribe had to be honored.

"His name was Theodore Pendleton. And old Theo was killed in a bar fight in 1960 behind his own bar. So, yes, I'm afraid he did get away with it."

"Oh, my God! So three people died here on the Promenade. Like, right here!"

"Friar Tuc's was down another block and a half, Rhea. They didn't die right here."

"But someone did," Rhea added.

I couldn't argue that. Someone did. Right at that front door.

We all sat in quiet contemplation over the chilling story and Rheas' closing comment. Then the front door swung open and you'd have thought a bomb went off in the place. Everybody jumped a good two inches off their seats. After the split second it took to assess that it wasn't a bomb, just a person entering the room, all three kids went into a huge belch of laughter.

"Oh, my God! I totally just wet my pants!" Rhea exclaimed.

Jesse jumped down off of the work counter and the girls went about their business, Tina busing her dishes and heading for her purse and coat, Jo adjusting her apron and stepping behind the counter, Rhea bouncing over to the cash register for quarters she quickly popped into the jukebox. Carroll sauntered

back toward the kitchen trying to look like he, too, hadn't just wet his pants. I just stayed in the booth.

Our new guest was Selene, Crow's girlfriend. She walked over to the back booth but didn't sit down. "Julie, what's up? Were you guy's having a meeting or something?"

"Hey, Selene. We were just taking a break. Sit down."

"No, that's okay. Crow wanted me to find you. You gonna be here for a while?"

Crow. I know I told Frank I wouldn't talk to Carroll or Charlotte or anybody, but Crow seemed like someone I should be telling about an attempt on my life. He didn't know who my enemies were but he knew the neighborhood. Maybe he could help protect me. Maybe.

"Well, I need to leave pretty soon but I'd like to see him, too. What does he need?"

"I'll go tell him you're here. Thanks, girl." And with that, she was back out the door.

A couple of swing kids and a trucker came in as she went out. It was as if the joint only stayed empty long enough for us to hear Jo's scary tale and now the campfire had been extinguished.

I got up and went into the kitchen. Carroll stood at the ticket wheel waiting for the first of the two new tickets to get hung. "Wow, Doris. Wow! That was some story. A real doozy! A lollapadoozy!"

"Yeah. Well, a place this old is bound to have a past. Carroll, did Tina leave out the back door?" He nodded. "I'd like to keep this door locked from now on, okay? They can knock or come in through the front. Is that cool with you?"

I waited for an argument or, at the very least, the questions that would follow as to why I asked him to keep the door locked, etc. But none came. The muscles in his sallow face pulled down and his already tiny eyes squinted into thin slits. Again he nodded. Then both tickets hit the wheel and he went to work.

"I'm gonna go see the Chads play tonight, Carroll. I probably won't drop back in here. Everything solid?"

While slapping two burger patties onto the grill and breaking eggs in a small bowl, he gave me his best assurance. "You go kick up your heels, missy. Will you do that?"

I considered the scene I'd be walking into at the Bait Shack.

"I don't think there'll be anybody there over twenty-five."

"You'll fit right in."

I chuckled on my way to lock the back door from the inside. The key to the deadbolt is on a large ring we keep hanging by the lockers. While I tried to remember which key it was, Carroll felt like chatting.

"Doris, I think I'm going to base my next book of poetry around the murders on the Promenade. The actual murders as well as abstracted ones. You know, I think that would be a pretty good name for it, *Murders on the Promenade.*

I continued trying keys, not commenting but noting how articulate my buddy sounded all of a sudden. "Uh-huh."

He pressed the burgers down while reciting, "She walks the length of the asphalt in the dark perpetually searching. Silent screams vibrate the midnight. Looking for things lost, things taken: Her lover, her body, air."

"That's great, Carroll." I started to walk out front when my insensitivity stopped me in my tracks. That wasn't a bad idea for a book of poetry. And, though he was just spewing off the top of his head, that wasn't a bad idea for a poem. How dare I dismiss my fry cook's art?

I walked over to the grill and took the spatula from his hand, tending to the meat and eggs, myself.

"You go write that down right now before you forget it. That was good."

I thought he was going to cry. Then he did.

"Well, that certainly means something coming from you, Doris. I'm speechless. I've got a pen. Let me just get a paper towel."

"Use a ticket book. There's some in the locker that doesn't have a lock on it."

He found one and perched the pen to write. "What did I say again?" We worked together to reconstruct the poem and then I handed over the spatula.

"Keep it up, Carroll. You have a gift."

He didn't respond to that. He simply wiped his eyes.

I grabbed my coat and purse on my way into the dining room. I hadn't passed the counter when I saw Crow. He was outside the joint, smoking by the curb, looking in. I don't know how he saw me from that distance but he subtly nodded in my direction as I raised one hand in weak acknowledgment. I said goodnight to my crew and moved to join him.

"Hey, Crow. Why didn't you come inside?"

"I thought we might want some privacy. And it's a beautiful evening."

The first waft of mist floated by letting me know it would be another foggy night but right then the Promenade was as black as my companion. He flicked his smoke out beyond where the lights from the diner could find it and maneuvered his generous mouth into a grin under deadly serious eyes.

"Let's sit down," he suggested.

"Sure." I started for the tiled planter box but he gestured to the curb, guiding me with his hand on my shoulder. Glad that I'd opted for the painter pants and tennies, I folded myself down on the ground as he did the same.

"I've got something I'd like to tell you, Crow, something I want you to know about. But it looks like you've got something you want to tell me first."

"Yeah, how 'bout I go first," he asked as a statement. I nodded.

"Anderson found a young man a few hours ago. He's been living in the gully by the tracks on the edge of town."

"He found a young man?"

"The neighborhood's been poking around, trying to piece together what might've happened here on our turf. You don't mind me calling this our turf, do you, JP?"

I didn't. "Is he all right?"

"Yes, he is all right. Street kids are like weeds. They grow and bloom through the smallest crack in the pavement. But sometimes it's hard to get them to tell you the truth about anything. Not this one, though. This one is very vocal. Hasn't been out there long enough yet. Anyway, after Anderson got him involved in some conversation, he offered up a hot meal if the young man would get in his car and come across town so I could meet him. Bad news is he was willing to get in the car. Good news is, this time anyway, it was Anderson."

"I'm glad it was Anderson. What does he know?"

"Well, JP, we know who she was."

My heart sank. Days and nights waiting for this information and now that I was going to hear it I had second thoughts. I guess I could keep her at a distance as long as I didn't know. Now, she was about to jump into my arms.

"Tell me."

"Okay. Her name was Bethany, Bethany Garrett. Girl was sixteen years old. She'd been living on the street since her mom passed about a year ago. I understand the stepdad didn't do anything to stop her from leaving. The young man seems to think she was going to ask you for a job."

I shook my head. The truth was almost insufferable.

"You gonna be okay, JP?"

I nodded affirmatively, still speechless. My breathing became labored. I reached for a pill in my purse and swallowed it with the fervor of a heart patient ingesting nitroglycerine. Crow waited for me to calm down a little then turned his head streetward.

"You need to slow that shit down, J." Nothing glib or defensible came to mind so I said nothing. But when I brought out a cigarette, he was quick to light it for me. People are so forgiving of their own vices. "You good to hear a little more?"

"Yeah."

"Eugene, that's the young man's name, Eugene says Bethany found a coat in front of the diner a couple days before she disappeared. It fit her and it hadn't been in the dumpster too long so it didn't smell too bad. She had it on when she came to see you that morning. She told him it would bring her luck asking you for a job. He never saw her again."

I took off my glasses to rub back the tears. "It was my coat. My old coat. I'd thrown it in one of the dumpsters."

"Mmm." Even Crow didn't know what to say to that. "Well, life's funny sometimes."

"Why didn't this Eugene tell me—or the cops?"

"He's nine."

"Nine? He's nine? Christ, he's just a little boy."

"No, he's a man."

"Oh, my god, Crow. Why does a nine-year-old kid know this shit?"

"He was her brother. She'd been taking care of him best she could for the past year. Moving him around, hunting out food and shelter. I told him she wasn't coming back. I told him she fought 'till the end and that he should be extremely proud of that."

I rocked back and forth there in the gutter. And were it not for the drug-inflicted damper I'd armed myself with, I would've been in hysterics. "I can't stand this. I can't. It's too fucking much."

"Yeah, you can. Everything's going to temper down pretty soon. You'll see. You should try to take in the righteousness of it, J. Eugene says she never done a needle, never even stole anything. And if she did, she never let him see it. She was in the process of turning it all around for herself and her brother. This was a noble warrior princess."

"Where is he now?"

"Eugene? We fed him and drove him back to his box."

"Oh, no, Crow…"

He guffawed and lit a smoke for himself. "Shit, J. You know how many dogs I got already. Crawling all over the furniture, eating my goddamn food."

"No, Crow. This is breaking my heart. We can't leave him out there. Bring him here. I'll take him in."

"Get tough."

"If I was any tougher, I'd be jerky."

"However tough you are, it isn't tough enough."

"Just for a couple of days until we figured out what to do for him. Maybe Frank knows of an agency or something."

He didn't reply, just stared out into the darkness.

"Please, Crow."

"We'll see."

I didn't know this man well enough to know for sure what that meant but decided not to push what I knew in my heart would be rectified.

"Crow, I saw Frank last night."

He tilted his big orb toward the imperceptible stars. "And what did the detective have to share? I'm eager to hear this."

"He deduced she must've been wearing the old coat that I'd thrown in the dumpster because they found fibers from it in the bullet wound. He thinks somebody mistook her for me that morning."

He turned his head hard right watching my face carefully. "You saying what I think you're saying?"

"Yes. He told me not to tell anybody…but I'm telling you. I can't imagine who wants me dead but you know this hood better than anybody else, and I want you to know what's going on."

"Well, well." He sought direction from the silence. "You can't think of anybody, J?"

"No, man. Not like that."

"Yeah. You haven't told Carroll or Charlotte?"

"He asked me not to. Besides, why freak them out, too?"

"Okay. Okay, it's our little secret, you and me. I'll keep an eye on things. Just don't be stupid."

"I'm going to make every effort not to be."

He rose, then helped me up, straightening out the lapels of my black peacoat for me. "This certainly came in handy."

"Not for her."

"Don't do like that, now. I'm sure she was thankful to have that old coat of yours. It's cold out there."

CHAPTER FOURTEEN

He walked away and I stood there watching. The heavy black curtain of night closed behind him only a few feet from the diner. It's like that on the Promenade, beyond Nighthawks, past the blinking beacon Owl. You're completely invisible once you leave the Owl's domain.

I turned and walked in the opposite direction toward the dirt lot. A car full of beatnik babies swooshed past keen on getting a table in a hurry. As I made my way around them, I wondered if that's how it'd happened for Bethany; a car from out of nowhere comes swooshing by, and the next thing you know you're down on your knees clutching an exit wound.

As I approached the back lot I thought I saw someone standing next to the Cad. But in that I could barely see the Cad I wasn't sure. I had no sense of panic about it. No additional sense of panic, that is. I just figured it was a customer admiring a vintage car or somebody waiting for a private moment with someone who hadn't shown up yet. As I approached, I realized there was no one there at all. Just my eyes playing tricks like they do now and then.

Again, I had trouble getting the key in the lock and decided I really should put a light somewhere along the brick wall if I was going to keep parking back there.

Mounting the great beast, I did my usual thing: hit the lock, hit the lighter, and adjusted the rearview mirror. As my hand landed on the mirror, I saw someone standing behind the car, close behind. I gasped and turned over my shoulder to see who it was but there was no one there, not right there, anyway. But a person could easily hide in the darkness that hangs on that strip. I wasn't going to get out to check into it further.

My heart raced as I checked each of the locks, and turned over the ignition. I asked myself why hadn't been afraid when I thought I saw someone standing near my car.

Someone tried to kill you. All you can think about is that someone tried to kill you yet you were more than willing to walk into a coal-black lot behind a building adjacent to an alley toward something you perceived as a person. What's up with that?

Crow's words flooded over me, a tsunami of logic and foreshadowing. "Don't be stupid." Man, I'm so fucking stupid.

As I pulled out onto the stroll toward Damien, a million thoughts ran through my rattled brain. Maybe I shouldn't have built the diner here. Maybe I didn't belong here. Maybe the ghosts of the Promenade were trying to get me to leave. After all, they'd paid their dues. They truly belonged to this place, as integral as the broken cement and as ageless as the dirt. Maybe when my murderer finally took me down, maybe then I'd fit in. I wasn't even making any sense. Nothing was.

But as I drove across town toward Third, I thought how the Hermes 3000 was right. I did know. Somewhere buried in my subconscious I knew who tried to kill me, and who did kill Bethany Garrett. There was just a piece missing. I was one puzzle piece away from the picture. Clues had been given but I must've been ignoring them. Why would I do that?

The street signs were difficult to read. Everything was a blur. When I'd pull up to a stop light, it seemed I was on an incline, then when I'd pull away, the road became level again. I started to reach for a pill then remembered

I'd taken one when I was talking to Crow. Had I taken one before that? What did I take when I was with him, a Xanax or a Valium? I couldn't remember. I couldn't remember. I couldn't remember.

I got to the club at ten after ten. If those kids only knew what kind of day I was having they would forgive my tardiness. But they didn't know. All they knew that night was that lifc is good, friends are good, beer is good, and music is God.

My legs were not sturdy as I locked the car and attempted the trek to the door. A handful of kids pushed past me to clamor around the Cadillac. Here, as opposed to the doctor's office, my car served as a kind of passport to Coolsville.

The place was crawling with kids, a dozen out in front smoking and making out and talking, and another dozen blocking my entry. Finally, I made it up to the guy at the door.

This was a big, bald guy, with a Marilyn Manson T-shirt stretched over a big belly and tattoos webbing up both big arms. His eyebrow was pierced as were his nose and lip, and there was a little chain draped between them connecting all three. In my current state, I had to look at this configuration long and hard to make sense of it. I never did.

"Can I see your ID?"

My eyes, which had been taking in the chain on his face, quickly shot to his eyes. "Honey, are you serious?"

He was momentarily disoriented. "Oh. No, I gotta see it anyway. Sorry."

I found my wallet and produced my license. He gave it a cursory glance and handed it back. "Sorry about that." His sweet smile exposed teeth too tiny for the rest of him. "What band are you here to see?"

I couldn't remember the name of the band. Big Pink Tongue? No, that wasn't it. The line grew behind me as I fumbled for the flyer I thought I might have thrown in my purse.

"You want to step aside for a minute?" He guided me gently to his side like I was feeble, which I was.

Doug came rushing up to me and I dropped my open purse.

"Julie! You made it! Thank you! How you doing?"

We were both gathering the items that had rolled here and there.

"Oh, shit. What a klutz. Good. I'm good. I thought I was late. When are you guys going on?"

The Xanax bottle was right at his feet. My habits must be public knowledge because the embarrassment on his face would've made you think it was a tampon. His way out of this awkward moment was to pick up the phone, lipstick, and comb, as well, handing me a handful of stuff instead of just the elephant. I don't think the comb was mine but I stuck it in my purse anyway.

Once we were both upright, we stared at each other smiling and nodding. Then he held out his snowy arms and hugged me.

"We were supposed to go on at ten but the Butt Blisters went on late, so we're going on next. You didn't miss any of it!"

"Great! Hey, I'll get to catch a little of the Butt Blisters set, too. Aces!"

When we met back with the door guy, Doug yelled over the song that had just kicked off, "She's with The Chads! Julie Page! She's on our guest list!" The Chads, of course. How could I have forgotten that?

The guy nodded and jotted it down. As we passed, he grabbed my hand. For some ridiculous reason, I thought he was going to say something to me based on the quality time we'd shared before Doug showed up. So when he took my hand, I took his, in a politician's handshake. He grinned but didn't look at me as he stamped the back of it and sent me on my way.

The ink stain was large and red but I couldn't make it out. "Doug, what is this? What's this on the stamp?"

Again, he looked embarrassed but this time he smiled. "It's a worm with boobies! And that says Bait Shack! The color lets them know if you can drink or not! See, mine's blue!" He led me to the bar where the rest of his cohorts were.

"Julie!" shouted Girl Chad.

"Hey, toots! You look great! Hi, guys! I'm so glad you're going on late!"

The two boys smiled and tipped their bottles toward me as a way of saying hello without having to yell over the Butt Blisters. They both looked like they were about to take their first driving test, excited and horrified, but Girl Chad looked like she was seeing Disneyland for the very first time.

It was about a hundred degrees inside the Bait Shack so I slid off my coat in a hurry. Girl Chad gasped and lightly touched the shoulder of my blue sequined shell. "Pretty top!"

Before I could speak, Doug yelled, "Randy! Hey, you guys, Randy made it!" High fives all around, sans me.

Girl Chad jumped higher. "Randy!"

Doug put his hand on my elbow. "I gotta go say hi to Randy, Julie! You going to be okay?"

"Yeah! I'm fine! I'll see you after your set!"

"Okay!"

As he headed back toward the front door he gave me a little two thumbs up with an I'm-not-so-sure look on his happy bleached face. The other Chads fell in behind him and I was alone at the bar.

The man behind the bar was about my age, I figure. There was a kinship between us as he leaned to ask the inevitable question. "What can I getcha?"

I wasn't feeling very stable and the heat in there made me even less balanced than I would've been otherwise. But you can't smoke inside and I didn't know what else I was going to do with my hands. "A Manhattan, up!"

His eyes smiled but his jaw remained serious. "How 'bout a Bud?"

I handed over three bucks as he handed me a beer. "Thanks!"

I moved around the periphery of the room until I could see the band on stage. The Butt Blisters were giving it their all and the kids crowded in front of them dancing were doing the same.

They were singing something about home and mother and wide-open spaces. Not really. I don't know what they were singing about. Couldn't make out a word of it. But they meant it, whatever it was. Go, Butt Blisters! Go!

They ended their set by bowing to the crowd then turning around and dropping their pants before bowing again. Each of the four boys on stage had a letter painted on each butt cheek. That's four boys, eight cheeks, and that spells B-L-I-S-T-E-R-S.

Then they pulled up their pants and started tearing down their equipment in a very polite, organized manner, making way for the next band. The announcer/soundman chimed in over the din. "Let's have another round of applause for… the Butt Blisters!" More applause and whooping from the throng. "Don't go anywhere because The Chads are going to be up in just a few minutes and I know you don't want to miss that."

I found a place to lean on the counter ledge against the wall. It was a straight shot from where I stood to the stage with a pool table and dance floor between. The beer bottle served as a cooling device when rolled over my forehead.

As I watched The Chads assemble themselves and their equipment, I started to feel a little nauseous, weak and sweaty, but it passed soon enough. The warm beer moistened my dry cotton-lined mouth. Surely, I could pull it together long enough to hear them play and congratulate them. I'd already accomplished the Herculean task of getting there. This should be cake.

Someone somewhere in the vicinity asked if I wanted to shoot a game of pool. I declined, hoping they had, indeed, been talking to me.

So this was the lineup, Black Chad on drums, Doug on electric piano, Girl Chad on bass, and White Chad front and center manning the guitar. The white kid (Black Chad) was shirtless and had dyed his hair and soul patch pink for the event. Girl Chad wore an Emily T-shirt, a Catholic uniform skirt, and Doc's over fishnets, and the black kid up front (White Chad) had a large hair pick displayed to one side of his fro and sported a mechanic's jumpsuit with the name

Alberto stitched over the breast pocket. Doug had on a white T-shirt and jeans. Being an albino, he was automatically the most outrageous person on stage.

From the soundboard, the MC announced, "Ladies and gentlemen...The Chads!" Mostly polite applause followed with a few cheers from the friends in the room, myself included.

They looked just mortified, and the first song started out tentative and unimpressive. They maintained this level of banality through the two songs that followed. No one addressed the audience. No "How's everybody doing?" or "We love you Berle!" or anything.

By the fourth song, the crowd had stopped even pretending to listen and I needed to sit down. Finding a seat was easy as some of the people had already gone home and others were hanging outside until the next band came on. From my new location by the dartboard, I was further to the side of the stage but a good deal closer.

I watched their expressions change from "Oh, God, they're looking at me." to "Who you lookin' at?" Talking amongst themselves, some decisions had been made. White Chad approached the microphone.

"This next song is sort of an homage to the Bait Shack. We call it 'Shark Bite.'"

Doug kicked it off with a Jerry Lee Lewis glissando down the keys, cheap but always effective.

Girl Chad made with a baby doll squeal spinning around one time before approaching the microphone for her back-up vocals of "Oh, oh, look at the blood. Oh, oh, pack it with mud." White Chad went for broke, and for one win-some moment, I was reminded of the B-52s and the good old days. Then Girl Chad dropped her bass. But she picked it right up.

Yes, the tone had shifted. The Chads were making points with the crowd that remained. I noticed a couple of people giving the band the once-over twice. The rest of the set held that high energy and the twenty people left in the bar stayed. They weren't bad, The Chads. They weren't brilliant but their potential was now apparent when only minutes before it was not. What changed? Did they just stop caring about pleasing the audience? I don't think so. I think they finally got desperate enough to try.

When it was over, their friends gathered around the foot of the stage as they started to tear down their equipment. The soundman piped in. "Are you ready for another band, little fishes?" No applause. Apathy had taken over the room. "All right, we've got Shelley Is My Neighbor coming up so stay put!"

I ambled over to the stage myself, stage left, by the piano. "Hey, Doug."

He kept winding cable and breaking down mic stands but worked his way downstage. "Hey, Julie. I know. We sucked."

"Yes, I came over to tell you that you suck. No, you didn't, Doug. You guys are great. Give yourself a chance. It was your first show. And, I don't know about you, but I thought this audience sucked."

"Really? You don't think we stunk up the whole room?"

"No, man. I really don't." Though I was standing still, I lost my balance and, for a moment, my train of thought.

"Julie, are you okay?"

"I...I don't think you stunk up the room. The first few were sort of, you know, like you were nervous. Big deal. Then you guys got loose and it was swinging. I swear to God."

He was smiling and nodding. You could tell he liked what I was saying but wasn't quite sure he believed it. "So, you'd come back and see us again, huh?"

I thought about everything that was going on in my life right then, about how unhealthy and overwhelmed I was. But the Chads were fresh, their vinyl unwarped. They had become for me the embodiment of all things hopeful. "Yeah, Doug. I'll make it a priority."

CHAPTER FIFTEEN

Back in the car, the weight of the day came crashing down on my battered psyche. I had held it together for the Chads but now the show was over and every cell in my body knew it.

The encroaching fog further complicated my ability to see things clearly. Had I done the right thing, telling Crow about the attempt on my life? Should I warn Carroll? The crew?

There was a little boy living in a cardboard box whose big sister wasn't coming back. I had no right to think I understood his dilemma, but on some level, I felt I did, both of us targets for different reasons. That sinister element, that only half-hidden cancer at the core of humanity is ever-present. Around every corner, some demon-possessed puppet is scoping out the weakest of the pack. And, of course, the easiest marks are always the ones who step away from the pack entirely, by choice or circumstance.

I headed for Vincent. It took me a little out of my way but then it would be a straight line home. Again, my depth perception wasn't calibrating correctly. I couldn't remember if I'd taken something at the club. The fog in my head was equivalent to the foggy blanket wrapping itself around my car.

And as I drove, each streetlight only a dull glow dotting the highway, my mind wandered back to another foggy time in my twisted little life, a time when the fog grew so thick that the only perceivable way out was to shut down completely. I remembered the last time my addictions had me by the short hairs: losing my job, sleeping in my car, alienating everyone who cared about me. That was years before a book about Maxine Montego changed everything, when celebrity was something aimed for instead of something to hide from. I remembered.

Only the last time I was that fucked up I was still able to write, albeit nothing of any consequence. To an audience of one, myself, I wrote with the passion of yet another pedestrian artist willing to bleed for her craft. And I did bleed over that mediocre work, clinging to each page as if it were a life preserver cast in an ocean of my incompetence.

I truly believed I had something to say. I'd have bet my life on it. Turns out I didn't have anything to say and I had bet my life. And that was the first time I got serious about drying out. The process was excruciating and messy. Then I met Felix.

He became the life preserver. The grandeur of his chi allowed me shelter wherein I could heal my self-inflicted wounds. The only man strong enough to survive my distorted affections. And he, in turn, needed someone to need him. I must have been an answer to a prayer because no one has ever needed anyone more than I needed him then - and now. But this time, he couldn't save me. This time, he didn't even know I was dying. How could I let this happen again?

The fog grew so thick along the coast that I thought about pulling over but I wanted to get back to the apartment, back to something that seemed real because nothing did.

I knew I was approaching the corner of Vincent and the Promenade as I could see the bus bench and mailbox that mark the spot a few feet past the intersection. I thought I saw someone standing by the bench. Because I could not trust my eyes any longer, I tried hard to focus on the form.

Was there someone there or was I just imagining things? Was it another hallucination, or another ghost?

When the car went over the curb, my head hit the roof of the Cad knocking off my glasses. When the car hit the mailbox, my chest folded around the hard thin steering wheel knocking the air out of me. When I woke up, my neck was reclined against the back of the old tuck-and-roll and the door of the Cad hung open. Someone was leaning inside, talking. "Julie. Julie. Julie."

The form remained difficult to distinguish, partly because of the fog, partly because of the drugs, and mostly because I couldn't find my glasses. "Where am I?" I asked, just like in the movies.

"Thank you, Jesus! She's alive. Honey, don't move. We need to find out how badly you're hurt." The voice was familiar, deep and silky.

"What happened? Where are my glasses?" I automatically began feeling along the car seat with my right hand in search of the plastic appendage.

"I'm serious. Don't move. You might have broken something. Let me." As she reached across, her perfume assaulted my nostrils like smelling salts bringing me around to the situation at hand. Long blond synthetic hair brushed over my face on her way in and on her way out.

"Here. Here are your glasses. Goddamn, girl, I don't think they even got scratched." She started to put them on for me but if you've ever had anyone do that you know it's easier said than done. I was willing to take a chance that my arm wasn't broken and relieved her of this duty. "Careful," she said, complying.

"Peaches, is that you?"

"Yes, honey. Who else would be stubborn enough to think they gonna make some money on this corner in this weather? Girl, you almost killed me. Now that I know you're alive, I think I'm gonna slap you silly."

"Peaches," I said as if telling myself who it was. Once the glasses were back where they belonged, I faced my champion with a weak smile.

Peaches is one of the she-men (as Peaches refers to herself and sisters) who only recently relocated to downtown Berle from Wilmore. The working girls monopolizing the Tuk-U-Inn are actual women and I hear there's a little bit of a club mentality between the two factions. So the she-men continue to scuff up their knees until an area has been defined as theirs alone or until the other team evolves enough to embrace their co-workers. Vive la différence!

We met shortly after Nighthawks was under construction. I'd bought her a couple of fast-food lunches during that time and a neighborly respect was established between us. It was Peaches who first introduced me to Crow.

She stands about 5'11" in her stocking feet but I've never seen her in anything other than heels. Her black skin sparkles, literally, from under a huge blonde wig, and the makeup on her wide, charming face glistens like oil paint on velvet. The tits are real (she showed them to me in front of the Taco Den one afternoon) but the ass is illusory. According to her, she snoops out ladies' rooms in hotels that have settees. Then when no one's looking, she slits open the cushions and cuts out the foam needed to create just the right butt.

Her lipstick ritual is awe-inspiring, liner under tube color under sealing wax under gloss. When she thinks she has it right, she opens a compact and faces the closest streetlight. If she can see the reflection of the streetlight on her lips, she's done. Chantilly is her scent and she fancies Monet jewelry. But what she's got under that short skirt, well, it just ain't feminine. No, she hasn't shown me but I have no reason to doubt her.

I understand some Johns don't quite understand what they've purchased before buying it. There is an occasional miscommunication. Personally, I think a guy would have to be in a real hurry not to notice the expanse of her shoulders and the enormity of her hands. Quite a girl, Peaches.

"Christ, what did I do? I hurt all over."

"You tried to run me over with this big ol' thing. You was off-roading." She purred her insolence softly while pulling the hair back from my face.

"You look like hell, Julie."

"Yeah, I hear that a lot lately. Did you call the cops?"

"Nooo. Last resort, girl. Let's you and I figure out if we need to call anybody. Seems like you doin' pretty good. You want to try to move a little?"

"Yeah, can you help me out?"

"Well, you just sit there for a minute and try out your parts."

"What?"

"Go on and move your little feet around some. See if they work. Bend your knees, move your arms around some. That's it. I'll be damned. I don't think you broke a thing." She offered me her hand. "Okay, let's get you out of there."

I was standing. I hurt but I was standing. I took a slow, painful walk around the Cad, which wasn't too badly damaged. The bumper took a horrible beating but the rest of the car, miraculously, came out of it relatively unscathed. The mailbox, however, looked like an aluminum can accordioned against the head of some frat boy.

"How the shit did I manage that? Aren't these things fairly sturdy?" It was bent in half and two of its girdered legs had been lifted about four inches off the ground.

"Oh, Peaches, this isn't good, my friend. I've got way too much going on right now to be dealing with the destruction of public property."

Words were flying out of me but they were all thick and slurred.

She observed me suspiciously. "You loaded?"

Lying to her seemed pointless.

"Was it my eyes or my ability behind the wheel that gave me away?" I dropped my head and leaned on the car.

"You ain't a stupid woman. What you doing that kind of shit for anyway? Loaded behind the wheel. And aiming at me! Lord, have mercy."

I took a moment to ponder the gravity of what had just happened.

"If it were me, I'd drive myself home and get myself to bed. Last thing you want to be doing is calling the cops right now. You do, loaded as you are, you won't be sleeping at home tonight. They don't need to know who hit this box. Ain't nobody seen anything."

"You don't think I should report it?" I mumbled, almost unintelligibly.

"I ain't deciding. Hell, I'm not even here. I'm just saying if it were me, you know."

"Yeah, I may as well add vandalism to my list of credits." I shook my head. "Man, no matter how low I go there's still someplace lower."

"Girl, you preachin' to the choir." She climbed into the driver's seat. "Come on now. Get your sad self in here. I'll drive you up the Promenade."

The ground spun underneath me as I limped and stumbled around to the passenger side. She popped the door handle from the inside. We didn't talk for the two-block ride we shared. I pointed to where she should pull in.

Looked like the joint was jumping. The lot was half full and folks were milling around out front.

"That's Crow's bunch. Maybe I'll drop in for a cup of kindness when I get you upstairs."

She came around and got me out of the car, locking it for me, as well.

"No need, Peaches. I've got it from here," I tried to say. I think what I actually said was, "Noonoonpeeesh. Mmm gottahar."

"What the hell did you just say?"

I didn't try again. As we walked around the building and I looked up those dark concrete steps, I was less inclined to go alone.

"Say, Peaches, maybe, if you don't mind, could you walk up the stairs with me after all?" I sputtered. Everything coming out of my mouth was indistinguishable but this time, she followed the gist.

"Sure, girl. You lean on me."

Of course, she thought I asked because I was having trouble walking, not because I was afraid of bogeymen. That was best, I figured.

I did lean on Peaches, her strong arm supporting my waist. She patiently let me take one slow, weak step at a time until the mission was accomplished.

When we finally got to the top of the landing, I found the key, which she graciously took from me, opening the door. "Peaches, you want some coffee?" I said, barely above a whisper. I was hoping she'd come in, not at all sure I was ready to be alone.

"You're barely moving. You're barely talking. Just get yourself to bed and sleep it off." She retracted the key from the lock and placed the key ring in my open purse. "And, girl, you need to be more careful. No foolin'. Don't be drivin' if you gonna do that shit, whatever it is you doin'."

"I'm not usually this fucked up," I mumbled, as if it were justification.

"It only takes once," she answered, intelligently.

"You tell Dom whatever you want is on the house."

"What?"

"He can call me if he wants to. Tell Dom. Thank you, Peaches."

"What the hell words are you saying? Girl, take those marbles out your mouth."

With all my might I worked to articulate, "I owe you."

She gave me a little hug before descending the steps. "You don't owe me nothin'. I know you got my back. We take care of each other 'round here. A'ight?"

I shouted something in slurred agreement as she disappeared.

It was empty in the apartment, empty and quiet. I thought back to a time when I was a kid and we had been robbed. For months after, every time we'd come home, my mom would walk into every room checking to see that everything was as it should be, and now, I did the same thing. Flipped on every light, looked in every closet, leaned out of every window. After completing my examination of the premises, I determined that I was very much alone.

As I entered the bedroom, the bed made an overture I nearly couldn't resist but my head, my mushy, rattled head wasn't able to calm itself. Spinning, spinning. I needed more air.

Frantically muscling out of clothes and dropping them as I went, I made my way into that big chenille robe then threw open the bedroom window and climbed (fell, more like) onto the fire escape. There I sat, dazed, bruised, limp, staring out into nothing.

All at once, there was a great racket downstairs. I could hear people yelling over one another even from the back of the building where I sat motionless. Then, cars began skidding out of the dirt and peeling off down the road, one after the other.

Evidently, something bad had happened but I didn't move. I formed thoughts like maybe whatever it was had happened inside the diner. Maybe a grease fire. Maybe a fight. I thought about how I should check on it, at least call down there, but I didn't move. My altered state of consciousness kept me tucked inside the metal cradle, removed and detached. I considered wrapping my robe around me more tightly because I was cold, but I didn't do that either.

Both arms hung heavy and boneless to either side and both legs stuck straight in front of me, feet pointing east and west, like a humongous marionette that's strings had been severed.

Then from somewhere underneath me, I could hear two people talking in hushed tones. The woman's voice conveyed urgency. She spoke quickly and passionately. When the man spoke again, I knew it was Crow. Crow and Selene were having a private conversation under the fire escape.

"Anderson's no racer. He's my right hand. He facilitates."

"I'm telling you he was alone. He wasn't racing nobody."

My head remained pressed against the brick wall. I couldn't see them from this position but their conversation transmitted clearly as they moved closer.

"Where are they taking him?"

"Community. He wasn't moving when Jamal and Tony found him."

"How much damage?"

"I don't know, baby, but he went through the concrete embankment before the car hit the sand."

"He just couldn't leave that motherfucking Chevy alone."

"I know, baby."

"Had to be a big man."

"I know."

"What the hell is that?"

"What, baby? I don't see nothing."

"Looks like we've got some company."

The conversation stopped abruptly and I sensed movement.

"J? JP, is that you?"

I lifted my head from the wall and blinked.

"J, answer me."

I wanted to. I tried. But all that came out was a tiny, "Crow." I tried again, this time attempting to use my lungs. "Crow."

"Shit," he whispered. "You look like a pile of laundry. Are you conscious? You been listening to our little conversation?"

Again, I wanted to participate but my mouth betrayed me. "Anderson," I managed.

"J, you didn't hear anything." My phone rang. "Don't get it," he warned me. Not that I was inclined to get it. Then it rang a second time. "You slept through everything, understood?"

"I'm okay!" I shouted, as if he'd asked.

"Yeah, you're about as okay as Lady Day. Go to bed. Keep your mouth shut. Shit."

The stillness let me know that he and Selene had, indeed, removed themselves as the message machine picked up.

It was Dom. I don't know what he thinks is going on upstairs, like maybe there are several offices up here or something, but the message went, "This is a message for Julie Page. Julie, this is Domenic, the cook, and there's been some trouble out on Vincent, an accident I think. Anyway, I didn't get any details 'cause everybody ran out of the diner at the same time but I thought you should know. It's, uh, it's about 1:30 and the number here is 438-9559."

He actually gave me the number of the diner. The message asks you to leave the time you called and your number and that's what he did, by golly. This is precisely why he's a great employee.

Getting inside was no easy feat. I flailed one arm up toward the sill yet couldn't quite get the oomph to stand. But within every functional junkie, there's a little reserve, some stashed adrenaline, a dose of willpower, and with that, I eventually managed to crawl back through the window I should have never crawled out of.

I didn't make it to bed. I remained right on the inside of the bedroom window like a pile of laundry and gave up for the night.

CHAPTER SIXTEEN

Incessant banging on the front door brought me around. Overcast sunlight assaulted my blurry eyes as I pried open each sticky lid. The room was like an icebox, cold as a meter maid. My hand, which was directly in front of my face on the wood floor, looked blue and I could actually see my breath in the air that filled the room from the night before. But nothing could compare to the dramatic pinch I experienced getting up. Each contracted muscle, every inch of battered flesh screamed a reminder of my dangerous escapade. That, along with the fact that I'd slept on the floor under an open window, made me a very sore girl.

My visitor continued banging vigorously on the door. "Just a minute," I yelled. Seemed to work because the knocking stopped. With inflexible fingers, I pulled the robe open a little to look at some of the damage that dictated each cautious movement. My chest was the most beautiful palette of purples, greens, and yellows, one large mother of a bruise, the steering wheel's impression nearly definable. Both knees and ankles rebelled as I tried to rise. Throwing on real and imaginary brakes prior to the collision had noticeably impacted the leg muscles being called upon.

I gently retied the robe and using the windowsill as a crutch, got myself up as the banging resumed. "I'm coming. Just a minute." Once again, it ceased.

Hobbling the best I could, rediscovering each joint along the way like the freshly lubricated Tin Man, I eventually got to the door. Fumbling with a deadbolt that hadn't been turned in the first place, I reached for the knob and opened the unlocked door.

On the porch, he seemed bigger than usual, and blacker, his leather jacket over wife beater thing finally striking me as imposing. He filled all available space. I was reminded of the game Mystery Date. Spin the doorknob and open the little plastic door to reveal your mystery date. Crow stood there staring at me with this clichéd bad boy outfit on. I don't recall there being a bad boy in Mystery Date but if there was, he could've been it, tucked between the dream-boat and the dud. This bad boy was holding two cups of coffee. "Morning, sunshine."

I walked back to where I thought my glasses might be while he closed the door, put the coffee on the kitchen counter, and pulled off the plastic lids.

"You doing some better today?"

I had rejoined him, extending a cigarette for him to light. "Oh, sure. I'm tops. What time is it?"

"It's about seven."

"And you're here?"

"I brought coffee."

"Better be really good coffee."

"How you feeling?"

I thought about it before answering. "My neck hurts."

He brought out a small bottle from his jacket, popped it open, and handed me two pills. I took them with one stiff hand, trying to recognize the shape and texture. "What are these?"

"They're called aspirin. You should check 'em out."

Smiling was an effort but I managed. Then I got the sugar out of the fridge and a spoon from the sink. "How do you take your coffee again, Crow?"

"Cream, thanks."

Being a gracious hostess, I rummaged through a box near our feet and produced a jar of Coffee-mate, placing it on the counter. He slowly pushed it away from his cup and took a swig, creamless. I threw the aspirin in my mouth and took a swig myself.

"Why am I up at seven o'clock?"

"Consider me your wake-up call, J. I figure in the next hour or so, you're going to be very busy. I thought I'd give you a jump on things."

"And why am I going to be busy again?"

"You remember anything about last night?"

My mind shuffled through mental note cards outlining the evening. "I saw the Chads…and then I was in an accident. Somehow, I got home."

"Peaches brought you home."

"Right! Peaches."

His expression was one of focused anticipation, like a parent watching a kid during a spelling bee, and the word is *prestidigitator.*

"Peaches, I remember," I reiterated, hoping he'd stop staring at me like that.

"J, let's you and I sit down. That be okay with you?" He started for the front room, coffee in hand, so I followed with mine. "You storing raw meat up here?"

"What does that mean?"

"You got some windows open?"

"Oh, yeah. It is cold. Sorry. I think I opened them before I went…went to bed." I trailed off, trying to remember why I'd slept on the floor. "I'll close them."

"I'll help you."

There are only five windows in the apartment, and every single one was open. Crow closed them all while I shivered and smoked.

I'd already settled into one of the easy chairs, gingerly folding my legs to one side of the big cushion, as the big guy came back through the dining room.

"This is a nice apartment, JP. They did a good job."

"Yeah. Thanks."

He came around in front of me and placed his cup next to the other easy chair near the flamingo lamp.

"By the amount of time it took you to answer the door, I was under the impression I woke you up."

"You did."

"Mmm. You take a minute to make the bed before you let anybody in?"

Cat out of the bag, I confessed. "Okay, I slept on the floor last night. I don't quite remember why."

"Could've been worse. You could've slept on the fire escape." Again with the hard stare.

"The fire escape, yeah. I was on the fire escape, wasn't I?"

He brought out the aspirin bottle a second time.

"Thanks, I'm okay," I declined what I thought was an invitation.

"These are for me," he grumbled, tossing back the bottle and swallowing. "Let me help you because this isn't moving along as smoothly as I had hoped."

"Why *was* I on the fire escape, Crow?"

"Only the good Lord knows that. I reckon that's where you thought you could clear your head, sober up. Here's how I heard it. Peaches says you had a run-in with the mailbox on the corner of Vincent and the Promenade last night. She says you were knocked down loaded. Says the Cadillac was airborne when it hit the curb and that the mailbox is the only thing that stopped you from hitting her. This ring a bell?"

I drank more coffee and took a long drag. "Yes."

"Yes, what?"

I was lost. "Yes, sir?"

"No, J, what do you remember?"

"I remember hitting the curb, and the mailbox. I also remember Peaches telling me she wouldn't say anything. I feel a little violated that she'd tell you."

He crossed his jean-clad legs. "You feel a little violated? You're gonna make me old, J. Peaches told me what she had to tell me to keep all of our asses out of a sling, if possible. And saying you're not going to tell anybody and not telling me are two different things. Hell, I know you know that already. Peaches did the right thing. Understood?"

When he said "understood" I flashed on another portion of the evening.

"I saw you last night. We talked. There was another accident. Oh, my God, Anderson was in an accident, wasn't he?"

Crow's face went a little ashy. "It's better your memory return while you're with me and not DiAngelo." He gulped down the rest of his coffee and gestured for one of my cigarettes. I handed him the pack.

"I'm right, aren't I? Anderson was in some kind of accident last night."

"Here's the irony of it, JP. Our buddy Anderson decided to try out a new engine he'd been working on for somebody else. He ran over, or I should say through, the cement embankment that divides Vincent from the surf.

"Oh, no. Where along V did he lose it?"

"Now that's the funny part. He lost it about a block past where you mowed down the mailbox. What do you think of that?"

"I think Peaches ought to find a safer place to work. Is he going to be okay?"

"Well, I've been at the police station for the last several hours – answering questions. But on the ride over here, Selene called from the hospital and he's still out."

"How bad is it?"

"I don't know. I'm going to head on over there in a little while when I get everything straightened out here."

We sat in silence for a moment, his eyes glued to me, mine darting here and there, trying to tamp down the strong sense of guilt welling inside me. What I felt guilty about, I wasn't sure, but I did.

"So, you've seen Frank?"

He turned to face the window, recrossing his legs in the opposite direction.

"A couple of BPD were waiting for me when I pulled into the driveway. I told them I'd been here, at Nighthawks, and that I hadn't heard anything about an accident."

"Then they let you go?"

He laughed, butted out his smoke, and leaned on the arm of the chair to address me directly. "No, that's not when they let me go. That's when they took me in."

"Oh, Crow. I'm sorry. Then you saw Frank, I'll bet."

"Then I did. Uh-huh."

"He's not a terrible guy, Crow. It's his job to figure out what happened to Anderson." I sounded like the love-struck secretary in every old movie defending her crooked boss. "You know what? I don't know what I'm talking about. Was he a bastard to you?"

Crow clenched his hand into a fist then wrapped the other hand around it before releasing both and placing them casually on the cushioned arms.

"Let's just say your favorite detective isn't exactly the model of civility you think he is. He does have an overly developed sense of right and wrong, that's for sure. And he will go to any lengths, and I mean any lengths, to protect what he feels needs protecting. But Frank's particular brand of vigilante bullshit justice tends to find me and mine on the unfortunate side of his highly personalized set of laws."

I shook my head, trying to understand.

"What beef does he have with you? There was only one car over the embankment. It wasn't a race. It was an accident. What, exactly, is the problem?"

I could see that he debated answering but decided to give it a go. "Well, JP, I guess it's something like…you remember that old man in the papers a few months ago? The one who worked that death camp during World War II?"

"Okay."

"Now, for the better part of his life that old man raised a family, ran a business, paid taxes. A real upstanding citizen by all accounts. But he did something in his twenties that folks find difficult to forgive. And even though it happened over sixty years ago, some think he should still stand trial. Maybe I haven't been a perfectly upstanding citizen, far from it, but it's something like that."

My head hurt as I tried to follow my company's lengthy exposition.

"What the fuck are you talking about?"

He harrumphed and offered me another smoke. "Don't matter. Let's just

say Francis and I have some history you don't know anything about. And the Marlboro Man isn't going to forget it. Therefore, I ain't gonna neither."

I grasped what he hinted at, and I didn't like it one bit. The line between good and bad was thinning.

"Please leave me the naive sap that I am, will you? I don't want to know one more goddamn thing." He gave me a half-grin and nodded.

I rose to throw out our paper cups and get some water.

"Yes'm. You're feeling better this morning. Much, much better shape than last night."

I drank some water, tired of rethinking the ugly depths I'd plumbed the night before. "I have a way of bouncing back."

"So far, so good." There was an addendum in his quip.

"What? Just say it."

"One of these days, when you least expect it, you may not bounce back so easily. That's all."

I leaned on the counter facing my unlikely conscience.

"Let's get some breakfast, man. I don't think I'm eating right lately."

Rising slowly, he walked over to the counter. "Sure. But first, we need to get a couple of things straight."

We were both in the small kitchen now, Crow leaning against the counter, me leaning against the sink. In this configuration, I couldn't leave without his permission. Were it anyone but Crow, I might've felt threatened. And, in fact, for one split second, I considered the precarious position I'd put myself in. But it was Crow.

"I'm a little surprised Frank hasn't called on you already, J. When he does, you need to know what you're going to tell him."

His demeanor told me, in no uncertain terms, he was serious. Everything discussed up to this point was just chitty-chat, and what he was about to say was the actual point of his early morning drop-by. I heeded the shift in tone, adjusting my spectacles for better comprehension.

"The fact that the concrete wall and a mailbox were destroyed last night aren't going to be seen as unrelated events, understand? The cops are looking at those two incidents as one and the same. You can't blame them. What are the odds of both happening within feet of one another on the same night, right? Anyway, as long as there's no other car they really can't nail me or my posse with anything."

I removed my hands from deep chenille pockets and crossed them in front of me, defensive of the answer that would follow my next question.

"How do I fit in?"

"The Cadillac, J."

"What about it?"

"Look, maybe if Anderson hadn't been playing Mighty Mouse last night nobody would question why your car's bumper is all curled up like it is. But Anderson was playing Mighty Mouse last night. And you had to complicate matters by taking out that mailbox. Get it?

"No."

He walked around to the other side of the counter and sat at one of the two stools there.

"Frank may try to put your car at the scene of the accident. Make like somebody ran somebody off the road."

"Why would Frank think I ran Anderson off the road?"

He dropped his head then lifted it as if duty dictated he must. "I need you to try harder to follow what I'm saying."

"Honestly, Crow, nobody's going to think I could run anybody off the road, except maybe Peaches."

"Frank won't think you ran Anderson off the road, but he might think somebody using your car did."

I guffawed. "That's a ridiculously long reach."

He gave me a steely look.

"You watch how far he reaches. Besides, that little scenario works great for you. That way, you don't have to explain the mailbox incident. Not so good for me, though, unless we can prove your bumper got damaged some other way."

I looked up and down the counter and, like magic, Crow produced a cigarette from his jacket for me. While he got his lighter out, I thought how this couldn't be as complicated as he was making it.

"This is crazy. If he notices my car at all, though why he would, I still don't follow, if he does notice the bumper, I'll just tell him I…I'll tell him that I hit that mailbox."

"He won't buy it, not with Anderson's nosedive."

"Oh, man. What am I supposed to tell him if he asks?"

"You know those three cement pillars in the parking lot, the ones you got chains between marking the edge of the property?"

"Yes."

"You hit one of those."

"But can't they check that sort of thing? The dent in the bumper won't match up with those pillars."

"It does now."

"What are you saying?"

"While you were sleeping, I had Darren take care of it."

"Darren ran my car into a pillar? How'd he get the keys?"

"Darren don't need no keys."

It was like science fiction. And I was sober. "Crow, I'm speechless."

"I doubt that."

He got up and walked toward the door, removing the sunglasses that had been on top of his bald melon. "So when asked, you hit a pillar, the last pillar, closest to the back lot. You were coming into the lot after seeing the kids play. Understand? Coming *into* the lot."

My mouth hung open as I stared at tile then wood flooring as I followed him to the door.

"Julie."

I'd never heard him call me by my name. Our eyes locked.

"Can you do that? You lie well enough and neither one of us goes to jail. You good with that?

I breathed in deeply and exhaled the same way.

"JP, in case you haven't figured it out yet, there's a code around here. You cover me, I cover you. It's all good."

He gave me a big generous smile, adding, "I know you got plenty on your mind right now. I haven't forgotten. Now, you may not see me around too much for a little while, until this shit settles back down, but you got people watching your back 24-7. Don't you worry about that. Ain't nothing going to happen to you, J. Word."

He opened the door for himself. "You should put some clothes on before you go downstairs for breakfast."

I grabbed at my robe. "I'll meet you downstairs?"

"I need to go check on Anderson. I'll catch you later. Hang tough."

"Okay, cowboy."

I stepped out onto the porch as he headed down the concrete steps. Then, something stopped him in his tracks. It was Frank. Frank was waiting at the bottom of the steps, leaning against the whitewashed bricks looking up at us.

CHAPTER SEVENTEEN

Moving away from the wall and looking up at the landing, he fell into the "at ease" position that never meant he was at ease, feet apart, hands clasped in front of him. Crow's exit was now blocked.

An uncharacteristic shyness flushed my cheeks, awkward, as though one lover had just run into another. There I stood in my robe, the first mystery date facing off with the next. I wanted to spin the plastic doorknob again, but this was no game.

As the two stared silently at one another, I tried to remember why I felt as though I'd been caught in a lie. I hadn't lied to anyone. Then, of course, it occurred to me that I was about to. This was pre-guilt guilt.

From somewhere deep within my bag of survival arsenal, I broke the silence with a voice that sounded as buoyant and relaxed as an out-of-town conventioneer at a hotel bar.

"Frank! Well, good morning. Come on up and I'll get you some coffee. Crow was just leaving."

Nobody moved.

"Come on, you two. Let's give it a rest. It's early."

Frank unclasped his hands and slowly pulled back his unbuttoned coat to slide them into pants pockets. Still, nobody moved.

"Okay, I'm tired of this shit. I'm going back to bed. You fellas can play Stare-Down without me." I shook my head in disgust.

"Hey, magpie, shut your cake hole."

Finally, Frank spoke. And though he was seven different kinds of serious, I almost laughed. Only Frank in a moment of anger would snap, “Hey, magpie, shut your cake hole.”

Something in his ludicrous command gave me confidence that I could handle this, after all. I pushed past Crow and walked down the stairs restraining a smile. It hurt like hell, walking down the stairs, but Detective DiAngelo wasn’t going to know that.

My intention was to put my arm through his and lead him back upstairs while sharing my concern over the accident Crow had just told me about. But I didn’t get that far. When I hit the bottom step and pivoted to place my arm through his, he backhanded me, clipping the side of my face. My glasses were pulled from their mooring.

I froze, facing the direction the glasses had flown, not truly hurt but stunned and frightened. This was a very different Frank, indeed. All inventive options on how to manipulate the impending conversation vanished and a somber dose of submissiveness set in.

Francis looked like he’d just run over a dog as he reached for the face he clearly didn’t mean to hit.

“Julie, I only meant to push your hand away...” he began. But Crow was already coming down the stairs to intervene. Before he could take three steps, Frank had his gun drawn as we all heard the small yet penetrating sound of the hammer being cocked.

He had one hand gently resting on my assaulted cheek and the rest of his attention aimed up the stairs. Again, no one spoke. I was too frightened to pull my face away from his hand, so while balanced there I attempted to calm him down.

“Frank...Frank, what are you doing? Relax. Please, put that away.”

I was careful not to cuss. Frank doesn’t like it when I cuss and right then I wanted him to like me. He removed his hand from my face and placed it over his other on the handle of the gun. "Your glasses are right there." They hadn't fallen far. "Are they okay?"

I quickly grabbed them up from out of the dirt. "Just a little dusty, Frank. No problem." I wiped them clean with the tie of the robe and pushed them on.

Crow wasn't grinning but there was something in his expression that seemed wrong given the dramatic circumstances. His eyes were twinkling and the muscles in his face pulled up. It was the expression you see on a wild animal before it attacks. He kept his lips together, I imagined, to keep from baring his teeth.

"Everybody, calm down. No one's going to die today, right Frank? Frank?" I said, waiting for confirmation.

He uncocked the hammer and slid the gun back in its holster. "No, not on my shift. All right, Mr. Big Shot, come down here and let's the three of us have a little talk. Keep your hands where I can see them."

Crow made his hands visible and cautiously descended the rest of the concrete steps. I'm sure my heartbeats were audible as the tired muscle banged against my battered chest. This was way too much excitement to bear on one cup of coffee and aspirin.

We were all together at the foot of the stairs, everyone's arms crossed in front of them.

"So, this is where you run, huh? Crow? Now, why is that?"

I wanted to spring to Crow's defense but I wasn't sure how.

"You two must be closer than I figured. Real good friends."

Frank shot me a look that hurt more than the back of his hand, and I turned my face to block it. He reached for me and I gasped, recoiling even further. "Geez, Julie, I told you

I didn't mean to hit you before. I'm just trying to get you to look at me. I need your full attention."

I looked him square in the eye, uncrossing my arms and placing them on my hips. "You've got my attention, Frank."

"Good. That's real good. Now then, who wants to tell me what exactly happened last night? Your boyfriend here's already given me his version, so why don't we hear from you, Ms. Page? Where were you last night?"

And now it was time for the lying. My brain gave one last cursory look around for another way to get out of this, but no alternatives were found. Crow's script would have to do.

"I…I went to see the kids play, the band that hangs out here, the Chads. They were playing at The Bait Shack."

"And when did you leave the club?"

"I don't remember exactly."

Frank's face got all screwed up like he was yelling obscenities at a slowpoke in the fast lane but he wasn't yelling at all. Very quietly, he whispered, "Try."

"It was like maybe midnight," I stammered, feeling a little faint.

"You come right back here?"

I inadvertently glanced at Crow. Frank lunged toward the drag racer and threw him against the wall, pressing his large face against the whitewashed bricks. "You don't need to get any information from your boyfriend right now. You just need to tell me the truth."

"Jesus Christ, Frank! What the fuck is wrong with you? Let go of him right now!" Oops. I lost my cool.

He swung around redrawing his gun, so frustrated he didn't know where to aim it. Crow started to turn around but Frank repositioned him with the full weight of his own body. Now they were stacked, one, two, on the bricks, like a wrestler pinning another against a vertical mat.

"Don't move. Don't move even a little bit. Don't move until I tell you that you can move. Understand me? I'm not feeling very centered right now and I'd hate to make a costly mistake. Got it? You got it?"

Crow nodded.

"Let me hear you tell me that you understand."

"I understand you, detective," Crow obliged.

The victor peeled himself off of his opponent and slid the gun away a second time. Then he turned back to face me. I couldn't even grasp the drama tactics being wielded around on my property, on my time. And better judgment took a backseat to wrath.

"You know what, Frank? You pull one more motherfucking stunt like that and I'm gonna call a real cop, you understand *me*?"

"You're not in authority, Julie. I am. Now you're going to answer my questions, here or downtown."

"Bullshit. This unwarranted look-at-me-I've-got-a-gun show is over, man. You pull out that fake penis one more time and you can talk to me through an attorney. Do you understand me, Frank? I want to hear you say it."

He looked up to the heavens, then at me. "You stop talking like a sailor and I'll leave the gun where it is. Deal?"

I thought I heard Crow chuckle. Frank heard it, too. But this time he didn't lose his mind. He just got that screwed-up look on his face again and calmly asked, "Something funny, pal?"

Crow responded more jubilantly than before. "No, detective. Nothing funny at all."

During this brief exchange, a tow truck rolled through the dirt lot toward the back of the building. I was hoping that he'd just come in for a cup of coffee but I had my concerns.

"There was a bad accident on Vincent last night, Julie. Seems our friends, the drag racers, were playing catch-me-if-you-can and somebody went over an embankment. The victim can't answer any questions right now because he's brain-dead."

Crow slowly turned around to absorb this newsflash more directly. Frank allowed it. The two held each other's gaze while Frank went on. "Yeah, I just came from the hospital. Looks like he'll be a vegetable for the rest of his life. Hope somebody's gonna get him some proper full-time care. Hate to see him in

the County hospital for the rest of his worthless life. Taxpayers get stuck with the bill. It's just not right."

Crow got that wild animal thing going again, but he kept it contained, making him a much nicer party guest than the Robert DeNiro impersonator. DiAngelo waited a couple of beats to see if he could provoke a physical response with his cruel remarks. He couldn't.

"So, anyway, whoever was racing with this idiot took out a mailbox, the mailbox on the corner of Vincent and the Promenade. Oh, yeah, there was a lot of activity out here last night, Julie. You didn't hear any of it, huh?"

My blood pressure had my ears ringing, I was so mad at this brute. Lying seemed not only doable but justified. I'd simply stick with the truth as long as possible, then veer off a little, as Crow suggested. But did I want to tell the cop about the pills? Nah.

"I got drunk last night."

"Really? Somebody drove you home?"

"No."

"You drove home drunk, huh?"

"No. The bartender will second that. I only had one beer at the club. I got drunk at home. When I got back here. Real drunk. Then I passed out."

"That's pretty."

"That's none of your business."

"The vegetable and the mailbox are."

"I didn't hear a thing. When I woke up this morning, there was a message for me from Dominic, my night cook, letting me know something happened out on Vincent but he didn't know what. I was here when he called. I just didn't pick up. Crow was good enough to drop by this morning to fill me in."

So far, so good. But while telling my tale, the tow truck rolled back in the other direction, my Cadillac hitched to it. The bumper that had taken a bad blow because of my nasty habits was now mangled, as was part of the nose and hood. My car. My beautiful car. I stopped talking long enough to yelp and cover my mouth. Frank took in my reaction with interest but not surprise.

"You sure you didn't loan the Cad to anybody else last night?"

"Where are you taking my car?"

"Hey! I'm asking you a question. You loan anybody the Cad?"

"I…No, I didn't." I was shaking and twitching, my eyelids batting like a debutante on a third date.

"Like I said, I was drunk."

"But not until you got home. Isn't that right?"

Shaking, twitching, batting.

"You want to tell me what happened to your car?"

"I ran into one of the poles in the parking lot, that one, there. I…I hit it on my way to the club. I hit it twice trying to pull out. The fog was thick and I was in a hurry. I didn't realize how badly I'd damaged it until now."

"On your way *to* the club."

I realized too late that I fucked up the one crucial element of the lie. Instinctively, I started to turn toward Crow but remembering what happened the last time I looked to him in Frank's company, I fought the urge, looking nowhere but directly at the cop.

"Yes."

"Oh, sure. That makes good sense. We're going to check that out, run some tests, talk to some people. Meantime, we're impounding your car."

"Oh, Frank."

He didn't touch me but he got right down in my face. "You forget we're trying to solve a murder? I thought you were pretty focused on that. You forget? You think I got time to play footsy with these thugs, these friends of yours? I'm not dancing with you, Julie. I'm dead serious. I find out any part of your little story doesn't add up, and it sounds like a bunch of hooey, I'll be taking you to a real-live jail and putting you in a real-live cell."

He turned toward Crow. "You got all that? Your girlfriend could be in a heck of a lot of trouble if I find out she's lying for somebody or that she's in any way connected to last night's festivities."

The dragger chose to bite his upper lip with his lower teeth as a response.

"You know, it's touching how you two protect each other. It is."

There was a lapse in the conversation. I didn't look over at him but I assumed Crow was pretty disappointed with my costly mistake. Okay, I messed that up but he wouldn't want me to retract now. I would hold steady. Perhaps I could still make it swing. I'd offer up another lie, and another, until the story made better sense. But before I reopened my mouth, Frank had a thought.

"You know, there's so much going on around here, murders and races and everything, know what I think I'm going to do? I think I'm going to blockade part of Vincent and the Promenade for forty-eight hours while we have a chance to investigate things. Julie, you tell your crew they're not to come to work until I say so. Crow, you tell your buddies it's rainy-day session for a while. No playground privileges. How's that?"

My scriptwriter and I both lit up at this suggestion.

"You can't just shut down her business like that. That's not right at all."

"Come on, Frank, that's not necessary."

He smiled a maniacal smile while his brow remained furrowed.

"Really? You think that's too much? Get out of here, you piece of trash, before I take you in for not cutting your toenails."

He gestured for Crow to skedaddle and, reluctantly, Crow took off. Then there were two.

He grabbed my elbow and led me upstairs. I struggled to keep up, as stiff and bruised as my legs were, negotiating the whole while.

"Frank, you don't even know what happened last night."

"You want to tell me?"

"I don't know what happened. But for all we know, Anderson just spun out of control. It was so foggy last night. Accidents do happen."

He practically pushed me inside my living room. "You think it was an accident, huh? Maybe he took out the mailbox on one side of the street then kept going another block and took out a concrete wall. You think that's it?"

I tried to remain nonchalant, though being upstairs with him in his current mindset made me a tad antsy.

"Could be. Look, maybe the two things are unrelated. That's possible, isn't it?"

He pulled out a dining room chair then pulled out another one and sat down. Julie, let's talk for a minute, okay?"

I cautiously joined him.

"I'd like to think you got nothing to do with any of this but, you know, you're making that harder and harder."

"I'm not trying to make things harder for you, Frank. Come on, it's me."

With laced fingers, he placed his hands behind his head.

"And who are you, again? Because I think I know you and then I find that piece of trash coming out of your apartment. I gotta say, I like Felix a whole lot more than this one and I can't stand Felix. You've got very peculiar taste in beaus."

I thought about telling him to fuck off then quickly reconsidered.

"He's not my boyfriend, Frank. He just dropped by to tell me about the accident."

He nodded, swiveling his head left and right as I spoke.

"Hearing you say that does relieve some of the anxiety. Now, go get your clothes on. You're going to shut down the diner while I'm here. And turn off the neon, too. I'll have officers at both entrances but we don't need to be attracting business for a couple of nights."

"Please don't make me close the diner, Frank."

His body language softened some but this newly devised plan of his was not open to discussion.

"Go get dressed."

I did.

"Turn off the Owl."

I went to the fuse box where the timer lives and fiddled with the dial.

"Better get your coat. It's cold."

I grabbed my coat and he grabbed it from me, holding it open for my convenience. He slid it up my arms, paused, and rested his hands on the stiff wool shoulders. "Wish we could find that other coat," he mused. I wasn't feeling chatty so I let the comment go unaddressed.

"Okay. We're going to go talk to the crew and then I'm going to leave. I'd rather that you stay here tonight so I can keep an eye on you but if you're going to go, to stay with Charlotte or something, do it. Once the barricade goes up nobody's going through it."

"I'd like to stay here."

"Good. I think that's good."

We were standing at the open door. As I started to walk through he did the same, catching my arm in the process.

"Look, Julie, shutting down a couple of days is a good idea all the way around. You don't want this place to become a morgue. That can't be good for business." His hand gently squeezed my woolly forearm.

"In the past two weeks, we've got a dead body and a half-dead body within three blocks of one another. Maybe they're related, maybe not. But I need to regain control of the situation, okay? This is crazy."

To push past him would be to push against him and that seemed wildly inappropriate. So I remained in the frame and waited for him to clear the way. In that tight confine, tight enough to smell the starch in his crisp white collar, it struck me that I had caused all of this.

If I hadn't hit the mailbox and run, it wouldn't have looked like a drag race. Now, while Frank tried to figure out who wanted me dead, he had to stop and figure out what happened to my car. And by creating that situation, I'd thrust him head to head with a guy he hated, a guy he already had some serious vendetta with. And I didn't know anything about that. Truth to tell, I could not easily tell the good guys from the bad. At that moment I nearly forgave his rage.

"Look, Frank. Whatever you think is best. And I do want you to catch whoever killed that kid. I haven't meant to complicate the investigation. You know that. In your heart, you know that."

"Mmm, yeah, I do. You're a good girl. You're just a very bad judge of character. I know you don't see it now but I'm trying to watch out for you. Anyway, you'll be safe here for a couple of nights. This place will be crawling with cops, don't worry."

I started through and he did as well, stopping me a second time. We were kissing close.

"But please don't think I won't play hardball with you. Please don't think because we're…pals…that I won't do whatever I think is right to protect this neighborhood, because I will. I can shut down the diner for forty-eight hours just like I can shut the doors permanently. There are plenty of ways to do it. So don't push me, Julie. I'm begging you. Don't push me."

CHAPTER EIGHTEEN

My legs worked some better going down the stairs this time but I was compelled to hold my chest just under my boobs as the pain there continued to be notable.

It's a longer walk than you might think from the front door of the apartment to the front door of the diner, which gave me time to debate what I should do next. Couldn't I just tell him I'd hit the mailbox? That probably wouldn't work in that Crow had somebody run the car into a pole to cover for me. I didn't want him getting into any more trouble than he already was, not on my account.

By the time we entered the diner, I'd decided to stick with the story as I'd told it. Though it occurred to me that if Frank snooped around enough, one of those kids from the club last night would surely report what a beautiful Cadillac I had. What a beautiful, perfect, cherry car. Not a nick on her. The medication I took while getting dressed had yet to weave its magic.

We had a nice breakfast crowd that morning, all six coffee pots in use. Jesus and Craig were covering the kitchen. Most of the crew at Nighthawks I'd known before hiring them. Many came to work for me from The Coffeehouse, a joint I used to frequent with Felix. But I didn't know Craig. He got the job on Rhea's recommendation. He used to work at the 7-11 she frequents and had recently decided to explore other career options. Nice enough guy. A little old for the company he keeps but nice enough.

As I nodded hello to him from the customer side of the counter, I thought how this was probably the guy who tried to kill me. I didn't know that guy. Yeah, it was probably him. This is the kind of joke you tell yourself when you think your life's in danger.

Jesse was pulling plates from table twelve as Frank and I assessed the room. "Hey, Julie. What are you doing here so early?"

"Hey, Jess. What are you doing here at all? This is where I left you last night."

"I know," he grumbled while nudging the gypsy with a wet towel. "I need the money."

Debbie put down a plate of eggs and hash browns in front of a gal with a mullet, then walked over to greet us.

"Morning, Julie," she offered, pleasant and professional. "Morning, Frank," she continued, sultry yet demure. He attempted to maintain his official posture but the suggestion of a grin threatened to blow his cover. He didn't look at her, choosing the floor instead, and I thought I detected a little extra color wash over his prizefighter features as he responded.

"How are you, Debbie? You look well."

She giggled. Extending one Lee Press-On nail, she gently placed it against his tie. "How do you know how I look? You're not even looking at me."

She had the nerve to giggle again. He cleared his throat, choking back the urge to giggle, too. I turned ugly.

"Are you kidding me, Frank? Seriously, are you fucking kidding me?"

He got very serious very fast, straightening his tie and adjusting his belt. "Debbie, I'm afraid I'm here on official business this morning."

He shook his head in agreement with himself.

Now, this is where Debbie would say something like, "Oh, yes, sir, detective. Will you need to frisk me?" But she didn't. She lost all the "lady in red" shit immediately, staring pensively at the big lug, then me, then him again.

"Well, take care of it, Frank. And be careful."

Sounded like a girlfriend. Sounded like…like a wife, for Christ's sake. Then she went about her business grabbing menus and leading a family of four to a booth.

We stood in the middle of the floor without clear direction.

"So, how do you want to do this, Frank?"

"I think we should tell Carroll and let him take care of telling the rest of the crew. He's your manager."

"Carroll doesn't come in for a couple of hours."

"Is Jesus your second?"

"No, he's my first but don't tell Carroll. You want to talk to Jesus?"

"Yeah."

He led me into the kitchen where Jesus was sprinkling grated cheese over an omelet.

"Julie! Que pasa? Como esta?"

"Hey, Jesus. Listen, I need to talk to you for a minute."

Wiping his hands on his filthy apron, he stepped away from the workstation to join us, eyeing the trench coat-clad intruder with vague curiosity.

"Hola, detective. Your order taking too long or something?"

Frank assumed the "at-ease" position.

"Good morning, Jesus. There was some activity on the highway last night very close to the Promenade. We're going to have to shut down the diner for a couple of days while the department has a chance to investigate."

My comrade looked genuinely stunned. "You're closing down the diner?"

"Just for a couple of days."

"This got anything to do with the murder?"

"That's police business, son. Nothing for you to worry about."

"Son? Oh, my God, are you my father? Because I imagined you differently."

Sometimes Jesus has a problem with authority. And for somebody inclined that way, Frank can prove to be a tremendous source of consternation.

"Okay, no need to get cute."

Jesus crossed his arms and stepped up close to me as if this would exclude Frank from our conversation. "You want to close the diner for a couple days, boss?"

"No, I don't. But more than that, I don't want to interfere with any police business, if you dig. Let's just do what Detective DiAngelo wants us to do. See if we can break this bad luck streak."

Jesus shrugged his shoulders and turned back toward Frank.

"What am I supposed to do?"

"Go ahead and put the closed sign on the door and finish up with the folks who are already here. By then, we'll have the barricades in place. We can keep the west end open until everybody's had a chance to leave."

"Barricades?"

I put up a hand to hopefully moderate a string of questions. My hand did not do the trick.

"Why do we need barricades?"

"So that no one travels this strip for a while."

"Ay, this is extreme, Poncho. And this is all because a guy ran off the highway last night?"

"You know all about that, huh?"

"They already got that part of V closed off, right up to the mailbox. Why you got to close down the Promenade, man? Nothing happened here."

The detective didn't like being interrogated, especially when his reason for shutting us down was so – personal.

"Well, there was a murder. Remember?"

Jesus walked back to the grill and flipped some sausage patties.

"Oh, yeah, I remember. That was like a week and a half ago right at the front door. You didn't shut down the diner then."

Frank stuck his hands back in his pockets and stared at an air vent over the grill.

"What about Julie? She lives here. She got to leave, too?"

Frank's impatience was palpable.

"No, she's going to stay. Look, Jesus, I need you to call Carroll and the crew and tell them they won't be able to get to work for the next forty-eight hours. And any delivery people you might be expecting. Can you do that?"

Jesus looked to me for my opinion. I buried my ambivalence with a reassuring wink then added, "Tell everybody I'll pay them for their full shifts for the next two days."

Frank rubbed his chin, turning slightly to the left where I was standing. "Now, that's nice, Julie. It is."

I wanted to yell, "You should be paying them, you big jerk. You're the one messing with their jobs." But I said nothing.

Jesus looked very unsure of this whole thing as he started to move toward the swinging door. We followed, sitting at the counter in front of the register. Jesus procured the address book and schedule from the shelf above the Owl souvenir drawer.

Debbie came up to us with two cups of coffee. "Can you tell me what's going on?" On some instinct, she was looking to me for a straight answer, not her love interest. I passed.

"I'll let Frank tell you." We both turned to him as he drank some coffee, buying time.

I don't know if Deb heard part of the conversation in the kitchen or if she just trusted the vibe that was emanating from Jesus and me but she got a little testy with Francis.

"Yes, tell me, Frank. What is going on?"

Just then, Jesus, who was on the phone, interjected. "Hey, boss, Mr. Sharkey wants to talk to you."

I took the call and explained the situation in abbreviated clarity. Carroll asked questions of abbreviated clarity. The only thing he was able to articulate distinctively was that I shouldn't stay at the diner if Frank thought there was a problem. I wasn't in a position to share that Frank was the greatest part of the problem. I just assured him I would be well protected.

Debbie stopped working for the length of that call, making her own assessments. She uttered a tsk-tsk while turning off the pots. "Something sure smells funny in here. Hey, Jesus, you smell something funny?"

My dark knight agreed while dialing the next number. "Si, Deb. Something stinks."

Frank got up and started for the door. I leaped off the stool to stop him.

"You can't blame them, Frank. This is nutty."

"Okay, it's nutty. I'm a kooky guy. Just give me two days, will ya? Two days. Maybe I can close the door on some of this stuff. I can't get much done when it's Party Central around here, okay?"

The phone rang. "Julie, it's for you."

"Frank, just wait a minute. Don't leave yet."

As I went to take the call, I saw Frank make a call himself on his cell. In no time the barricades would be up. Jesus handed me the phone. It was the dreadful receptionist from Doctor Stewart's office.

"Mrs. Page?"

CHAPTER NINETEEN

"It's Miss Page," I hissed. "What can I do for you?"

"Yes, ma'am. Doctor Stewart wants to know if you can come by and see her today around noon. Is that possible?"

Marjorie had never asked such a thing. And the fact that I had just seen her made this request even stranger.

"Do you know what she wants to talk to me about?"

The receptionist had a kind of acerbic containment to her voice, like a hornet in a jar.

"No, ma'am. I don't know what she wants to talk to you about. Can I let her know that you'll be here at noon, Mrs. Page?"

I put on my best Roseanne Barr and screamed into the receiver, "If for nothing more than to see your smiling face, yes, tell her I'll be there with bells on," then slammed the phone down so I wouldn't have to hear her retort.

Why would Marge want to see me?

While pondering that, Frank approached. "You okay?"

I sat down on a counter stool as something about that call had me feeling a little shaky. "I don't know, Frank. I don't know if I'm okay. That was my doctor's office calling."

We looked at each other for information that neither had and then his cell rang. A waitress whose name I can never remember was taking the order from a family of four as Deb sidled up next to me.

"Hey, is he being an asshole?" She referred to Francis.

"Little bit."

"And that was your doctor?"

"Yeah."

She went back to dropping salt and squeezing lemon into each of the empty coffeepots to give them a good cleaning. "Well, Julie, none of this is worth you getting sick over. You want a refill?" She picked up the one remaining active pot and waited for my answer.

"Thanks. It wasn't a GP. It was my psychiatrist."

She replaced the pot and went back to swooshing the salt around. "See if they can fit me in. I've definitely got some holes in my head."

That made me laugh. Most people act as though you've just farted when you say the words "my psychiatrist," but not Debbie.

Frank joined me at the counter. "You got to get to your doctor's today?"

"Marjorie. Marge wants to see me. Isn't that odd?"

"Oh, that doctor. I don't like her, what she did to you. And while you were in the hospital, too."

"Felix is a big boy. She didn't force him to do anything he didn't want to do. Anyway, let's not revisit that right now, all right?"

He shuffled his feet apologetically. "So what could be so urgent?"

"I can't imagine. I just saw her. Are you going to let me go or not?"

He rolled his head in a circle and raised and lowered his shoulders before answering. "What's the point of a blockade if people are coming and going through it?"

"I have to see her, Frank. She might know something about...about something I need to know about."

"What? Never mind. Yeah, go. But get back here and stay put. Deal?"

"Okay. Hey, Frank..."

"What? You need to pick up some dry cleaning, maybe get a manicure? What?"

"You impounded my car."

Debbie, Jesus, and Jess shot each other emergency glances, none of them willing to ask why the police had the Cad. Frank rubbed his eyes hard with the palms of his hands.

"All right, I'll take you. When do you need to be there?"

"Noon. But it's only a quarter past ten."

Just then, a cop walked in with Richard in tow. "Richard, I've been expecting you," I said under my breath.

My agent looked like he'd just been in a fistfight, eyes bugging, hair loosed from his ponytail going every whichway. The cop and Richard stood just inside the front door, one disoriented, both pissed. Frank and I moved to join them. The cop spoke before anyone else had a chance.

"We're in the process of getting those barricades up, sir. Should be taken care of within the next few minutes. But this man says he has urgent business with Miss Page. Says it can't wait. You want me to escort him out, or what do you want to do?"

Richard unbuttoned his coat and swiped his hair out of his face. "What was that? What the hell was that? Julie, what's going on here?"

"Hey, I'm truly happy to see you, man. Just don't ask me for pages. There are no pages. Richard, this is Detective Frank DiAngelo. Frank, this is my agent, Richard Randall." They shook hands. "Frank, can Richard stay?" Frank nodded.

"Can I stay? What have I walked into? Do I want to stay?"

"Richard, don't have a fit. Go back to my booth. I'll be there in a minute."

With flapping of arms and loud mutterings, he moved toward the booth in the back.

"Frank, maybe I can get Richard to drive me to see Doctor Stewart. I'll need to stay open for another hour or so anyway. Those folks haven't even gotten their food yet."

"Okay. That sounds good. Just remind him to use the west-end exit. I'll leave word so he can get you out and back." He looked awkward and tired. "I'm gonna go solve some crimes now."

"Yeah, go solve some crimes. Just be careful to get the actual bad guys, okay?"

He shook his head and left without even throwing Debbie a glance.

I hate Frank. I love Frank. I have so many emotions about Frank, from compassion to disdain, that I sometimes can't sort through them all. Every time I want to beat the crap out of him I realize I could never beat him up as badly as he beats himself. And beyond all evidence to the contrary, he truly does try to do the right thing. In his warped, muddy head, he does. Why the war with Crow? It wasn't any of my business. But maybe my blind trust of this racer should be reevaluated if Frank felt that strongly about it.

I joined my discombobulated guest.

"Richard, there's been another situ on the midway, so to speak. They're going to have the Promenade closed off to the public for the next couple of days and my car's been impounded. Meanwhile, I need to get to Peavemont in a bit because my psychiatrist wants to see me, and before I go see her I got to close the joint.

"I'm sorry, are you talking to me? Because I'm still reeling from having survived the border crossing two blocks from here."

"Man, they got there fast. Was it awful?"

"Dealing with the militia? Well, let's just be thankful that I had my passport with me and my papers in order. They may as well have asked that I bend over and cough. What's going on?"

Before I could answer, he placed a finger to my lips to keep me from it. "If you say words like *there was a situ on the midway* I'm going to explode."

I gave him an expurgated version and finished by asking if he'd drive me to see my shrink. He had a chance to calm down while I told him the story, growing contemplative, even grave.

"They impounded your car? Did you do something... naughty?"

I neither confirmed nor denied, which was certainly a clear answer.

"Sounds like you've had a wicked day already."

"You know, unfortunately, it's not that different from the last several."

"Yeah, of course, I'll drive you to Peavemont and back. Go take care of whatever it is you restaurateurs do. I'll eat. May I eat?"

"I'll send Debbie over. Get whatever you like. I'll hurry up." It occurred to me that I should at least acknowledge the uniqueness of his visit. "Richard, I'm sorry. I've usurped the point of this impromptu visit of yours. What's up?"

He was fanning and shuffling a large stack of business cards pulled from his pocket, a habit I'd observed before. "Nothing too pressing. It can wait a little longer. We'll talk on the way to the doctor's. How's the halibut?"

"The halibut's great. But, Rich, it's ten thirty."

"I'll put syrup on it."

CHAPTER TWENTY

I sorted out checks while Jesus tried to quick-thaw a piece of halibut. During this, the girls dropped the last of their tickets and bused around the remaining customers. After the halibut was served, the grill was scraped and the fryer turned off as my confounded crew and patronage filed out one at a time.

"Remember to exit on the ocean-side, you guys."

Now it was only me, Richard, Jesus, and that party of four. As the family rose, the guy came up to the register where I greeted him to take his money.

"Say, we understand there was a murder here a few days ago. There hasn't been another, has there? Is that what this is about?"

I deliberated over what would be trendier, more murders or fewer. In that these shiny, faceless folks were clearly from a city unlike Berle, I opted for the truth. "No, sir. No more murders. Just a bad accident down on Vincent. Here's your change. Come see us again."

"Uh-huh. How long are you going to be closed for?"

The baby started crying and the agitated mom chimed in. "I'll meet you out front. Let's go. This place gives me the creeps."

Nice.

"Just a couple of days. We'll be open next week. Take care."

With a to-go container in one hand and a toddler in the other, he still managed to look like a kid in line for his first roller coaster ride, eyes wide open, a half-grin crawling around his bleached teeth.

"We hear drag racers are frequenting this area all of a sudden. Those are some tough cookies. That can't be good for business."

"Oh, business is very good. Bye now."

He wasn't done.

"You know, we've thought about opening an eatery ourselves as a side business. We were thinking crepes. If you don't mind me asking, what's a place like this bring in on an average day?"

I pretended to be invisible but the gentleman saw through me. Fortunately, the wife poked her head inside, baby still wailing. "Tim, come on. It's like a ghost town out here. And it's dirty."

He minded the mommy. "Gotta run. Good luck. We love the vintage motif."

"Hold on." I grabbed a Nighthawks postcard from under the glass and stuck it in the to-go hand. "To send to the folks back home."

"Oh," he chuckled, "we just live in Irvine."

"I thought I recognized the accent. Enjoy your stay."

He left with a quizzical look on his face that I found quite satisfying.

By the time I located which key locked the glass door with the scripted *We're Always Open!* painted across the front, Jesus had pulled Richard's plate and wiped down both booths. "Richard, this is Jesus. Jesus, Richard Randall, my agent." We exited together.

"So, you're Jesus. I've heard so much about you."

They shook hands in transit. "From Julie, I mean, not the New Testament. I'm not feeling clever enough to riddle you with a bunch of bad one-liners you've no doubt heard a million times."

"Damn, dude, you talk a lot."

Richard smiled while sliding on his Raybans. "Yes, I get paid for it."

Once in our respective cars we rolled slowly toward the west end exit of the strip, the family of four, then us with Jesus right behind.

Driving toward the blockade I could see three police officers patrolling in front of wooden foldout sawhorses, the kind you see at fairs or raceways. We stopped as a cop approached the family of four and the man fished for his identification. Richard felt around for his wallet, muttering, "You think you can bully me? You can't bully me, you big mustached cartoon. I'm with William Morris."

We were next.

"Yes, I'm Richard Randall, with William Morris. We spoke no more than an hour ago." He was willing to keep talking but the cop waved him through without comment. "Well, that's a cold how-do-you-do. Not at all the reception I received on my way in."

"You're so 'an hour ago,' Richard. They're bored with you now."

"Apparently."

Additional police guided us forward past the mutilated mailbox, and a half-block further, past the shattered embankment. That was a grisly sight, a gaping, ragged hole in the dividing wall framing a covert view of the ocean. What could've taken such a vicious bite out of something so sound, so resilient? Oh, right, Anderson's car. Anderson, who could locate the kid with the answers one minute and drive his brains through cement thc next. A hubcap and paint fragments scarred the broken concrete. "Oh, my God," I whispered. Guilt deep enough to drown in threatened to take me down were it not for the medication.

The pill I'd taken in my apartment did nothing. Maybe I had inadvertently taken a vitamin. But the one I took in the diner was just starting to rock me steady. And by the time we left the quarantined area, I felt numb and ready to face the day.

"So, my drug-addled friend, how do we get to your shrink's?"

"You're going to stay on V for another fifteen minutes or so. I'll warn you in plenty of time. Richard, maybe you should tell me why you came out here today."

He stared straight ahead, occasionally glancing at the surf to his left. The marine layer wasn't completely gone but the sun made a valiant effort to represent the heavens and the whole scene was beautiful, as usual. When the mist glides back and forth across the breaking waves like it did that morning, it's majestic. You can almost hear Van Morrison singing every time you stop to take it in.

"I lost my contract, didn't I?"

He frowned from behind his dark glasses, lips parted in an attempt to speak. Finally, he did. "You knew?"

"I deduced. You showing up, finagling yourself through a barricade and all. They called twice yesterday, the publishing house. I think it was yesterday. The days kind of blur together. Anyway, I didn't take either call."

"And why was that?"

"Because I figured they were going to tell me I lost my contract and I don't like any of them. I wanted to hear it from you."

"You know, for a hophead you're sharp."

"That's sweet."

He was at a stoplight and turned to face me, removing his sunglasses. "You make me very angry, Julie. You make me so goddamned angry I

could scream."

I knew how he felt. I let it ride.

"It's not that you lost this book or that you refuse to fork over pages. It's that you stopped trying. Why? Why did you stop trying?"

I stared past him at the mystic surf, looking for solace that didn't come. *Have I stopped trying?* I pondered internally.

The light turned green but he didn't move. "Is getting high more important to you than writing anymore? Is it?"

He hit the gas. We rolled along for a good three minutes in silence but for the sound of my lighter.

"I read that other book of yours, you know; the novel you wrote before 'For the Record.'"

I guffawed. "That was a silly waste of time."

"Why?"

"Because it sucks. They wouldn't even publish it while I was number one on the best-seller list with Maxine's biography."

"And that makes it a bad book?"

"Pretty much, yeah."

"God, you're naive. You know why they wouldn't publish it?"

"Enlighten me."

"Because a group of square, gutless bankers make those decisions. Your success was with a biography and you handed them a novel. They were scared. It isn't a bad book. On the contrary. It's fresh and edgy and.... Your voice... it's very unique, Julie. Whether people like it or not is another matter, but it is unique."

He shook his head and gestured for me to give him a cigarette. "God, listen to me. I kept Patrick up all night boring him with this same tirade. It's not my life. It doesn't matter."

"It matters," I interjected with dark sincerity.

He took a hard drag then filled the car with it before cracking his window.

"Well then, do something about it. Write. You're letting every boorish literary hack who ever had a dicey opinion about you win. Don't let those sons-o'-bitches win. You're gifted. How dare you throw that away. How dare you."

I gave him a mock scowl.

"You're pissed about losing that fifteen percent, aren't you?"

He threw his head back against the rest, then forward again. "I'm not even going to dignify that." Under his breath, he added, "And fifteen percent of what? I could make more money waiting tables at your diner."

I laughed for the first time that day.

"There's a pothole right here. Watch it."

He hit the pothole. We both came up off our seats and then back down, regrouping at the next stoplight. I massaged my bruised ribs with one hand.

"Thanks for the warning," he snarled.

It's a notoriously long light there by the tracks, allowing you a moment to adjust to the factory skyline ahead. A smattering of independent businesses line up shoulder-to-shoulder like a collection of beauty pageant drop-outs still hoping someone will notice them amidst the sexy, vital power plants that monopolize the landscape from there on. The tiny, glamourless Nails of Love Salon is butt-up against Alberta's Bail Bonds, both promising fast, easy service. A van pulled into the driveway of the Holy Trinity Heating and Air Conditioning Company as a tamale vendor walked slowly by pushing his wares and ringing the little bicycle bell attached to the handle of his cart.

As all of this nothingness played out in front of us, Richard tentatively reached over and tapped my knee.

"Hey, how are you taking this? You okay? I can't read you, no play on words intended."

This garnered a smile from us both but the laughter was gone along with the ocean view.

"I don't know. Like I say, it isn't altogether unexpected. I am a little rough these days, a little fragile. It's funny, yesterday I felt like I could write for the first time in a long time. But circumstances kept me from it. I swear to God,

Richard, it's like something or someone wants to keep me from writing. I know you think I'm making that up but I'm not."

"Like a curse?"

"Okay."

"You're crazy as a loon, you know that?"

"Really? My psychiatrist says I'm perfectly sane."

"It is a curse. They call it writer's block. Just write. You don't need that house. There are other publishing houses, believe me. And don't let everything else that's going on derail you so completely. I know you have to deal with the murder and this accident and God knows what else but somewhere in there," he pointed to my head, "you've got to save a little space for some inspiration to work its way through."

I lit another smoke and stared at nothing out the passenger side. "You know that kid, the one who was murdered at my front door? She'd dug my old coat out of a dumpster and was wearing it. They pulled fibers from the coat out of the bullet hole in her back. The cops think somebody thought it was me. They think somebody might still want me dead. Isn't that wild?"

I turned to make eye contact while Richard abruptly pulled the car over to the side of the road. He exhaled twice, shallow, quick puffs, like he might be about to hyperventilate. "Well, I guess that trumps losing a book contract." When the engine was silenced, he took the pack from me and lit another.

"Hey, man, that's a premium brand. Leave some for me. I thought you quit."

"Me too. So, do they have any suspects?"

"None they've shared with me."

"Wow." He shook his head in the direction of the soybean plant to the right. "What's that feel like, anyway, knowing somebody's trying to kill you?"

"I love the attention. Makes me feel special. What kind of fucking question is that, Richard?"

He guffawed, flicking the ash onto the highway. "Sorry. I've just never known anyone..." He trailed off, exhaling a couple more times out the driver's window. Then, as if he'd finally come up with something that would make me feel better, he triumphantly exclaimed, "You know, when this is all over, you're going to have another blockbuster on your hands."

I winced. He didn't hear how barbaric he sounded.

"Well, let's not book any promotional tours yet, you mercenary bastard. I might end up dead."

Finally, he saw himself in all his steel-cold splendor, first embarrassed, then amused. He modified the smile on his face, turning the ignition over. "You're right. You might not make it. Do try to leave me something I can shop posthumously, won't you?"

"You're a regular Noel Coward. At the next light turn right. You know, I just saw this twat yesterday. What could be so important? And whatever it is, why couldn't she just tell me on the phone?"

"No idea?"

"No. But something's up, I can feel it."

CHAPTER TWENTY-ONE

The showroom parking lot out front of the three adjoining medical buildings was standing room only, as usual. There was even a Bentley on display for Richard to enjoy. His shiny little Cooper fit in a degree or two better than the Cad.

"Wow," he assessed, "They sure know how to live in Peavemont. Weren't we just driving through electrical plants and oil refineries?"

"That was Wilmore, son. This ain't Wilmore. Let me have my cigarettes."

The Mini glided to a conclusion right in front of Dr. Stewart's door. My agent fished out a smoke from the pocket of his leather bomber jacket and struck a match. "You want me to go in with you?"

I cupped my hand around his, taking advantage of the flame, then considered the offer while staring at the doctor's nameplate.

"No, it's cool. I'll be okay. I don't know why but I've got a creepy feeling about this. Isn't that weird? Hell, I probably dropped something out of my purse yesterday and she wants to give it back. No need to dream flat tires, right?"

He was studying me with quiet concern. "Right."

"Of course, under the circumstances, no one could blame me for being jumpy. Every time the telephone rings, or the doorbell, or..."

"Right." He had turned to position himself toward me. "Julie,"

"Yeah?"

He leaned in a little more, spreading his fingers out across the corner of the bucket seat, somehow connecting us without any physical contact. His intuition served us both because had touched me, I'd have broken into a million tiny pieces.

"You're going to get through this. Whatever you've done, whatever's happened, your contract, the murder, everything, in three months you'll still be here and all of this will be nothing more than a bad memory."

I could feel my eyes well up but the rest of my crying gear was dulled and relaxed under a downy soft narcotic blanket. "I want my car back," I said, sounding more like a little girl than the weathered crone that I am.

"We'll get your car back. And we're going to see about suing somebody. How's that?"

On that note, I grabbed my purse to face the task at hand. "Making friends wherever I go. Listen, stay put. I'll be in and out faster than a freshman after curfew, okay?"

"Your similes suffer when you're tense. Take your time. Hey, Julie, I know you pretty well. You think this has something to do with Felix, don't you?"

I was already out of the car when those words left his lips. I swung around braced between the door and frame. "Yep."

Four separate sets of eyes attached to me as I entered the waiting room. Yes, the good doctor was making the rent that day.

The joint smelled like a perfume counter at Christmas, all those distinctive designer scents co-mingling into one suffocating bouquet. Mixed with the refrigerated air, it made me think of a funeral home.

Another set of eyes made brief contact with mine before averting their gaze. From behind her uncluttered desk, the receptionist looked my way just long enough to communicate disdain then continued placing stamps on envelopes.

I signed in without comment. She allowed me to, without comment.

I wedged myself between two of Dr. Stewart's more gilded patients. The gentleman to my right wore yellow-gold cufflinks and a yellow-gold pinkie ring. The lady to my left carried at least ten pounds of jade and coral around her neck, wrists, fingers, and ears. This museum-quality bling hung heavy around her laser-treated skin. Faint Musak filled the room with a string version of "Laura's Theme" from Doctor Zhivago. Every face, drawn and empty. A David Lynch adaptation of Dante's Inferno. Understated horror. I recognized this place as hell.

The office door finally opened and a patient came out with Marjorie directly behind him. She crossed her arms when she saw me, tried to smile, then gestured for me to join her. As I rose, I could almost hear the other patients groaning subdued protests as I took cuts.

Marjorie looked tired and even smaller than usual. The green in the angora sweater she wore made her skin seem somehow sallow, and though her honey-blonde locks were neatly anchored with what looked like a real pearl barrette and a good deal of lacquer, her usual back-home freshness was notably missing. *Funny*, I internalized, *I thought you were supposed to glow when you were in a family way.*

"Julie. Thanks for coming on such short notice. May I take your coat?"

"No thanks."

She drilled through me with bloodshot, cosmetically dusted eyes.

"All I've heard on the radio since late last night is about that horrible accident right by the Promenade. What happened?"

I raised my brows deciding whether or not to tell her.

"Well, they're trying to figure that out. The diner's been temporarily closed while they dig for clues."

We were standing just inside the doorway. Realizing we were exposed to the waiting room, she closed the door and gingerly reached for my elbow. I knew she was about to hug me and that wasn't going to happen so I made for one of the high-backed chairs, eliminating the possibility of her joining me this time as she had on the couch the day before.

Stunned by the news about the diner, she crossed to her desk where a cup of steam waited. She dunked the teabag that was resting in it a couple of times before throwing it out. Then she brought the cup to me and placed it on a cork coaster of the Mona Lisa just to the side of the chair. "You take it. It'll warm you up. I'll make myself a cup later."

She plopped down in the other high-backed chair with no finesse at all, legs slightly apart, arms on either armrest. More than her polish was missing. There was something raw about her, something jagged.

"Thanks," I said, with no intention of drinking it.

"Julie, what's going on? Did someone connected with the diner have something to do with the accident?"

"Not that I'm aware of. It'll be over in a couple of days. It's proving to be an inconvenience more than anything else. So, tell me, what's on your mind?"

Reluctant to move away from the topic but obliged to stick with her schedule, she let out a weak laugh without smiling.

"A great deal. A great deal has been on my mind since you left here yesterday. Kept me up all night."

I crossed my legs and snuggled into the back of the chair thinking to myself there are times to speak and times to listen. I was all ears.

"Julie, I've always prided myself on giving my patients the best care I possibly can. Their concerns are my concerns. My job is to stay detached but I believe empathy is an important component of successful therapy."

We sat staring at one another in silence. I gathered it was my turn to speak but didn't know my lines, so I just nodded.

Realizing this, she repositioned herself a little and continued.

"I've failed you, Julie. And I've failed you from day one. In fact, I think I've made matters worse." Her voice got thin and her cheeks flushed. "I guess I can be pretty self-righteous sometimes. I truly thought I could help you get back on your feet after the fire. I thought I could help you adjust to the pressures of celebrity. I convinced myself that I could, knowing, knowing all the time…"

She trailed off, fixed on the box of Kleenex between us. I slowly slid it a couple of inches in her direction. Again, she laughed without smiling. "Now, that would be a new one. Thanks, I'm fine." She picked up where she'd left off.

"...knowing all the time that your past with Felix was always going to be between us. Even if I was the most compassionate, progressive, insightful psychiatrist in the world, I could never tear down that wall. And with it there, I could never really help you, not substantially. But I just kept ignoring that."

Her piddling remorse was pissing me off. Was I supposed to console her? What was this *really*? I continued to wait it out. Then, she lowered the boom with all the force of a bulldozer on a plywood shed.

"Julie, I've turned your file over to Dr. Rosenberg. Irving Rosenberg is a very good man with forty years of experience in human behavior. I've filled him in on everything, including Felix, though I think it would be beneficial for you to reintroduce the subject from your perspective. He's in L.A. but he's worth the drive."

She stroked her lacquered hair making sure it was all in place then readjusted herself in the other direction, crossing her legs and arms simultaneously.

"I want you to know I've never turned a patient over before. This is very uncomfortable for me. I hope you'll be understanding under the circumstances. I truly want to see you get the right help. Believe me, if I could give it to you, I would. But I can't. I know that now."

I could feel my face muscles go slack as my vision blurred from behind insufficient lenses. My lifeline to Felix had just been cut and there was nothing I could do about it. I just kept thinking it's over, it's over, it's all over. Then I picked up my purse and fished out a Xanax. I didn't give a shit. She gave them to me. She could watch me take one.

I picked up the cup of tea and took a swallow. Before I had the cup back on the coaster, Marjorie had gotten up and was squatted directly in front of me, one hand on her right knee, the other on the arm of my chair.

"Julie, I've also suggested to Dr. Rosenberg that your meds need to be adjusted. You know the Valium was never on your chart and I think he should consider tapering you off the Xanax, slowly. Of course, that's up to him now but you should know that's my recommendation."

She looked down and tilted her melon kind of pensive-like before continuing.

"I thought about that all night, too. I'm not going to question whether or not you've really been losing pills and such but it could be that you've, inadvertently, developed a dependency. I wanted to wean you off the medication a long time ago but there never seemed to be a right time. Since the fire, you truly have had to thrash your way through an extraordinary series of circumstances. And now a murder investigation, not to mention the accident on Vincent, which, for some reason, you're having to deal with, as well. But you can't live forever on Xanax and Valium. It's been a little over a year. You'll be better off without them. Please trust me on this."

My mind shut down momentarily. The crushing horror of my addiction not being fed jammed every synapse. I felt like one feels when blocking out a particularly horrific memory. You sense that it's lurking somewhere in your head but you can't access it, you won't. Like suffering physical pain so great that all at once, there's no pain at all, just white light, nerves in denial, coping, coping.

Gradually, things came back to me, the room, the situation at hand. She was still talking, saying something about my well-being.

A chorus of desperate affirmations wailed against the back of my forehead like a dozen banshees prophesying a dozen brutal deaths. *Not to panic. Don't panic. Don't cry. Are you going to cry? Don't. Get out of here. Don't run. Don't let her think you need to run. Don't panic.*

She remained kneeling before me, this compassionate, professional mother-to-be, waiting for a sign that I understood, that I forgave her, maybe even that I appreciated her tough love.

The self-protection tactics I possess, fundamental and hardwired, eventually presented themselves as they always do, in words. But each syllable dripped out thick and sticky over my tongue, as would an unsuccessful attempt to yell during a nightmare, which is exactly what I was doing.

"You are one passive-aggressive piece of shit, you know that?"

She remained crouched but her mouth fell open.

"You need to get up before I knock you on your ass."

She scrambled to her feet crossing her arms again while shaking her head.

"You're just feeling a sense of abandonment. That's to be expected. But nobody's abandoning you. I'm helping you. You'll see. Julie, wouldn't you like to have someone with whom you can talk about your unfinished feelings for

Felix, someone other than me? This is going to be better, I promise you."

I wanted to deck her and nearly did, but remembering she was pregnant kept me from it, that and the fact that I couldn't have managed the muscle coordination right then.

"You're an icy bitch, Marjorie. God help that baby."

The door seemed miles from where I stood but I made for it with slow, measured steps. I didn't run.

She flapped her arms in disgust and took off for her desk.

"I'm sorry you feel that way but if you have nothing more intelligent to offer

than that, then we have nothing more to say to one another," she shot off.

"Promise?" I shot back, as I closed the door between us.

My vision remained blurred and selective. I didn't see the waiting room or the patients. I didn't see the receptionist. I didn't see anything except the front door. It seemed to be hanging at a Hitchcock angle and a little off the ground. Pride and anxiety nudged me toward the twisted goalpost. I took baby steps so I wouldn't fall, slow and steady, masking my hysteria, little baby steps, just like I took while walking through Bethany's blood.

Then, as I reached for the knob, it seemed the door fell open, though I think someone got up and opened it for me. Once safely outside, the crisp air cleared away some of the mirage-like clutter from my glassy eyes.

Richard stood directly in front of me, leaning on the hood of the Mini smoking my cigarettes. The expression on his face made me think the expression on mine must've been pretty bleak. He got to his feet and dropped the smoke.

"Julie, what is it?"

He took my elbow, as one would an elderly woman's, and walked with me to the passenger side then opened the door. I clung to the metal frame and cloth seat for the balance necessary to climb aboard. He got in.

"Are you all right?"

Relieved to have escaped and thankful to be in a friend's company, I uncoiled and let the medication begin to do what it's supposed to do.

"No, I don't think so," I whispered. "And you know, man, you're right. I'm not that nice."

CHAPTER TWENTY-TWO

My buddy wanted answers. I told him I'd give him answers as soon as he found a liquor store and got me some more cigarettes. As we reentered Wilmore, I directed him to the Del Rey Liquor and Junior Mart just off V on Ramona. I thought he graciously bought me three packs but he threw two in the glove box. Life took on a veil of normalcy.

Relaying the crux of the conversation in parenthetical spurts, I filled him in on other things, such as the good doctor's delicate condition, and mine. He began talking, trying to give advice when he knew he had no solution. Just talking to fill the car, to snuff down my quiet hysteria, but I couldn't hear him. For the past several months, my hearing and vision had straddled the ebb and flow of frayed emotions, chemical absorption, and fluctuating tolerance for both.

All I could hear were my arteries pumping fluid through my veins, rhythmic squishes of life force somehow keeping me going, keeping me conscious. It played in my ears like the sound of the ocean through a conch shell, faint, hollow echoes.

The medication had not yet quelled the typhoon raging through my psyche but the bad weather was completely internal. Externally, I had no desire to shout or hit or even talk.

I looked over at the man sitting next to me for a moment, my agent. "*How had I earned myself an agent?* I asked myself, struggling to remember. *It was that book. That's right.*

It seemed that book about Maxine Montego and the success accompanying it were ancient history but it had been only been a year and a half. And in that brief passage, I'd gone from there to here."

My thoughts spun out to a time when I was maybe thirteen or fourteen. I was standing at the half-counter in the abandoned Woolworths with my friend Renee. She practiced French-kissing techniques on a half-eaten orange while I pored over a worn copy of *The Lion, The Witch, and The Wardrobe.* Between citrus kisses, she asked, "Julie, why do you read that same book over and over?" I said, "You know how some books you love and some books you hate? I'm trying to figure out why that is." Then she said, "You're going to be a famous writer someday. Everybody thinks so." I put the book down, intrigued. "Really? Everybody?" The boys walked in and my future was no longer the focus. "Well, not everybody."

I always wanted to be a writer. When I was a kid, my gift with words won me many awards and much attention. Labeled a writer early on, I grew into one, clichés and all. And you may think we artistic types don't have to work any harder than anybody else to do what we do but let me just say it's no fucking cakewalk. Plying one's craft and paying the phone bill are almost always exclusive pursuits, and except for those occasions when your Muse withers under the cruel light of public opinion, it's your phone service that will suffer.

Ground down to blood and pulp, I ended up a deadbeat, an outcast, and an addict, as listed under the word "writer" in the dictionary. Then, purely by happenstance, I caught a break, made some money, and in doing so, a name for myself. It seemed I'd rewritten my personal profile and the world was buying it. I almost bought it. Almost.

But I fucked that up.

I reflected on this as Richard talked. I studied the ocean when it finally came into view thinking how it had been a long time since I considered killing myself, a real long time. And as I considered it, the irony that someone else now wanted me dead did not escape me.

"Richard…"

My agent, shocked and encouraged that I had chosen to speak, practically yelled at me, "Yes? Yes, what is it?"

"Nothing," I retracted, sleepily. His disappointment was obvious.

After a moment of consideration, he bellowed, "Honest to God, Page, get a hold of yourself. You're pathetic, leaning limp against the window like that. I'm serious. If you're scared, scream. If you're angry, yell. Do something, even if it's wrong. Where are you?"

That successfully retrieved me from my enervations as adrenaline was instantly produced and distributed. And it struck me as being pretty funny.

I started to laugh but he didn't.

"I'm taking you to the hospital."

"Oh, no, man, I can't take another doctor right now. Richard, I'm sorry. I truly am. Allow me to be a little self-obsessed today, okay? Forgive me?"

He grunted and shook his ponytailed head. "Just pathetic."

Something about his way with words made me like him from the day we met. I think because he's nearly as nasty as me.

Approaching the Promenade, we noticed the police were gone. The barricades remained but there were no uniforms to contend with.

"Rich, drive around the other end, would you? Let's see what's up over there."

He did. Same thing.

"Well, what do you want to do? I don't even know what I'm supposed to offer to do right now. This whole thing is very far from my usual agenting duties. Shall I stay? Would you feel safer if I stay? Or, what if you come with me? Patrick is much fonder of you than he is of me. You can stay with us at the condo tonight."

His frustration spoke volumes. It was touching.

"Honestly, Julie, I don't understand this whole thing. Tell me again why you're barricaded in here. And if they're watching you so closely, where are they? I don't like it."

I agreed. But I was so done with everything right then, I didn't even care. "Let go, let God," I said, doing my best Stewart Smalley impression. I hope he found the humor in that. I didn't check.

We'd both gotten out of the car and were looking down the expanse of the Promenade from the paved side of the blockade.

"Take care of yourself, Richard. And thanks. Thanks for everything."

I hugged him, which is something I'd never done. Not only did I hug him but I held on until he hugged me back.

"Birds of a feather, Richard."

He pulled far enough away to speak to me directly.

"Perhaps. But somebody wanting you dead is news. Somebody wanting me dead is all in a day's work."

I stepped around one of the sawhorses onto the dirt that would lead me home. "Keep in touch."

He just stood there as I took off down the stroll. I didn't look back but after a moment, I heard the engine turn over and wheels roll away.

Now it was just the Promenade and me. Traffic bustled on surrounding streets but I stood in a vacuum, a broken time machine clogged with memories. My balance once again became difficult to manage so I moved with caution through the trash and gravel.

There would be a good three hours before nightfall but the air felt wet already so I maneuvered the collar button of my stiff, new peacoat. The street reverberated with a spooky kind of "High Noon" vibe, desolate and dusty. It was a perfect scene for another murder, and I was all but eager to tempt fate. I'm not too sure I didn't welcome the idea. At least I'd know who and maybe why. There would be some resolution, some closure. My hands would be clean. Let someone else do the dirty work. And I was so tired. Death didn't seem all that ominous. Making more mistakes did.

As I languidly made my way toward the diner, I thought I saw someone off in the distance, someone walking toward me from the ocean end of the Promenade. This didn't seem particularly odd. Someone simply stepped around the barricades, as I had. I rehearsed my "I'm sorry. We're closed," speech continuing forward. Then, all at once, she stopped. And I stopped. I recognized the blue army surplus coat, my old coat, my lucky coat. It was Bethany Garrett. She stood several hundred yards from the diner in one direction, and I in the other. But even from that distance, I knew it was her.

At first, just like in my dream, I felt happy and relieved to see her. But then reality crawled over me like a snake and relief turned to fear.

"There's nobody there. She's dead. She's dead," I muttered, beginning to shake and rubbing my eyes to break the illusion. Sure enough, when I looked again, she was gone.

I couldn't remember how many pills I'd taken but my thoughts were loose and gummy like they are whenever I'm loaded. I needed to get inside, to just get inside, lock the door, and make some coffee. I'd call Charlotte. She'd talk me through it. She could keep me company on the phone until…until it was time…

As my subconscious waited in the wings and my conscious mind took a final bow, I wobbled toward the empty diner allowing the great Owl to guide me in. Even unlit he is pervasive. I stood reverently observing the neon god above with a mother's pride, a disciple's ardor. "But who would take care of Nighthawk's if I were dead?" I asked him.

While trying to come up with an acceptable answer to that question, I saw something move out of the corner of my eye. I shifted my attention to the stairwell in front of my door. It was Bethany. I hadn't noticed before but she wore a colorful wool cap on her blood-splashed head. She didn't look my way, she merely turned the doorknob and went inside. This time I had no fear. This time, I knew I was supposed to follow her.

Climbing the stairs on rubber legs, I kept my eye on the landing, just in case she tried to leave. I arrived at the top and saw that the door was closed. I turned the knob and found it locked. She had locked it from the inside. But why? She knew I was right behind her.

I found the key and eventually the lock. Once inside, I began looking for her, confident she would appear. "Bethany," I called out as I searched the bedroom and bathroom, the fire escape and walk-in closet.

She doesn't want to talk right now, I thought. *She just needs a place to be for a while. I'll make some coffee and unpack a few of these boxes.*

It was about three o'clock. At a quarter to five, I found myself leaning against the large picture window, a half-empty box of books and an unbroken coffee cup at my feet. I don't know how long I had been standing there but I couldn't remember anything after checking through the apartment. I don't scare easily but that freaked me out.

This time, I did make a pot of coffee while reflecting on the whole Bethany thing. Hallucinations weren't my usual trip, blackouts either. The last couple of days illustrated new and devilish aspects of my addictions. This was uncharted territory, and a bad trip at that, and I was troubled by it more than I care to admit.

I turned on the wall heater, radio, and flamingo lamp, planted myself in an easy chair and lit up. Even though my thoughts remained loose and gummy, I felt some better, more comfortable anyway.

Whatever had been playing on the radio ended and the DJ announced a request he'd just gotten for the Maxine Montego classic, "Nobody's Fool." Maxine Montego. Maxine. Mythic. Muse.

As I listened, I began to locate emergency exits unexplored. Charlotte would find Felix. Of course, she would. Marge wasn't necessary for that. And she wasn't the only drug dealer in town, either. Not my town. Crow would help me if I needed pills. Surely, he could hook me up. And if not Crow, somebody else. Someone new. I'd do what I had to do.

Going without wasn't even an option. I had money. I could give a blow job as well as the next gal. I had no reservations about picking up a few fleas if lying down with dogs was necessary. I love dogs. They're loyal. They're ferocious. I'm part canine myself.

But before turning to strangers, I'd knock the dirt off of each jewel scattered in my own backyard. From Peaches to Cecil, I made a mental list of every street warrior and dark angel who might help keep me propped up if need be, as "Nobody's Fool" continued to fill the dusky room.

I was, after all, living in a subterranean battle zone. These people, these friends of mine, were trained in the art of survival. How thorough my own training had been was all that remained to be seen.

CHAPTER TWENTY-THREE

The phone rang and I picked it up. "Julie? Julie, honey, are you all right? I must've left fifteen messages on your cell and at the apartment in the last couple of hours." The vibrato in Charlotte's voice sounded tight, bird-like. "Julie?"

"Charlotte, I was going to call you. It never rang."

"They both rang. Rang and rang. Your answering machine must be full by now. Just what in the wang dang doodle is going on over there? Carroll says Frank put up some kind of barricade?"

"Frank. Yes. Frank." I sounded like a child's programmable robot, and not a very expensive one.

"Oh, Julie, something is wrong. You don't sound like yourself a-tall."

It occurred to me that Charlotte knew nothing of what had transpired in the past 48 hours. She didn't know I knew Bethany's name or that the doctor cut me off or about my publishing contract disintegrating. She didn't even know the murderer had made a mistake.

I thought about filling her in but there was no way of doing that without scaring her to death.

"Don't worry. Everything's cool."

"It is? Are you sure? It seems all hell broke loose since I've been in the studio the last two days. Girl, Carroll is worried sick. He thinks we need to get you out of there. You need me to get you out of there?"

"No. Don't come over here."

Now, that sounded frightening. I made a concerted effort to lighten my tone while handing her a bunch of optimistic assumptions.

"I mean, I'm fine for the night. Frank's got it under control. The Promenade is being patrolled. By tomorrow, things will be back to normal. I can't imagine they'll keep this up for another day."

"You think so? Carroll says there was some kind of rumble and that somebody ran off the highway last night and that Frank thinks the drag racers have something to do with it. Any of that sound right? Not that I doubt him but I'd like to hear it from you."

"Yeah, that's pretty much it, bless his heart. They shut down the Promenade so they can figure out what happened."

"Uh-huh. Okay. Now, why did they impound the Caddy?"

It became progressively more difficult to keep up.

"Right, the Cad. Well, I...I hit a pole in the parking lot."

"So, the Berle Police Department is gonna fix that up for you? Sugar, I'm willing to have conversations like this with Carroll but let's you and me try for something more fluid, okay? What happened to your car?"

I couldn't think fast or clearly enough to run any circles around her logic. The pause gave her reason to venture a guess.

"Julie, did you have anything to do with the accident on Vincent?"

The continued silence on my end gave her reason to panic.

"Oh, my sweet Jesus! Lord, have mercy! Girl, what did you do?"

"Charlotte, calm down. No, I didn't. And the guy isn't dead, just…just hurt real bad. Look, if they thought I was involved I wouldn't be here, right?"

Through all the glue in my head, I still sounded so rational.

"Okay. That's right. That's right." Her words simmered down to a low boil. "So, what did happen?"

As I went to answer, I saw someone run across the doorway to the bedroom. I'd been all through the bedroom. There was no one there. My guts cramped. "There's no one there. Nobody there."

"What? Nobody where?"

I scrunched my eyes shut as hard as I could, praying I wouldn't lose it again, not while talking to Charlotte. "Nothing."

"Julie, you got company?"

I wasn't one hundred percent sure. Part of me hoped there was somebody in the bedroom, that my mind wouldn't betray me so viciously twice in one day.

"Charlotte, could you hold on for a minute? Don't hang up, okay?"

"What's going on over there?"

I didn't want her to panic and I didn't want her to leave me yet. "It's nothing. I think I left the window open in the bedroom and it's freezing in here. Let me run and close it, okay?"

I gently placed the receiver on the table, all the while staring at the doorframe, even though on some level I knew it was nothing more than a shadow cast by the last throes of twilight or, more likely, another delusion.

I rose and timidly made my way across the floor to quell my fears.

The bedroom was dark and icy cold, much colder than the rest of the apartment. I angled cautiously in, observing my breath hanging in the sub-arctic air. The silhouette of a standing lamp was visible in the corner so I turned it on. Of course, there was no one there. No one in the closet, no one on the retracted fire escape, but there was fog out there; a thick sheet of billowing, exaggerated, marshmallow fog positioning itself precariously close to the building. My eyes fixed on this moving wall of milk, altering my depth perception just as it had the evening before. But no dragons emerged. Nobody there.

I walked back to the phone, disoriented and uncomfortable. My descent into madness seemed to be advancing rapidly. But I wouldn't let on. Nothing to be done, not right then. Besides, maybe it would pass. Maybe it would.

Not wanting to inconvenience my friend any more than I already had, I tried to pick up the conversation with renewed focus.

"Thanks, Charlotte. Uh, the car is being checked out by the police because Frank thinks somebody might've borrowed it last night or something crazy like that. But nobody did. Their little lab tests will prove I'm right. It'll all pan out. Go to work. I'll talk to you tomorrow."

"You sure?"

"I am."

"Well..." She weighed her concerns against my assurances and, eventually, I won. "All right. I'm gonna go ahead and eat something and get ready for work. Will you call if you need anything?"

"I will."

"You got the number for The Capri? That's where I am tonight."

"I do."

"Okay. You cozy in then. I'll talk to you tomorrow. Oh, Lord. Sugar, you and I must have plenty on our minds because you haven't even asked me what I found out about Felix and I nearly hung up without telling you."

"I already know. His pregnant girlfriend told me all about it. Japan, right? Touring in Asia."

"No, he's in Mexico. She told you he's in Japan?"

My sticky brain tried to grasp what had just been said, but ultimately couldn't. "Char, did you say Felix is in Mexico?"

"Yes, honey. I just got off the phone with him, couldn't have been ten minutes before I called you. When I got home there were two messages, one from Carroll and one from Felix. I wanted to call Felix first so I'd have something to tell you. Then I called Carroll and got sidetracked by all this barricade business. Anyway, I gave him your number. He said he'd call you as soon as he got on the road and that was more than two hours ago. You should be getting a call anytime if you haven't already."

"He's going to call me?" I got choked up. "Charlotte, what did he say?"

"Don't cry, honey. He was real glad I found him. Real glad you wanted to talk to him. I had to call Jimmy who knew to call Benny's wife. Benny's on the road with Otis right now and..."

"Charlotte, for the love of God..."

"Sorry. Felix has been in Mexico building a studio with Coastal Eddy. They've been there for the last eight months. They're way down in the bowels of Mexico, somewhere off the beaten path. He only has his cell and the connection's rough."

"Coastal Eddy, the club owner? Doesn't he own the Belmont Capri?

"Honey, that cat owns them all. Listen, Julie, I told Felix you weren't seeing anybody."

I could feel my cheeks flush with embarrassment. "Why? God, Charlotte, why would you tell him something like that?"

"Because he asked."

"He did?"

I felt giddy for a split-second, like in the Quad the day before my high school graduation when Becky Green told me Dave Farwell liked me as much as I liked him. Then I remembered I was a delusional junkie and that this man hadn't seen me in over a year.

"Probably just idle curiosity on his part."

"Uh-huh. Well, according to him, he's not seeing anybody either."

Now I was just confused. "Did you tell him his girlfriend has a different take on things?"

"Something like that. And you know what he said? He said the last kind word he had with your doctor was over ten months ago. Said he only went down to Mexico to get away from her and to..."

"Tell me."

"Well, to get over you."

The information being shared seemed less real to me than the visitor in the bedroom, but my heart was beating so loud I had to raise my voice to be heard over it.

"Is that so? Then how'd he get the good doctor pregnant?" I asked with suspicion.

"That's a damn good question, honey."

"You think he's lying?"

"Somebody is. Seems to me you two have a lot to talk about. I'm going to get off the phone now in case he's trying to call. You tell me all about it in the morning."

I stood at the front window stretching the cord as far as it would go, looking out at a scrim of fog so thick that not one city light cut through.

"Yeah, okay. Hey, Charlotte?"

"Yeah, sugar?"

"Thanks for finding him."

"You're very welcome. Sometimes those instincts of yours are dead on."

"Sometimes." Still at the window, I turned to face the bedroom, and there she stood. Wool cap, my lucky coat, blood bubbles dried across her neck. Staring at me. Staring. And I stared back.

"Charlotte?" I spoke quietly, earnestly.

"Yeah, Julie?"

"Carroll's a real good man. You guys need to always take care of each other, okay?"

There was silence between us for a moment.

"What made you say a thing like that?"

I got choked up again and this time, she did, too. "Nothing, I just love you and Carroll loves you and I wanted to say it. That's all."

She blew her nose. "I love you too, you damn fool. In a couple of days, you and I need to go shopping."

This is how Charlotte relieves stress. Never my forte, I had accompanied her on only one previous shopping excursion. She came home with so many bags it took us both two trips to get it all into her apartment. I came home with a three-pack of cotton underwear and a headache.

"That sounds great, Charlotte. It's a date."

We said our goodbyes. I hung up but didn't move.

"Oh, Felix," I lamented, staring at the little dead girl who was standing in the bedroom doorway, "where would I start?"

I didn't have an opportunity to figure that out because the phone rang in my arms breaking apart my thoughts like a mallet crushing ice, shattering my delusion, scaring my ghost away. Four rings before the answering machine would pick up. Four rings to figure out how I was going to handle this.

He doesn't need to know you're seeing things. He doesn't need to know how sick you are. You just wanted to know he was okay, remember? That's what this was about. You wanted to check in on him, that's all. That's it.

I considered that it might not be him at all. He may not even call. But I knew better.

Putting the phone back on the lamp table, I sat down then picked up the receiver with a hand so unsteady I had to brace it with the other, pressing the phone to my ear, waiting.

"Julie? Jules? Baby, it's Felix. Are you there?"

And with that, the weight of thirteen months broadsided me, pitching me against the past, hurling me forward present-day. No seatbelt.

When I went to speak, it came out much louder and more uncontrolled

than I would've preferred. Kind of a yell/cry/speak, child-like and unedited.

"Felix. Felix, I miss you so much. Why aren't you here? Oh, God, Felix, you don't know how messed up I am. Everything has gotten so messed up. Please come home. I'm so scared. I'm so fucking scared."

"Jules? Whoops, I lost you there for a sec. What did you say? Can you hear me?"

Truly, the Lord works in strange and mysterious ways. I pulled it together, found the volume control in my throat, and tried to sound unfettered. "Yes, I can. Where are you?"

"I'm down in Mexico, baby. Like, nowhere. Way down. I'm with my pal, Angel, right now. He has a truck. He's taking me to the nearest airport but that's another three hours from here. I've been building a recording studio with Coastal Eddy. You remember Eddy?"

There was a horrible racket going on and the connection was tenuous. "Is someone screaming, Felix?"

"No, it's chickens. That's just how they sound. Angel and I are going to get this truckload out of here. It's not safe for chickens down here. Look, I'm catching the first flight out. I should be in Berle sometime tomorrow afternoon. Charlotte tells me there's been some action there. A murder?"

"Yeah, she's...right here…she's…it happened right here at the diner. I thought it was weird you didn't call. It was in all the papers. That's why I had Charlotte check on you. I hope you don't mind."

"Nah. Mind? Come on. You're the one who wouldn't take my calls, remember?"

I didn't remember much, not clearly anyway. And I wasn't going to get into a pissing match with so little ammunition.

"We can talk about it when I get home, Spider-Girl."

"Or now," I added, not wanting to lose his deep baritone so soon after relocating it. Not wanting to be left alone with my ghost, or myself.

"Well, as long as you're hip to talking and the connection holds out. Like I told Charlotte, I only came down here because you sent me to the cornfield."

"What about Doctor Stewart?"

"Oh, man, that weirdsmobile? That was bleak. My blue period. Then Coastal Eddy made me this offer and I figured why not? Maybe I could sort some things out. So, I canceled a couple of sessions, packed my sax and huaraches, and split. But if I'd thought you were in any kind of trouble, I'd have been there. I'd have at least seen if there was anything I could do. You know that, don't you, baby?"

He sounded so much like he always did. Like nothing had changed at all. But, of course, everything had changed.

"Felix, a lot's happened over the last few months. I'm...I'm not...feeling very well these days."

"Jules? Julie? Jeez, I can barely hear you over the chickens. They're in the back of the truck and Angel's making like Speedy Gonzalas. Yes, I'm talking about you, lead foot. Ease up. Julie, can you still hear me?"

"Felix, are you still seeing Marge?"

"Marge? I only ever saw her for, like, two months. Jules, believe me, I haven't talked to her in the eight months I've been down here. And the only talking we did before that was me telling her to get lost and her telling me how much I loved her. Way gone. She broke my fucking hand. It was an accident but…baby…Julie… Aghghgghgh! I don't want to talk about her. I want to talk to you. I want to see you. Let me come see you when I get home. Are you good with that? Whoa! Angel, how did this one get in the cab? Pull over. Pull over! Hello? Jules, can you hear me?"

Water cascaded down my cheeks as I tried to understand the situation better. But before I could ask him to clarify, the phone went dead.

"Felix?" I jostled the receiver button, waited, then realized we'd lost our connection. I hoped he would call right back. Another thirty seconds and that possibility seemed slim. I decided to call Charlotte. She had his cell number. But when I picked up the receiver, there was no dial tone. The trouble was on my end.

I squeezed the pack of cigarettes next to me while trying to locate the truth. I couldn't. Why would the doctor lie to my face? Was it her pride? Was she just fucking with me for sport? Could I hold it together until Felix got home? I wanted to make every effort to do so. We could talk it through together.

In an uncharacteristic move, I chose against the smoke and rose instead to get the cell from my purse, but I was stopped by a knock at the door.

CHAPTER TWENTY-FOUR

I pushed my glasses back to the bridge of my nose while moving toward the door, wondering if someone *had* knocked or if I imagined it. After all, who would be visiting? It might be Frank checking in. I could certainly do with the company, even Frank. Or maybe Crow. Those flimsy barricades wouldn't keep him out. They wouldn't keep anybody out who wanted in.

Running both hands across the smooth wood, I remembered considering a door with a little peek-a-boo window in the middle, but I didn't get that one. A second round of knocks urged me to respond. "Who is it?"

"Julie, it's Marjorie, Marjorie Stewart. May I come in?"

Speak of the devil and the devil appears.

With my hands still resting on the wood, something came over me, something dreamlike. I slowly turned my head toward the bedroom. I knew she was still in there, my delusion, my ghost. No longer visible but undeniably there. I could feel it, just beyond the bedroom door, just out of sight. And she was waiting. And she was scared.

I turned my head back to face the front door feeling a deep resolve about something. But what? As my hand tightened around the knob, a cavalcade of indecipherable images flashed in front of me like lightning splitting open a Midwest sky, out-of-focus photographs from someone else's hidden shoebox. It didn't matter if it was some blurred insight or another shot of madness, the information was too fleeting to grasp.

I opened the door with as much disgust and venom on my face as would fit. "What do you want?"

She didn't speak right away, allowing me time to take in the weird image there on the landing. Standing bundled, as anyone would've been in the weather, her wide-brimmed hat and long, loose coat made her look like a tiny priest. And a freakishly heavy cape of dry ice fog completed the ensemble. It draped over her shoulders and head in thick velvet folds, swirling around her gloved hands as she repositioned them from pockets to sides.

"Julie, I didn't know if you would even speak to me after today."

"Sure. I think we've got a lot to talk about."

She appeared timid and skittish. Mustering a smile, she broke our Indian standoff. "May I make my apology inside? It's freezing out here."

I moved back to allow her entry. She took only a couple of steps in, keeping her head tilted down, omega to my alpha.

"This is going to sound silly but I could've sworn I was being followed out there."

I thought how maybe it was her conscience or past following her but relocked the door behind us as she made her way further into the apartment.

"Things got so out of hand today at the office. I don't even know where to begin."

"Why don't you begin by telling me how you got in here? Didn't you notice the barricades?"

She nodded. "Certainly I noticed. I spoke to one of the officers positioned on Vincent."

"There was someone there?"

"Yes. He wanted to know my business so I told him I was your doctor and that you had asked me to come by. I guess I told a fib but I just needed to clear things up tonight, if possible."

Relieved that police were once again present, I made my way around the dining room table without asking her to join me, without asking her to take off her coat. "A fib? You?"

She followed me over. "What does that mean?"

"Even money says that's not the first fib you've ever told. Is that a safe bet?

Not knowing what to do with that, she stammered, "Julie, I didn't come here so that we could get into another argument. Let's just have a civilized talk, woman to woman. Can we do that?"

I took a seat, determined to see if I could get her to tell me the truth about Felix before I told her.

"So, what did the cop say when you told him you had a hall pass?"

She pulled out a chair across from me and nervously perched there, stiff and twitchy.

"Nothing. He let me by. I parked somewhere close and walked the rest of the way. With the outside lights off, I could hardly find the place through this fog. I've never seen fog like this. Have you?"

I thought about how I'd navigated through plenty of fog, some real, some in my head. But truly, no, I hadn't seen anything like the fog outside that night. And without benefit of the great Owl holding it at arm's length, it clung to the sides of the diner like a lover saying goodbye.

"What is this? Are we buddies now?"

"What?"

"I said are we supposed to make like buddies? You come here to talk about the fog and shit? Because I'm thinking you've got some other agenda. You got another agenda, Marge?"

She didn't scoff at my impudence, which surprised me somewhat. Instead, pity washed across her tense face, relaxing it a degree or two.

"Yes, actually I do have some unfinished business with you, business important enough to come out in this weather." She shook her head. "You truly don't know when someone is trying to help you, do you, Julie?"

"Help me? I thought we determined you were unable to help me."

The pity remained but her eyes flickered with a dash of curiosity, as well.

"Maybe I can help you now if you'll let me. Julie, it's just you and me here and I'm not your doctor anymore. No bond of ethics to respect. What happened out there on the highway last night? Are you in any trouble?"

I placed both elbows on the table and folded my hands in the prayer position under my chin while studying her concern.

"So, that's what fucked up our relationship – ethics."

She waved her hands in exasperation, leaned back in the chair, and tried to mask her agitation with an oversized smile.

"You are quite a little firecracker, Julie Page. I give up. You're right. It's not my business." Then adding a seemingly sincere addendum, "But I do care. I do."

Placing her purse on the table with one glove and unbuttoning her coat with the other, she suddenly gasped and grabbed her stomach, rocking back and forth rhythmically. "Oh, God, not now. This morning sickness happens at all hours of the day and night. Could I trouble you for a glass of water?"

Her machinations continued as I looked on. I had nowhere to go and was more than interested in whatever the doctor wanted to share. So even though I knew there was no baby (at least not Felix's baby) I rose to get her some water.

"You're hilarious," I said under my breath, glancing over my shoulder toward the bedroom on my way to the sink.

I watched her from the kitchen while filling a glass. No longer cradling her questionable womb, her hands gently drummed the table as her head swiveled to one side then the other.

I rounded the counter corner and grabbed the smokes next to the flamingo lamp on my way back to the table, placing the water in front of her. She didn't touch it. She just stared at it, growing still and focused as if the Flintstone glass in front of her was a mystic orb.

"What? You expecting the good crystal?"

That broke her meditation. She blinked and guffawed simultaneously.

"Before I forget, one of the things I came here for was to give you Dr. Rosenberg's address and number."

She reached inside a coat pocket and produced a page from one of her prescription pads, sliding it toward the center of the table. I took another couple of drags contemplating the absurdity of this whole scene.

"You didn't come here to give me that guy's number. Cut the crap."

Whatever had been ticking in her subsided, and once again, the muscles in her face relaxed. Only this time, tension wasn't replaced with pity. This time, her pretty eyes took on a sinister droop, corners down, pupils pushing against her upper lids. Signs, perhaps, of not appreciating my directness.

"Yes. Yes, I think everything's in order," she sighed.

Standing up, she removed her hat revealing a shaved head. Smooth as a cue ball. The black coat, vile new expression, and absence of hair made her look far less priest and much more Nosferatu. Sure, I was shocked, maybe even scared, but I couldn't think of any particular reason for fear. So I laughed.

"Bad hair day?"

Pulling her coat open, she produced a gun from an inside pocket, aiming it my way. "Nothing more incriminating than a stray hair," she said.

I sat there dumbfounded, caught between horror and disbelief.

"Don't worry, Julie. It probably won't have to go off. Just take a breath."

Someone pulling a gun on you is creepy. Someone shaving their head and pulling a gun on you is Manson-creepy. Besides, I wasn't positive any of this was real. For all I knew she was still sitting across from me with a full head of hair and no gun at all. But she looked bald. And the gun looked real.

"Poor Julie. Such a troubled girl. Well, you take heart. This is the last bit of trouble you'll have to endure."

Like every sleuth in every film noir, I took a last drag from my smoke, slowly, so I wouldn't startle her, and butted it out. Real cool, just as if I wasn't urinating down my leg.

"Marge, what are you doing with that thing? Put it down."

She cocked her head dramatically to the right, holding my gaze all the while.

"I've been planning this for a long time, honey. Nobody's going to rush me. And by the way, there are no cops on the Promenade. Didn't you hear about the bomb threat at the airport a while ago? I think every spare cop is busy with that right now. Aren't I clever? Thinking to call in a bomb threat? We'll just have to keep each other company."

Still standing, she placed her gunless hand on the table leaning in to share a confidence.

"I've planned and replanned this evening. Gone over every detail in my head a million times in the last couple of weeks. But today when you told me the diner was going to be closed it was like receiving God's blessing. And now this delicious fog. Every circumstance has come together to create the perfect opportunity for me to do what's right. You're not supposed to be here. Even heaven agrees."

My self-destructive mind fought for self-protective solutions but was too fuzzy to help. Telling her I knew the truth about her and Felix might just finish her off—and me with her. She was already as unsteady as her prey. I'd just have to step delicately toward the subject.

"And this is about Felix."

Her face puckered as she slammed the barrel of the gun into the tabletop hard enough to leave a mark. "Shut up."

"Okay, Marge. Okay. Just put the gun down."

The deadly weapon in her little hand became the focus as her tone lightened considerably.

"Crude, isn't it? This is a Rossi 38-caliber revolver. I got it from a pawnshop right here in Berle. It was so easy. Of course, he wanted me to fill something out and wait for clearance but another hundred dollars and he was content to simply hand it over, bullets included. It was nearly as easy as it had been a year ago when I bought the first gun, a Glock 9-millimeter. I got that one in Denver while attending a convention. I thought I might need it."

"Need it for what?"

"To kill you."

My hands inadvertently went up in a gesture of inconsolability but my assailant brought them down again with a grimace and by extended her shooting arm an inch more.

"Marge, this is crazy. I left Felix, remember?"

"Yes, I remember. I remember how he turned to me and how I was there to console him, listening ad nauseam about how much he loved you, how he didn't think he'd ever love anyone again. That's when I bought the first gun. Seemed like the simplest solution."

"You thought that would make him stop loving me?"

"No, I just thought it would make you dead."

She casually walked around the table toward me.

"You won't ever understand the connection Felix and I shared while you were in that hospital bed. Oh, he stayed loyal, right by your side, and I wouldn't betray my professional obligations. But it was there and it was real. The day you were released I thought, great, she'll be back on her feet in no time. Then, when she's stronger, Felix will let her down gently and we can finally be together. But you don't get better, do you, Julie?"

The closer she got, the more I felt I should say something nice.

"I'm no threat to you, Marge. I haven't seen him in over a year."

Directly behind me now, she pulled back my hair with gloved fingers.

"But, finally, he did fall in love with me, and killing you didn't seem very important."

Bending down so that her lips were very near my ear she whispered, "Then things changed."

She pressed the hard barrel of the gun to my soft temple as a sharp pain ran from my neck down to my ankle.

I tried to inch my head away from it but she placed her other hand on the opposite side of my head and pressed, creating a vise. My doughy brains were trapped between a .38 and a velvet glove. *Oh, Felix*, I thought, *you fucked the wrong girl this time.*

I could smell the metal as she shared the exposition I'd egged her on to share. Only now, I didn't care so much.

"He claimed I was too possessive, too controlling, that what we had was nothing more than a fling."

Removing the gun from my vulnerable flesh, she walked back around the table opposite my chair and reseated herself. I slid my glasses off just long enough to wipe the sweat from my forehead and massage my third eye.

Then she crossed her arms, as if not holding a weapon at all, and got sort of conversational and girly.

"So, one night we ended up arguing in some parking lot. I know he thinks I meant to break his hand but I didn't. I swear to God, it was an accident. I only meant to slam the door. It all happened very fast." She looked disgusted with herself. "Whether I meant to or not, a horn player with a broken hand isn't terribly marketable."

Regaining her center, she straightened her spine and placed both arms on the table, gun poised directly in front of her on the Ikea pine.

"In case you haven't put it together, no tour of Asia. And no baby, either."

"So why lie?"

Her stare was as hard and cold as the barrel of her gun.

"I wanted to hurt your feelings before I killed you."

She shook her cue ball with great melancholy.

"Don't misunderstand. He does love me and he is somewhere. He's just mad about his hand, that's all. He hasn't forgiven me. We haven't spoken in months. And I won't have him running back to you. Besides, we can never truly make a life with you lurking in the shadows. I knew what I had to do a long time ago. It was just a matter of figuring out how. That girl...that was a terrible mistake."

Tears filled my dilated eyes. "Of course, it was you. You killed Bethany Garrett. You thought it was me. It was supposed to be me," I sobbed quietly.

"You know her? Huh. That explains why she was wearing your coat. You know, it was supposed to look like a random act. I wasn't even going to leave my car. But you wouldn't lie down. The Glock with the convenient bullet clip jammed when I took a second shot. So in a moment of desperation, I grabbed the keys from the ignition, ran up behind you while you gasped on your knees, and slit your throat. It was disgusting. Oh, God, it was horrible. Couldn't get the key to puncture the flesh. Couldn't poke it through your neck. But I had to. I had to. Finally, I got it in. Then it was a little easier, slitting you open. Easier but not easy. It's no way for anybody to die. But I did it. I finished you off. Then, you fell backward and it wasn't you at all. Just some child."

The murderer paused, nearly seeming remorseful, staring vacantly at her intended target.

I looked to the bedroom through salty emotion. Through running mascara, I thought I saw part of a blue wool sleeve. Then, as if the imaginary girl knew I saw her, the sleeve disappeared from view.

"The coat."

"What?" I broke her ghoulish reverie.

"Where did you put my coat?"

"Oh, I kept it. I thought it would be safer than trying to discard it. I figured someone might smell foul play with her wearing your coat and all so I yanked it off of her. And the hat because a hat with no coat…I don't know what I was thinking. The whole thing was sloppy and pointless."

Without moving the gun or her arms, she leaned forward as a devilish grin graced her face.

"I've got them under my bed in a zippered storage bag. It's pretty ugly, Julie. I don't think you want it back."

Loaded, exhausted, and unbelievably sad, I grasped at some comfort in my final moments. "Mind if I smoke?"

She readjusted herself in the chair while exchanging the wicked grin with a benevolent one. "Be my guest. We're going to be here for a while."

I struck a match.

"You know, I read in the paper that she was found at the front door reaching for the handle. That's not where I left her. The young lady was some fighter."

"I found her," I choked.

"I know. Isn't that ironic?" she quipped, sans emotion. "Well, the whole thing gave me time to reconsider your imminent demise. Once I started thinking clearly, an infinitely more logical choice presented itself. Suicide. You're going to kill yourself. And I'm going to help."

CHAPTER TWENTY-FIVE

The apartment was dark, very dark. With no outside lights and only the flamingo lamp illuminating the interior, things became difficult to see. From one dim bulb through murky eyes, I saw well enough to know I was about to die. And isn't that what I wanted? Wouldn't it be nice to let someone else take care of what I hadn't the courage to finish myself? The self-hatred was there, but not the courage. It's almost comical that at that moment when all control had been ripped from my hands, I began to measure the value of my life. But it didn't matter anymore. Any new estimate would be logged as too little, too late. Now, I was sitting about five feet away from a loaded .38 with nowhere to run.

"I know I pulled the rug out from under you today," the good doctor purred from the shadows. "No Felix, no drugs, murders on your doorstep. And all the while, your meager credibility as a writer steadily fading as you waste every decent opportunity you're handed. You're simply not thinking clearly anymore through all those drugs. Stealing that Valium from your doctor's cupboard? That's below you, Julie. My goodness, what's happened to you? Poor thing. No one will have to ponder why you killed yourself. Maybe only why it took so long."

Even without knowing about the book contract being dropped, her assessment of me rang true enough. Fresh tears rolled down my cheeks without the natural accouterments of pursed lips and furrowed brow. These tears fell all by themselves. And they weren't for Bethany. They were for me.

"I talked to Doctor Rosenberg yesterday and told him all about you. And clearly, I told you today because you have this dated page from my prescription pad with his info on it. See, I've thought everything through this time. Put it in your purse."

My medicated muscles and over-extended brain made no attempt to reach for my purse. She took this lack of discipline as an insult and pushed her chair out with some force, walking my way a second time. I was sure she was going to stick that gun to my temple again but she didn't. She gently pulled my hair back and stuck the barrel up my left nostril, cocking the trigger. My sweat-covered face contracted in spasms, as perhaps all people contract in the last moment before a violent death. I was shaking so hard that she had to pull the gun out a little just to hold it steady. After a good thirty seconds, she let go and uncocked the hammer, retracting another idle threat. But she remained behind me.

"Now, reach over there and get your purse." I did. "Now, stick that piece of paper in it." I did. "That's good. You know, you've been so accommodating up until now. Please let's not complicate a simple plan."

She took off toward the typewriter table while I pressed my hands against each precious feature on my face. I heard her yank a piece of paper from the dusty roller of the Hermes 3000 before reappearing and replanting herself across from me.

"You're going to write a suicide note. Something about desperation and disappointment, etcetera."

She pushed a pen across the table, one she'd nabbed along with the typing paper. I didn't pick it up.

She bristled. "Honestly, Julie, why the drama? You were never much of a writer to begin with. I mean, your only success was a fluke."

She coquettishly scratched the top of her neck as if there were still a hairdo to contend with.

"That's not going to happen again, I promise. No more flukes. Someone else is going to have to write this one."

I wiped my nose on my sleeve, sniffing back the rest of the snot. "Maybe I can be my own ghostwriter," I quipped, trying to appear as callous as my assailant. She seemed to appreciate my meager attempt.

"All right, let's get the pills from your purse. You can take them one at a time, that might be fun, or all at once. See how poetic that is? The thing you crave the most will be the thing that finally kills you."

"So the gun is just incentive?"

"Well, if you don't play along, you'll be shooting yourself in the head with it. I bought this one not only because I couldn't trust the Glock anymore but because I wanted someone in town to see me buy it. I wore a burgundy wig, called myself by your name, everything. I had to be thorough this time. I had to plan ahead. Wasn't that tidy of me?"

"Yeah, you did real good."

"And when we're done, I'll have plenty of time to lose myself in the fog and get back to the car."

I tried to figure out how many steps it was from the table to the front door and then I tried to figure the odds of reaching it alive.

"The pills aren't in my purse. They're in the bathroom."

"Do you think I'm stupid?

"I'm telling the truth. Look."

Between trembling digits, I fumbled the purse open to show her. She shook her head, embarrassed and disgusted.

"You're a worthless liar. And, more to the point, you're a junkie. Junkies keep their stash close."

She waited, I think, to see if I would produce the drugs without further prodding.

"Julie, what do you suppose will happen to you if you don't take the pills out of your purse for me?"

Without another moment's hesitation, I grabbed my purse and fished out the pills.

"Thank you. Okay, there's the Xanax. And there's a bottle that says vitamins. Why don't we pour those out?"

I did. And, God help me, I wanted one.

"Oh, how brilliant of you to put the Valium in a vitamin bottle. No one's ever thought to do anything so clever before." The sarcasm made neither of us smile. "Now let's write that letter."

Writing a suicide note would buy more time than getting shot in the head. And in that I was about to compose, I needed something to steady my nerves.

"May I take one?"

The doctor gave a sadistic grin and nodded.

I slowly picked up the glass of water and popped a Xanax. Next, watching her for stop signals while proceeding forward, I gradually slid out another smoke and lit it. Placing the cigarette in the ashtray, I adjusted my glasses and picked up the pen she'd placed in front of me. And all through this ritualistic exercise in stretching time I'm thinking, *"Why won't Bethany do something? She's right there in the bedroom. What is she waiting for?"*

"Well, what have we here?" Cecil's southern drawl rolled like thunder through the room and up my spine. The doctor got to her feet in such a hurry the chair went over in the process. "Please, don't get up."

Cecil barreled into the apartment undeterred by the circumstance.

Frantically, Marge debated on whom she should point her weapon. She chose me.

"Stop right there. I mean it."

Her demand sounded weak and pathetic but being the gentleman that he is, he conceded, remaining somewhere just inside the open front door. I went to look over my shoulder but she wouldn't have it. "Don't move a muscle. Not one muscle," she hissed. Then, to our company, "Who are you?"

"Never mind that, darlin'. I know who you are."

The doctor placed her hand to her ear, then ran the tips of her delicate fingers over the side of her fuzzy melon. She walked around the table right up to my chair. I wondered if she was going to show Cecil the temple or the nostril trick. Instead, she told me to get up and to do it slowly. I waited for Cecil to suggest something else but he didn't. So, slowly, I got up. She turned me around to face him. Wrapping one arm around my waist from behind, she rested the barrel, this time, on the back of my head. There I stood; a dopey, trembling ventriloquist dummy with dangling arms and a mascara-covered face.

"Hi, Cecil."

"Hush," she said before turning her attention to my most honored guest. "You picked a very unfortunate time to visit, whoever you are. We're all going to have to stay very calm until I figure something out."

The fog made its way in, hovering near the doorframe, creeping over the hardwood floor. It rubbed against Cecil's Cuban heels like a kitten as he began to unbutton his red snakeskin jacket.

"Put your hands up," she said. But Cecil wasn't minding. "Put your hands up or I'll shoot."

He continued unfastening buttons with his right hand, tracing his pencil mustache with the middle finger of his left hand.

"Now, you sound just like one of those famous Hollywood gangsters. You surely do. Put your hands up or I'll shoot. That's delightful."

"How did you get in here? I watched her lock that door."

"With a bobby pin." He produced a bobby pin seemingly from thin air (a carnival trick usually reserved for coins) then lifted his pimp-feathered cowboy hat and stuck it somewhere to the side of his pompadour.

With her arm still around my waist, she took a half step to the side and aimed the gun at him. He got the message, gingerly graduating his arms down from his head and into the surrender position, palms facing the killer.

"Now, I must admit this is not what I dropped by for." He gave me a long hard wink before shifting his eyes back to Marge. "But I heard your conversation from the landing front to back, informing me of the situation in full. So before this charming creature suffers one more indignity, I thought I'd better let myself in."

"Thank God," I stuttered.

Without warning and with the gun still aimed across the room, the doctor yelled in my ear, "Pow!" Yes, it was weird but it was also very frightening, much like her haircut. I screamed, dangling there in her embrace.

Cecil's face went dark, stony. He made a solemn recommendation while lowering his arms.

"Honey, let's put down the gun and talk this thing through before somebody gets themselves hurt."

There we all stood, waiting for Fortuna to move the next chess piece. Suddenly, my friend's attention swung a little to the left, toward the bedroom. His head shifted as if he saw something, maybe heard something. It was subtle but notable. The killer turned also. Not because she had the same instinct but because he had guided her to do so. And at that moment, he produced a knife from his shiny red sleeve. She laughed.

"What are you going to do with that?"

He flicked it open. It glimmered even in the half-light.

"Well, we're going to find out."

Skillfully flung, it met her cheek and stuck there. For more than a heartbeat, she remained as she had been, only now with the addition of a knife dangling from the side of her pink-gloss lips. A look of utter shock replaced arrogance. Upon realizing what had just happened, she dropped the gun and pulled the shiv from her punctured flesh.

Cecil took several great strides toward the action as I stepped away. She tried to grip the knife, prepared to accept it as her new weapon but he backhanded her before she could and it fell, landing only inches from the revolver. But she didn't fall, not until he backhanded her again.

Once she hit the ground, he kicked the gun with one green ankle boot, kicked it my way then dug that polished Cuban heel into the side of her neck holding her in a position he felt secure about. I stood back with both hands clutched over my mouth to keep from screaming again.

"Julie, darlin', would you get that?"

I stared at the pistol next to the bloody pearl-handled knife, then at the woman who wanted me dead. Cecil gently reiterated his request. "Go on, now, honey. Pick it up."

I found some of that courage I claim not to have and cautiously lifted the loaded .38 by the handle.

"Perfect. Now, you just keep that pointed right at our friend here while you and I make some conversation. How are you holding up?"

I worked my shaky palms around the gun, resting an index finger on the outside of the metal surrounding the trigger. It was compact in my hand, substantial. I thought about how this very gun had been pressed against my brains in pretty much every way imaginable, but my brains were still in my head.

"I'm okay."

"Excellent. And how many of your little helpers have you taken?"

I didn't know how far back in the day he meant. "Only one."

"That's very good. Very good. Hold your arms out straight, sweetheart. This here's real life. Not like in the movies."

I straightened both arms, cupping one hand around the other for support.

"Now, little sister, how do you want to handle this?"

He ground his heel deeper into the side of her neck as she squirmed, blood dripping from her punctured cheek.

"What do you mean?"

"Well," he spoke evenly, with a sweet curl to each syllable, as if he were talking to a child or a dog. "You pull the trigger, it's self-defense. When it's over, I let myself out. I think the television station that employs me would appreciate that. Then you call that strapping young detective and no one is any the wiser. On the other hand, if you don't wish to pull the trigger, well, then we need to let him know there's been a situation. In that case, despite my better judgment, I'll stay put to answer any unseemly questions that may arise."

You could tell the doctor found it difficult to breathe with her wounded face flat against the hardwood floor.

"Miss, you need to move your hand away from the knife a tad. Thank you. So, Julie, honey, what's it going to be?"

The question was too absurd to address. I simply kept the gun pointed at the ground on which my killer lay, waiting for inspiration. And if inspiration is truly born of desperation, it should've been right around the corner.

Cecil looked again toward the bedroom.

"Well, you think about it for a minute."

He removed his boot from Marge's throat, taking a step back and toward the bedroom while nonchalantly straightening the cuffs peeking out from his coat. He paused there, listening, not looking in, just fiddling with his cufflinks.

"Cecil? Cecil, she's in there, isn't she?"

He shot me a sober look that dissolved quickly to a not-to-worry grin, "You stay focused, honey. I'm going to take care of everything."

The doctor started to get up but Cecil returned in time to keep her from it, kicking her in the back hard enough to bring her to her knees. She rested on all fours trying to catch her breath.

"This is insane," she wheezed. I'm a respected doctor. No one is going to buy this."

The carny squatted down bringing them face-to-face.

"If it weren't for the complications you've jimmied into everyone's evening, I'd kill you myself. I could do it real fast and clean, tiny little neck like that. Yes, I could. And the way I'm feeling right now, you need to move ever so carefully so something like that doesn't happen. Because this is Julie's call, no one else's. She decides. This is a game, sweetheart; a game you brought to the table. And we gonna see a little sideshow retribution here tonight."

The doctor said nothing, remaining on her knees, holding the butt of her hand to her cheek.

Just then the Owl lit up, flashes of red rhythmically interrupting the lamplight shadows in the apartment. Like a code being transmitted across the Promenade, a mute siren, tenacious, demanding. I'd never adjusted the timer before. Apparently, I'd done it incorrectly.

"I must say, Julie, that Owl gives off a lovely glow," Cecil chuckled. "Unfortunately, we may also acquire some company before too long because of it. And when the cavalry arrives, we won't be able to deal with things the way we see fit. Now, Julie, I don't mean to rush you, sweetheart, but you need to make up your mind."

And time stopped there in my cherry red, pulsing neon cocoon.

I thought about everything, about how this woman took my self-respect as she fed my addictions, she took my ability to write as the drugs snuffed out each

flicker of creativity, she took Felix though that was only a loan, and she took my coat – when she killed Bethany Garrett.

"How do I do it?"

"Oh, now, that's good, honey. I'm proud of you." He pulled a linen handkerchief from somewhere, retrieved the pearly knife, wiped it, retracted it, and then slid it inside his coat along with the soiled hanky.

"Cecil, how am I supposed to explain that cut?"

He lifted her sullen face for assessment. "She cut herself shavin'."

With her face balanced in his hand, she made an observation. "I know who you are. You're that shyster from the cable show, Hearts from Beyond."

He was humored by the ill-timed recognition. "Well, yes I am," he said, jostling her chin back and forth. "I get paid for talking to the dead. And right now, I'm talking to you. Now the clock is ticking on our time together so before you reach the other side, do us a favor and apologize to that little girl."

She shook her head, confused by his command.

"What's her name, Julie? Bethany, is it?" He dropped her chin, staying squatted next to her.

"Yeah, Cecil," I said, readjusting the gun between sweaty palms. "Bethany Garrett."

His voice came down again as he picked up his conversation with the doctor from where they left off. "There you go. You killed a little girl named Bethany Garrett. Now, apologize."

"She's dead. There's no one to apologize to," the doctor said, unflinching.

His gold-capped tooth shimmered from a generous smile before he added, "But it would be a lovely gesture."

She turned her swelling face away from him. Again, he took her chin in his hand.

"Now, you may think that help is on its way. That the police are going to show up and you won't need to take care of this silly business." They were forehead to forehead. "But whether I hunt you down in some jail cell or whether I hunt you down in hell, you will be apologizing."

"You can't be serious," the doctor misguidedly said.

Cecil picked up the hand that wasn't pressed to her face.

"I'm going to count to three and then I'm going to snap each one of these pretty little digits back until you understand how serious I am."

All this and not a tear in her. No emotion beyond disgust. But when Cecil broke her first finger she screamed, grabbing her damaged hand with the blood-soaked one and curling into a fetal position.

He leaped up straightening the crease in his trousers.

"Damn it, I forgot to count. I'll remember this time. Ready?"

Curled up and moaning in pain, she managed, "I'm sorry."

"That's better. Now say it loud so God can hear it, because you surely offended him, too."

"I'm sorry. I'm sorry Bethany. I didn't mean to kill you. I didn't." She yelled. Then looking up at him with sincerity, she added, "Honestly, I didn't."

He nodded, satisfied.

"Julie, there's no safety on that little .38 so all you have to do is pull the trigger if you're sure."

Walking over close enough to communicate intimacy but not close enough to screw with my hugely unsteady aim he gave me a hard look, cool and commanding. "So, Julie, darlin', are you ready?"

Before I could answer, Frank stepped through the open door, gun drawn. You could see Cecil's disappointment but he made with the patter just the same.

"Well, good evening, detective. My, my. This is starting to look like the stateroom scene in that old Marx Brothers movie, all of us crowded in here. We've been expecting you for the longest time."

Frank assessed the room while holding his gun on Doctor Stewart.

"Thought I saw the Owl through the fog. Thought I better check things out. Looks like I was right. Mr. Valentine, Julie, one of you want to tell me what's going on here?"

Seeing this as an opportunity, the doctor finally got to her feet, one hand squeezing the broken one, both clutched to the puncture wound.

"She's crazy, detective. They both are. This is a woman with a very bad chemical dependency. They were going to kill me. And that man…"

"Shut your cake hole. I'll get to you in a minute." His brows lowered atop squinting eyes. "Say, don't I know you? You're Julie's doctor, right? The psychiatrist."

Voice dripping with pathos, the killer took her best shot. "Yes. And these people are dangerous. They're in this together. She called me here tonight. Out of the goodness of my heart, I came. My God, they've broken my finger. They used a knife on me. Look at my face."

"What happened to your hair?"

Cecil felt he could move things along.

"Seems the doctor thought our Julie was too much of a liability to her love life."

"This is about that horn player? Your ex?"

Frank was looking at me but I kept my attention, and the barrel of the gun, on Marjorie. "She killed Bethany."

He looked to Cecil for clarification. As always, Cecil had words to spare.

"The girl outside the diner. The murder you've been working so hard on solving. This lady mistook her for our Julie and in an effort to rectify the situation, came here tonight to finish what she'd started." Cecil winked at the killer. "I'll give her that. She's diligent. Got a strong work ethic." Then to Frank, "This time, it was going to look like suicide." He directed the detective to the table of evidence.

"Detective, please listen to me," Marge attempted.

"Shut up. We got proof of anything?"

"My coat," was all I mustered. My head began to throb and my breathing became erratic as all the furniture and people in the room began to float about an inch off of the ground. Cecil picked up the slack.

"If I understand it correctly, detective, Julie's coat and the little girl's hat are in a plastic bag under the doctor's bed. And perhaps you should investigate the doctor's car. Seems she used her car key on the child's throat before driving away."

"Jesus Christ," Frank muttered. "Okay, Mr. Valentine, how do you fit in?"

Cecil buttoned his snakeskin jacket like he was preparing to leave.

"Me? I just dropped by for a visit. Lucky thing I did." He produced the

knife and bloodied handkerchief from his pocket and handed them over to Frank. "I was able to finagle the gun out of this lady's hand and into Julie's."

Frank slid the knife into a pocket for safekeeping.

"I thought a barricade might inspire whoever wanted Julie dead to try it again, but if that Owl hadn't lit up…"

Cecil's expression was one of genuine surprise.

"Barricade?"

Frank looked like he was going to cry.

"I took too long. This is my fault. I should've figured this out," he muttered to himself, shaking his head and biting his lip. "All right folks, let's wrap this up. We'll deal with the details later. Julie, put down the gun."

I stood motionless, the gun still tenuously pointing at the doctor.

"I'm not going to go over there and cuff her until you put it down. She's unarmed. I'm here. You're going to be okay now, Julie. Julie? Jules, are you listening to me? It's over."

I was locked in indecision as the room started spinning. The gun that adrenaline had held steady was wavering in the air, loosey-goosey, as I tried to find my center. Must've concerned Marge a little.

"Do something, detective. Disarm her. They're both lying. I'm a respected doctor, for heaven's sake."

Frank made like she wasn't talking at all, pulling a set of handcuffs from the back of his belt and extending them toward Cecil.

"Mr. Valentine, you know how to use these things?"

Cecil straightened up like a soldier reporting for duty.

"Yes, sir, I believe I do."

"Here." The shiny bracelets exchanged hands. "Everybody move slowly, slowly. Julie, put down the goddamn gun. It's over. She'll stand trial. And with that coat as evidence, it shouldn't be a long one. She'll get what she deserves. Put down the gun."

The doctor sucked in air for moral support as her arms were brought back behind her and the handcuffs snapped in place.

"Cecil, step away," I whispered.

At first he froze but subsequently did as I'd asked as the furniture settled back down on the hardwood. I started to pull back the trigger with unsteady but determined hands. Then Bethany came out of hiding, timidly walking over to Cecil and standing at his shoulder, arms folded in front of her.

"There," I said, triumphant. "Now you can all see her. This is Bethany Garrett. Bethany, are you okay?" She nodded, nervous and shy.

The doctor sneered. "Perfect."

Frank looked at Cecil, and Cecil looked at Frank. Then Frank cautiously extended his arm in my direction.

"Julie, honey, you need to give me the gun. Everything's going to be okay."

He took a step, patiently coaxing me to comply. I just wasn't happy with this ending.

I fell forward toward the handcuffed, bald woman by the dining room table. With the barrel shoved against her torso, I calmly said, "*I'm* the writer..."

A spark appeared from the point of contact and my hand stung with the force of the shot as a deafening bomb went off in my head. Next, without cocking the hammer, I pulled the trigger hard as another bomb exploded. "…and *I* decide the ending."

Frank pulled me off of the limp body. I don't know where the gun went, must've dropped it. Cecil held me while Frank felt the killer's neck for a pulse that wasn't there.

Cecil saddled up to the lost detective to offer advice.

"You do still have time to make this right, Frank. You know what you need to do."

"Yeah. Yeah, I can make this right."

Replacing his own gun in its holster, he fished out the key to open the handcuffs muttering, "Holy Mother, forgive me."

"Okay, this is how it happened. It was self-defense. I got here a minute too late." He removed the cuffs and repositioned her arms. "Mr. Valentine, you weren't here. You need to scram."

The most by-the-book guy in the universe was plotting out our futures one lie at a time.

"Detective, we have company," Cecil said, my head still pressed to his chest.

Crow was leaning against the open front door. "I saw the Owl."

The two enemies stared at each other long and hard.

"How long have you been there?" Frank enquired.

"Long enough."

"Great. And what are you gonna do with your wealth of knowledge?"

"That depends. We even?"

Frank paused, finally nodding begrudgingly.

"Then just like this very well-dressed gentleman, I wasn't here at all. I'd say this one belongs to Julie. How you doing, JP?"

I tried to smile at him but had nothing to say.

"You'll be all right. Girl, you're part of the hood. You and that Owl."

Frank straightened his belt, reevaluating Crow's commitment.

"I've got your word?"

My ebony cowboy extended his great, black paw as his signature on the contract. "Honor among thieves, detective. Honor among thieves."

I watched through blood-splattered lenses as these two adversaries shook hands.

"Gentlemen start your engines."

Crow disappeared before Frank took out his phone to call for backup.

Still in Cecil's arms, I fuzzily asked, "Where'd she go? Where's Bethany?"

"I think she's sleeping now," he assessed, rubbing my back as he spoke. Then he pulled away, adjusted his hat, and gave me a peck on the cheek. "I got to run, sweetheart. You did yourself proud here tonight. Yes, indeed. I swear you must've been a carny in some other life."

He started for the door then stopped. "You see, little sister, you surely do have the angels on your side."

CHAPTER TWENTY-SIX

Things are clicking along smoothly enough at the diner, I understand. Peaches took in Bethany's brother, Eugene, at Crow's request, and she's guardedly enjoying motherhood. Jesus even convinced Carroll to make the kid a busboy part-time and Peaches got him enrolled in a transitional K-12 for homeless kids where there are no questions asked. I hear that Jesus renamed him Lucky and Eugene digs the fresh handle. I like it, too.

Charlotte and Felix got the few things I unpacked repacked and out of the apartment. I'll be moving back to Poppy with him when they release me. Felix and I have an awful lot to work out but we're willing to work it out under one roof. I'm looking forward to getting back to the Poppy house, back to something familiar.

I asked Carroll if he wanted the apartment. "Doris, you're good people. No dootabootit," he sobbed. Charlotte says he doesn't even mind the bloodstains and bullet holes. He did tumble down the stairs, though, so I think I'm gonna have somebody put in a ramp.

Random House wants me back but Richard says I should tell them to kiss my ass. He says I can go anywhere I want, hot as I am right now. I think I'll self-publish. That should piss off everybody.

I've already started working on the book in here, the one about the incident. Something to do. Hell, I've got more than a hundred pages already. And with all the press coverage, I've got more free publicity than mere talent could ever garner.

Frank brought my coat and Bethany's hat to Felix's. I asked him to do that when the police were done with them. Felix had the coat cleaned but it's pretty messed up. Maybe a happy face decal over the bullet hole. I just can't part with it. It fits better than the new one and it has saved my life – twice.

They say I may get out of here in a couple more weeks. It's already been three. No more hallucinations, no blackouts, either. And as far as treatment centers go, it's very posh. Many famous people have dried out within these walls. It's an honor, really. But I can't recommend a place like this to just anybody, not unless it's court-ordered. The rooms are nice but the patients are a mess. It's like having Annie Lebowitz shoot the Elephant Man for the cover of Vanity Fair. Great picture, but it is what it is. I guess I'm still a little tense, a little edgy.

You never know how close you are to the edge until you're already falling. Maybe you're falling in love, maybe you're falling over a cliff in a borrowed Chevy. It doesn't matter, if you slip, you're going down. And the climb back up gets a little steeper each time.

But as long as you're breathing, you've got to try. I mean, everybody's haunted. Just because you bury something doesn't mean it won't haunt you.

We tear down a lot of shit in our lives: careers, relationships, stability. Tear down until there's nothing left. Then, sometimes, we rebuild. Nighthawks is a testament to that. I'd say I've been pretty fortunate, considering. Could be Cecil's right. Could be I do have angels all around me. One thing's for sure, I've got a lot of ghosts.

Made in the USA
Columbia, SC
14 November 2022

71224858R00152